Mr. Lincoln's Wars

Perennial

An Imprint of HarperCollins*Publishers*

Mr. Lincoln's Wars

A Novel in
Thirteen
Stories

ADAM BRAVER

"No More Time for Tears" and "The Ward" first appeared in
Cimarron Review.

A hardcover edition of this book was published in 2003 by William
Morrow, an imprint of HarperCollins Publishers.

HarperCollins books may be purchased for educational, business, or
sales promotional use. For information please write: Special Markets
Department, HarperCollins Publishers Inc., 10 East 53rd Street,
New York, NY 10022.

First Perennial edition published 2004.

Designed by Nicola Ferguson

The Library of Congress has catalogued the hardcover edition as follows:
Braver, Adam.
Mr. Lincoln's wars / Adam Braver.—1st ed.
p. cm.
ISBN 0-06-008118-X
1. Lincoln, Abraham, 1809–1865—Fiction.   2. Historical fiction,
American.   3. War stories, American.   4. Presidents—Fiction.
5. United States—History—Civil War, 1861–1865—Fiction.   I. Title.
PS3602.R39 M7 2003
813'.6—dc21   2002023073

ISBN 0-06-008119-8 (pbk.)

04 05 06 07 08 ❖/RRD 10 9 8 7 6 5 4 3 2 1

for my grandfather

Thanks to family, friends, and teachers along the way;
my parents, who always told me everything I wrote
was good; Nat Sobel, not only for taking the time
to find me and then cajoling me into finishing the
manuscript, but also for his guidance and unrelenting
confidence; Henry Ferris, for his advocacy, diligence,
and infectious enthusiasm; Jerry Williams, for being a
great friend, as well as for reading most of these words
at least two times over; Alisson, for her nonstop love
and belief when there hasn't always felt like a reason to
believe; and last, Addison, for napping at just the right
times.

CONTENTS

No More Time for Tears

Passion has helped us; but can do so no more. It will in future be our enemy.

—FEBRUARY 22, 1842

*   *   *

 ime moves on, and each day ends with a curtain slowly being dropped, and every day seems like the one before. It can seem as if the only thing to make it better would be a quick stick of morphine into the veins and a skeleton key twisted in the lock, leaving the flame of a candle as the only other breathing thing in the room; and Abraham Lincoln was the sixteenth president of the United States. He sat in his second-floor office outlined in blue moonlight, kicking his feet high up against the wall, no shoes, just white socks with brown rings around the heels, folding his arms tight against his chest, looking out the window down to the gardens, at the rows of plants that were shaded in black from the quick close of the winter sky, and the gray outline that traced the edges of the leaves, bringing them forward like another dimension. His white shirt puffed out over his stomach, pushing out four wrinkles that rose and fell with each breath deep and constant. The air passed over his lips with a slight whistle that carried a tune all its own, yet as familiar and natural as the act of breathing itself.

His face looked sunken, cheekbones drawn out in a sharp cut, with thin jowls of flesh formed under his eyes that locked off to the distance. And his boy, Willie, had died three years ago at the age of twelve, and Lincoln had been right by his bedside and the night had been dark and the wind howled just as it should have, and not too far away, all up and down the seaboard, soldiers had been lying in infirmaries screaming and moaning and crying like boys with men's pains, and some cursed Lincoln and others called him a good man, none of them ever imagining their president falling to his knees and fighting for breath while his eyes stayed dry and the inside of his head seemed as if it would drown in a thousand different lakes. And even after three years he only occasionally came up for air, the rest of the time being spent holding on to his last breath.

And the battles were still being fought, though the war appeared to be near its end, if not completely over with, but endings could never make the beginning and the middle go away. Smoke was finally clearing and people on both sides were no longer shadow figures, they were tired and worn and feeling helpless. The bullets and the cannons would finally stop pounding, the war was ending.

Lincoln's secretary of war, Edwin Stanton, was due to arrive in the president's office at any moment. He was going to stand there in officious pride with his fists lodged into his hips and his feet a shoulder's stride apart. The mouth above his funneled gray beard drawn down in permanent disappointment, and his eyes magnified twice their size behind his thick-lensed glasses, breaking a smile like a bottle of champagne, and making plans with the president on how to bring this mess to a quick resolve and take back the South like a gentleman. Telling Lincoln the time is now, that you gotta ride out to Richmond tomorrow and declare victory by shutting down the rebel capitol. And don't hang your head so goddamned low, Abe, you're a hero and they'll be lining up halfway down the seaboard to see you putting an end to this, and please no more of your Richard-the-Third-Throne-of-Blood-Winter-of-Discontent bullshit, because war is war, and that's a fact, and acting in response to attack is not tantamount to responsibility for all the tragedy suffered in what had to be done, so pull your boots up, put a spit shine to 'em, and be ready to ride out tomorrow morning, and give my best to Mary and the boys. Then he walked over by the window and left Lincoln dropping his face into his palms, listening to the mechanical growl in his gut.

The office door pushed open again. Lincoln's youngest son, Tad, stood in a thin crack of light. "Mama won't eat again," and his eyes opened wide with the fear of the messenger before he shut the door. Abe pulled himself up from his chair, ran the edge of his finger below his eyes, and walked past Stanton down the hall to the room where Mary had secluded herself. "Mary," he said, giving the door a slight rap.

He heard scampering sounds.

"Mary." He knocked louder.

The door creaked slightly, revealing just the center of Mary Todd Lincoln's face puffing out like a fat moon. Her eyes in slits, with the green irises jumping from side to side. Sweated strings of dark hair shoelaced over her face. And her fingers wrapped around the door, red-and-white knuckles. "What is it?" she spit out. "What is it you want?"

Lincoln stood composed, holding his stare firm against hers. "I understand you haven't eaten today," he said.

"Don't need food," Mary growled. "I don't need anything."

"Now, Mother."

"And I don't need anything from you, you hear?"

"Please, Mary." He hushed his voice.

"If it wasn't for you . . ."

"Mary."

"You're a pox, Abraham Lincoln, you bring tragedy to everything you touch. Kill off all the boys in this country, as well as your own." And she looked deep at him with her eyes carrying a pierce of intentional hurt, rolling her lips into a grin and folding her arms across her breasts.

The mansion hall dimmed in green shadows, leaving no trace of light from the day. His eyes skipped along the hallway walls and settled on a mirror, then jumped from the fright.

Mary saw him looking away. Her pale complexion flushed to red. "And I'll tell you, sacrificing everything, all those lives, for the nigger. The nigger comes first around here. I can't tell you how that makes me feel."

Lincoln pulled his hands behind his back.

"I suppose you got a war to go and fight," she mumbled.

Lincoln looked down. "It's over and gone."

"What," she laughed, "the war?"

"I told you last night."

She glanced past him. "I don't listen anymore."

He sighed. "Well, it's done with."

"And I am happy for you, Abraham. You gonna go kiss some nigger babies now? Get on your knees and pick cotton and sing about Jesus with them?"

Lincoln put his hand on the door. "I gotta get some rest. I have to go to Richmond in the morning . . . Mother, eat your supper." And he started to walk away.

"I'm not eating alone," she called out.

He turned around. "I'll send Tad in to eat with you. I don't believe he's eaten yet."

Mary stepped back in the room. "No." Her voice wavered. "No. I don't want anyone coming in this room. It's safe now from all evil and I don't want you or anything you've touched to contaminate this room. Go ahead, go to Richmond. Dance with your nigger friends the whole night long for what I care. Just leave me alone, Abraham,

like you always do . . . like you always do . . . like you
always . . ."

She slammed the door.

The president walked down the hall, his legs hanging
like death. Knowing the goodness in Mary, knowing the
pressures that build up in a person when their son dies of
disease at twelve, and the oldest boy, Robert, graduates
from Harvard and enlists in the war, scaring his mother
halfway to Jesus, and Tad runs around the Executive
Mansion halls trying to smile and look so happy while his
big brown saucer eyes look so lonely and sad, and he's
scared to death to be in the same room with the woman
who bore him. And sometimes Mary tells Lincoln that
she's already an old maid, and Lincoln looks away, unsure
of words, because he himself feels like he's lived his life
before, and the doors slam and the valves are tightened and
the pressure builds. And Mary exclaims that she will never
enter the room that Willie slept in, and she wants to know,
Abraham, what do you think of that? And Abe just shrugs
his shoulders, as his stomach boils, unable to reply because
any thought of Willie sends him into a thousand thought
dreams that swirl like a hurricane wind. And Mary tells
him that it's clear he doesn't care, and what can he say to
that when the memories dull all his feelings.

And the Lincolns are one more family behind a set of
doors where a plague not seen since the likes of Pharaoh
has stolen a son from every home. On both sides of the
border, North and South, the bodies are piled high and the

tears of grieving parents wash the black from the night into their hearts. And the parents wander around accidentally bumping into each other as the grief and fear slowly drives them away from one another. And sometimes when they wake up in the morning and the sky is a silver-blue with the sun hanging in the corner, rays forming perfect points from the center, the mother and father look at each other and remember the love and kindness without the thought. And it feels like a new life is beginning, like the fence has been whitewashed.

The war is over, by God.

It's a fresh start.

President Lincoln walked down the hall. His legs felt like death.

The Undertaker's Assistant

Perfect relief is not possible, except with time. You can not now realize that you will ever feel better. Is not this so? And yet it is a mistake. You are sure to be happy again. To know this, which is certainly true, will make you some less miserable now. I have had experience enough to know what I say.

—DECEMBER 12, 1862

* * *

ometimes it's best to just get the particulars out of the way. My name is Seth Jackson, I'm fifty-four years of age, live by Dumbarton Oaks Park in Washington, and work as an undertaker's assistant dressing bodies for Drs. C. D. and J. Brown, Undertakers, on 469 Broadway. I guess I believe in Jesus, although it's not like I talk to him at my bedside or anything like that, but I do try to stay truthful, the commandments and such. President Lincoln, in my opinion, was a good soul, but the kind of man who seemed drawn to tragedy as a way of fixing things and shining sense on them—not necessarily for himself, but more for the rest of us imbeciles. And there is one more particular worth mentioning for the purposes of this telling: I was present for the preparation of both his body and his son's.

I met President Lincoln once before I fit his black suit to his slain body in the Executive Mansion's upstairs guest room. It was in the summer of 1862, not too long after his son Willie had died. Mr. Lincoln was walking in a country

stride down an alley off K Street NW toward Franklin
Square, leaving his bodyguard behind like they said he
sometimes liked to. The day was drowning under a
Washington humidity that could melt you from the inside
out. He wore flat black pants, and his legs rose long and
lean, but strong, like a fully matured poplar. He was
coming toward me and I couldn't help but notice the
almost circular rhythm of his legs. It was like they were
rolling with the grace of a brand-new wheel. And it was
just a plain white shirt that he wore, sleeves pushed up to
his elbows, striking me as kind of unusual, because I'd
never known the president to be out of his dress coat.

Lincoln kept his eyes held hard to the ground, but it
was no doubt due to my bug-eyed gawking that he rolled
those grays down until they met mine, and just held his
stare for an endless moment. His frame was massive, and I'd
have sworn to Jesus that the man stood eight feet tall. I was
struck by his poise. Sometimes when I'm done working, I
peek through the crack in the door and observe Dr. Brown
making the final arrangements. I watch family members
walk the floors, trying to find a reason that makes it all right.
Dead in shock with a lightning rod run straight through
their spines. But Mr. Lincoln looked strong. Like he had
flicked the weight of the world right off his shoulders.

"I'm sorry about your boy." I spoke first, although not
certain that anybody actually needed to talk at all. But still,
he had only recently lost a son.

Mr. Lincoln didn't say anything. He just kept his stare.

A draft swept across my face. And I noticed my foot was tapping. Sometimes I tend to talk when I start feeling a little uncomfortable. It's something about myself that I can't explain. Maybe it's pure nerves that set my mouth to moving, or maybe I've got some part of me that naturally wants to make people feel at ease.

"He was a nice-looking boy," I said. "A fine-looking boy. But sometimes folks aren't long for this world. It seems like they're placed here just long enough to be snatched up to a better place."

Lincoln drew his lips together, and I could see the thoughts running across his mind like a handful of photographs. He was breathing hard. And he brought his hand up to his face and started stroking his beard beneath silent eyes. I started babbling about how he should be proud that he was able to have his boy for the time he did, that some things are just meant to be a certain way. And I told him that his boy had had hair the color of the earth and maybe, somehow, that was where he truly belonged.

Mr. Lincoln cut me off. "You've seen my boy?" When he said those words I could tell he was falling back into another place where a one-eyed sun could still shine brilliantly on this piss-drenched alley.

In my position you're always in the hidden background. A family member doesn't even want to know about the idea of you. Not wanting even to fathom the notion of hands like mine snapping a radius in order to bend their loved one's arm back and forth and slip a sleeve on, posing their appendages to make them look as halfway presentable to death as they were to life. And in the case of the Lincoln boy, just like the others, I had anonymously dressed Willie for the casket. Buttoned up his shirt, applied the makeup, and ran the comb through his hair. Like he had done it all on his own.

"How did you know Willie?" Mr. Lincoln asked.

I bit down on the end of my thumb, calloused and cracked, though the flesh, like the rest of my body, had grown soft in my advancing years.

"How did you know him?" he pressed.

"Well," I said, "I work down at Drs. Brown, Undertakers," and I proceeded to explain the situation of my vocational circumstance surrounding the passing of his son.

I could only imagine the kinds of things he must hear being the president, what people must want or expect, and the graciousness and respect he must need to exude at all times. But at this I saw something in him change, like the flickering light of a fading candle, the strength draining from him. He reached out and held my forearm. I'm sure I jumped a step or two. But he held on. At least his fingers were warm.

"Tell me everything," he said.

I looked at him, shrugging my shoulders.

"I want to know." His voice barely sifted through his throat.

"What do you want to know?"

"Everything about Willie."

"Well, I don't know what . . ." Mr. Lincoln led me by the arm to a set of back-door steps, and instructed me to sit down beside him. He called me by my full name. A dancing light tapped up and down my spine. And a cold line of sweat wept straight across my forehead. I tried to look at Mr. Lincoln but my nerves swelled deeper.

"Let me tell you something," Mr. Lincoln said. "Since Willie died all I've done is walk the floors all night. Back and forth. One foot in front of the other. Counting off the steps until light breaks through the window and I have an excuse to be awake . . . seventeen hundred, Mr. Jackson, seventeen hundred."

I looked at him, unsure of what he meant.

"Seventeen hundred steps last night. See, the thing is, Mr. Jackson, every step seems to count for an isolated frame of Willie's life. My feet fall hard and flat to give me one more memory of him."

Being an undertaker's assistant I knew exactly what he meant. I see every face that comes through our doors, and though most of them just kind of wash away with the day, I recall the faces of every child I have ever dressed. I close my eyes and see their bloated cheeks and their pupils in a frozen look of confusion. And all the marks and scars. A little Negro girl with hoofprints branded into her face, looking up at the ceiling like she still has one more round of screaming to do. Or a boy so starved the bones are breaking out of his cheeks.

Lincoln was breathing hard. "I know every chapter, every single line, except one: I don't know what happened when Willie went to the mortuary. I stood there when the doctor said he wasn't gonna live much longer, pushed his head into my chest when he died, and sat by his side in the East Wing two days later and cried harder than I'd ever thought I'd known. I know it seems strange to have to know everything, like there aren't enough etchings scratched across our minds already, but I need to know. Willie was just passing through here for some reason, and I want to know that reason. I don't eat these days, Mr. Jackson, and I sure as hell don't sleep. And the boy's mother is reduced to a saddened state of . . . I'm in charge of a divided nation where boys on both sides seem to have been born to just pass through too quickly. Maybe that's why the Lord put them here, I don't know. But He included my twelve-year-old boy, and I don't understand. I don't understand. So maybe you can show me one more piece, Mr. Jackson. I'm just a grieving father. Please, tell me what you know."

I could close my eyes and see his boy, but I still wasn't seeing anything Mr. Lincoln didn't already know. The color of his hair, the texture of his skin, the slight rise of his upper lip, and his blue eyes set gently back behind almost-blond lashes. But I never saw answers that February night. No missing text that would complete the unfinished chapter. Just a twelve-year-old boy who'd been stripped naked by disease.

"Mr. Lincoln," I whispered, "I'm just the undertaker's assistant, I don't know much about anything except preparing bodies."

Lincoln bent over and ran his hands across the tops of his shoes. "Please," he said, "just tell me anything."

"He looked peaceful," I said, remembering Dr. Brown saying that truth can always be found in the ears of those who want to hear it. "Like he was resting on a heavenly bed." And while talking, I had the realization that sometimes saying things that aren't exactly truthful is not necessarily bad or evil. Sometimes it's even necessary. Just to keep somebody alive and standing on his own two feet.

Lincoln looked at me for more.

"It was strange," I found myself saying. "I could just tell that he wasn't alone. That he was in the company of others."

"Like who?" Mr. Lincoln asked.

My voice dropped to a whisper. "I don't know," I surmised, "maybe he was joining all them other boys on their marching." It just spilled out that easily.

Mr. Lincoln looked hard at me with that deep-set loneliness that always accompanies a grieving parent. "You think he knew what was going on? Do you think he knew he died?"

"Like I said, sir, he looked like he was being kept company was all."

He stood up, then fell right back down again. His voice still held to a whisper, though with a certain urgency that slowly raised it to full volume. "I'm just so confused." His face turned withered. "Mr. Jackson, do you believe in the connection of things?"

Now I was really deep into it. "Mr. President, I'm really just a simple man, you know. I mean, thoughts like that don't make a whole lot of sense to me."

Lincoln fixed his gaze across the alley. Staring at the white bricks that sat one by one on top of each other. "You see, Mr. Jackson, I often think that we're all in some type of relationship with each other that extends far beyond what we see. There's some part of me that believes Willie's dying was somehow a part of all the soldiers dying, and if that's the case, well . . ." His voice trailed into a thin breath.

"I guess I don't follow," I said. Truthfully.

"If what I'm thinking is the case," Mr. Lincoln barely uttered, "then I'm responsible for my boy dying. Just as I'm responsible for all those others boys going."

I reached up my hand to put it on his shoulder. I didn't look for tears (I'm trained for that). But I was lost, not knowing what lines I had crossed, where they were, or how to get back.

"You see boys all the time that are dead," he said. "What do you think? What do you think when you see them? Why do you think it happens?"

I left my hand on his shoulder, feeling the burdens he must have carried all the day long. I considered his question as best as I could, and tried to answer it with some degree of my own truth. "It's so hard," I began. "I mean, on one hand I do believe there is a God above who watches and protects us all. But then I see all those bodies that have no more sense of life in them than this stoop we're seated on. And I know those bodies are gonna be fitted in a pine box and get lowered into the earth where they'll do nothing but rot like compost and become feed for the worms and maggots. I mean, they aren't going anywhere. But then there's that feeling that I get, like the one I said about your boy. And it's a feeling, nothing that can be explained, but I get this creepy-crawly sensation that there's something going on around me when I'm dressing 'em up. Like there's some kind of welcome crew, or parade, or . . . Hell, I don't know. Now I'm talking crazy."

Mr. Lincoln leaned his bony frame toward me. "Keep talking," he said.

The truth is, all I was doing was talking, and of course I didn't know what I was saying, where it was coming from, or what it even meant. I was just connecting all the strange thoughts that have passed through my mind into one long sentence that might be meaningful to him.

"You know," I continued, "there's some bodies I just don't want to touch. I get an order to have that body dressed by a certain hour, and I start to pick up the legs, or something, and I get a feeling running right through me like a shock, like I'm poking around in some place I don't belong. And it's a little confusing, because there is something that still seems alive to the touch. So what I do is take the pair of pants and slice a razor up the back seams, then lay the open pant over the legs. And I back away, just letting it all take the proper form . . . Sometimes, I swear, it's like we're burying the living."

Mr. Lincoln leaned backward. The edge of the steps cut into the small of his back. He rolled his lips into his mouth and stroked his fingers over the ends of his whiskers. It was probably minutes, but I would have sworn it was hours. Like the thoughts were just working their way back and forth across his brain, and he just kept reading them over and over until they made the right amount of sense.

He finally looked up at me. "I think my boy walked out with the living." Mr. Lincoln pushed himself up and stood tall in the shadows. He scraped the dust off his legs and tucked the tails of his shirt back into his waist. He ran his hand through his hair like it was a comb and looked right into my eyes with a stare so intense I felt it in my stomach. "You've been very helpful for me, Mr. Jackson," he said. "I hope I can repay the favor some day."

I was entranced by his stare.

"You call on me anytime you need to," he offered, bent down and touched my arm, then turned and walked down the alley into the sun. Walking a little bit taller.

I never did call on him.

Didn't see him again until he lay dead on the table.

And I sliced the seam of his pant leg and laid it flat, just the same as I had his boy's.

Zack Hargrove

I believe it is an established maxim in morals that he who makes an assertion without knowing whether it is true or false, is guilty of falsehood; and the accidental truth of the assertion, does not justify or excuse him.

—AUGUST 11, 1846

＊ ＊ ＊

A mean sonabitch who'd grab you by the lapels, put his face right into yours, and then say he'd turn traitor and do the Confederate soldiers' job for them, and leave you out to rot with all the other whore cowards if you compromised his duty. That's what Zack Hargrove told all the new Union conscripts who looked to him with a green trail of fear in their eyes. "Milquetoasts," he'd say in a voice that dropped like a bullet-ridden rebel flag falling from the boom. "Cowards still holding on to Mommy. Well, I'm telling you that nobody is going to give a rat's ass how cute you were as a baby boy. I've fought alongside Grant, McLellan, Burnside, and Meade. I faced Robert E. Lee himself, even held his balls in my hand ready to be sliced and strung into some Chinese necklace until one of those half-cocked Confederate crackers came up behind me and took a swipe at the back of my legs with a dull, rusty-edged blade that nearly gave me TB and laid me up in a hospital for damn near two months. Nobody cared. That's how it goes. Nobody cares." And Zack Hargrove would bend at the waist, allowing a thin band of fat to hang over his belt, and reach his calloused hands down just far enough to tug at the bottom of his pant leg. He'd pull up slowly, making sure to watch the curious expressions of the young soldiers turn to fear when they saw the parallel cuts traveling up his calves, deep pink with thick brown ridges that looked like thick rubber worms. Then Zack would let go and the pant leg would slowly fall. "You hack little newborns will never know shit until it's streaming down your shaking legs. You'll be all alone out there. Looking for some way out. And nobody will care."

⁘ ⁘ ⁘

Zack Hargrove had always wanted a horse. As a boy he would sometimes sit cross-legged on a rotted stump beneath a brooding willow, looking out across the fence at the neighbor's collection of horses, their heads shaking from side to side, sloughing off yellow showers of spit in thick-headed laughter. The young Zack studied the faces. Not concerned with knowing a Palomino from an Appaloosa from a Mustang. Just watching their drawn expressions, eyes that bulged at the sides, and lips that ran the length of their jaws, rolling back and forth, exposing the long yellow teeth and the thick red tongue that slopped back and forth. What would it be like to ride one of them? To pull back on the reins, have the bridle set into

place, and just trot off while saddled at the top of the
world. Running free with all the power and strength in
the world, in a way he wished he might have. Running
away from an old man who ran a farm outside of
Newcastle, Delaware, who had one hand on a hoe and
the other around the neck of a bottle. An old man who
had ground a blade into his wife's stomach and claimed
self-defense by saying that she was possessed and was
trying to kill him, and the white-haired judge who feared
Satan worse than the dead of night acquitted the old man
and sent him back to his farm to raise his crops and his
boy, not even considering for one second the boy who had
held his mother as she bled to death by her own husband's
hand. And just once, with all the courage that he could
muster, waiting until one darker-than-usual night when
the old man didn't seem to be as liquored as normal, the
boy asked his father for a horse, and his father said that
men who rode horses all the time just did so because they
were small-dicked and needed to feel like they had more.
And he said he knew his boy wasn't like that, no, and the
old man reached down and grabbed the boy's crotch and
squeezed like a sonabitch, then gave a quick yank
downward, and letting go said, "None of us Hargroves
needs a horse, do we? Now you take that thought from
your mind, and if it should come back in, I'll just have to
reach down and grow your pecker myself."

Zack never talked about horses again with his father.

Hardly talked about anything with him. Just thought a lot to himself that one day he'd saddle up a horse of his own and ride off far away. And probably piss a golden shower down his father's throat on the way out.

❖   ❖   ❖

Outside of Beaufort, South Carolina, the clouds swelled into one thick shadow, portending snow. Icicles already hung from the skeletal trees, almost low enough to touch the river. There was not much sound except for the passing chatter of soldiers bundled in their threadbare coats, hands in pockets, and forcing laughter to keep warm. The fire crackled in the background with forgettable pops and hisses. A nothing lieutenant by the name of Simpson broke branches with his boots as he walked up to the fire, bent over to rub his hands, then sat down on a rotted log next to Zack Hargrove. "Well, sonabitch," he said. "I just been given word that the war is good as over. Sure as hell we can get off this watch and head back home."

Zack didn't say anything back. Didn't really think too much except for leave-me-the-fuck-alone, while the fire lit the hollows of cheekbones above his scraggly beard.

Simpson's eyes opened, carrying every ounce of enthusiasm and belief. "Didn't you hear me, Zack? War's good as over."

Zack shifted a little. He put his hands inside his coat and rested them on his belly for warmth. "I heard this all before," he finally said. "Always someone putting an end to the war." He laughed.

"I heard Lincoln's ending it," Simpson whispered.

"And you heard that from . . . ? Some little eighteen-year-old pack dog who's hoping the war don't go on 'cause he don't want to die never having had his dick anywhere but in his own hands?"

"No, I . . ." And Simpson hung his head and laughed. "Holy Jesus," he said. "Zack, you sure can spin them."

Zack grumbled, "Ain't no war coming to an end if we're out here shivering our asses off."

"The way I heard it is that once Sherman marched right on through . . ."

"Sherman? That useless soldier? I had to practically hold his hand just to get him up to the battlefield. Little baby doll girl."

"Anyway, it seems that old Sherman took straight through the South burning everything in sight including Atlanta, Georgia."

"Are you serious?" Zack cocked his eye suspiciously.

"Too much for Lee and Davis. They're surrendering, I hear. Lincoln himself is going to Richmond for the victory."

There was a true moment of silence between the two men. Then Simpson said out loud how nice it would be if the war ended so he could go back to his bride and baby daughter, and maybe even work in the general store again and try to forget everything he'd seen over these last couple

of years. Zack didn't respond, he just looked into the fire
and tried to forget about how empty he felt. How he
suddenly had no sense of home or place, and he wondered
what he would do when it all ended (if it was ending),
because he certainly wasn't going back to that farm in
Delaware to live with that crazy old drunk of a father. He
thought hard and he couldn't think of anything left for him,
because, after all, besides war, what other legal occupation is
there for a man who likes no other feeling flowing through
his body than the hot white fire of killing a man?

"What about the niggers?" Zack asked.

"I guess they'll be freed."

Zack shook his head. "You know, that's not why I
fought in this war, and I don't want anybody thinking I
did. I fought because I don't like the Southerners. I don't
like the way they look, don't like the way they talk, and I
don't like the attitude they carry in that pole stuck straight
up their asses. So it ain't about niggers. I don't care about
them."

Simpson scratched his head.

Zack's voice was getting louder. "Well, I just don't want
anyone thinking I'm doing what I'm not," he justified. "I
don't wanna go home to a bunch of backslappers who tell
me what I was . . . Look"—he stopped himself—"we don't
even know the goddamned war's over for sure."

"Well, we're supposed to ride out to Richmond
tomorrow. Can't think of any other reason why."

"Shit," Zack Hargrove drawled. "Shit."

❖   ❖   ❖

When Zack Hargrove was nineteen, he and his father took a train ride to Annapolis. It seemed the Hargroves had a relative who now held a seat in the Maryland legislature, and old man Hargrove sought to keep Zack from having to go to the newly declared war. On the train ride over Zack told his father that he wouldn't mind going off to fight. He'd go to war in order to protect the Northern way of life. Plus, he thought to himself, it'd be a good way to get away from the farm and split the old fuck, and take it out on somebody else.

The old man soured his face into a ball that hid behind a cancerous bulb nose that looked eaten by termites. "That piss honking war's about the Negro and if Lincoln wants it, he can fight it himself. Now you're my boy and I need my boy and his back plowing my farm. Don't need you trolling around with a rifle in your hand trying to pry open the welcome gates for a bunch of Negroes. And that's exactly how I'm gonna state my case. Gonna tell Senator Cousin, *Don't let my boy go, I need him to work.*"

Zack stopped listening. He saw the uniform and the gun. The protocol of war, of kneeling down and cocking the rifle and firing and tasting the metal smoke that rose from the weapon. Something about that made his legs tingle and his heart pound stronger.

They pulled into town and marched right up Main Street to the base of the Capitol steps. "Now go off and

entertain yourself for a while while I go talk to the
senator. Walk up and down them streets or something."

"I think maybe I'll walk on down to the water."

"I don't give a rat's ass what you do, just keep yourself
out of trouble." And the old man climbed the marble steps
and slipped his bony frame between the tall wooden
doors, barely opening them.

Zack Hargrove started down the hill toward the bay.
His feet creaking the planks of the wooden sidewalks
made him nervous, so he sat down on a bench under a
bleaching sun. He'd never been in a town like this.
Sophisticated. Fancy stores, and coaches pacing the streets.
Pretty women marching round with their heads perched
just perfect atop their necks, arms leveled at their sides,
clutching the dainty hands of sourpussed children, without
even an expression that might suggest that there was a war
going on, that just miles away corpses rotted face down in
meadows, the backs of their heads gnawed on by wild
animals, where once fine hair was now matted in brains,
blood, and dirt, while this whole goddamned town walked
around like they were given immunity from it all; and
Zack sat down, a curse on them all, wishing that the
goddamned war would spill into the streets of Annapolis
and bayonet their sightless eyes.

A husky man with a face torched in hardened
wrinkles struggled up the road tugging a pack of horses.
They were all connected at the neck by strands of white
rope in slipknots. They paraded single file for a few paces,

knocking their shod feet in an ugly rhythm against the bricks.

The man stopped the herd in the middle of the main street, holding all the horses by a single strand of rope in his right hand. "Open your goddamned door," he yelled out to the closed door of a brownstone business. "Open your damn door," he called again, as the horses jerked him off balance, driven by the shortened tone of his voice.

The trader kicked his foot into the dirt and cursed something under his breath.

Zack watched the horses, each one as singularly intriguing as the other. He rose off the bench and walked down to them.

"Goddamn welcher," the trader was mumbling.

Zack went up to touch the nose of a brown-and-white horse that stared cross-eyed at him, but right as he touched it, the trader snapped, "What in hell are you doing?" and the horse jerked her head, causing Zack to draw back his arm into a cocked position.

"Just wanted to give her a pet, was all," Zack said.

"Christ, just wanted to give her a pet, was all," the trader mimicked, then raised his voice. "Goddamn, son, you can get your head blown off for touching a man's horse . . . Jesus." He yelled back to the brownstone, "Now get out here, Jesse, I don't have all the day long."

"That room looks empty," Zack offered, looking up alongside the trader.

"That cheap bastard don't wanna hear me. Orders up a

half-dozen horses, then buries his head underground when
the time comes to pay." He yelled back out, "You ordered
them, you pay for 'em." He turned back to Zack. "He's
trying to tell me the war has set him back and I tell him
bull-the-shit, you got a debt to pay. I could've sold these
things a thousand times over, but I didn't because of him
and his word."

The trader looked up to the sky with his eyes rolled
back in prayer, then turned his head from side to side,
muttering, *Jesus Christ, Jesus Christ.*

"You really think it's the war that's keeping him from
paying?" Zack asked. "I've been thinking of going, but
my father . . ."

"Bullshit on the war. It's just a bunch of neighbors out
there having a brawl. Goddamn, from what I hear, out
there at Manassas it was practically a picnic. One more day
under the sun . . . Shit, boy, if you end up going, don't
worry about it. It's just Lincoln's chess match. Probably
wind up being one big howdy how-you-do, with nothing
more than a few fat lips and the occasional hurt
feeling . . . Now this one," and the trader broke into a
bellow, "he'd better watch it or I'll have his lanky frame
seared over the campfires of hell . . . Pay up, welcher."

Zack ran his palm over the long brown snout of the
mare in front of him, in time to incur the delicate smiles
of a pair of schoolgirls admiring a man and his horse. "I
can watch them for you if you'd like?" Zack volunteered.
"Maybe you want to go knock on the door."

"But how do I know I can trust you?"

Zack Hargrove told him he was Zack Hargrove from Delaware, and that his father was here in Annapolis to talk to their cousin, the senator (although he didn't say why), and that he knew horses. "And I ain't no welcher."

"Well, Jesus Christ." The trader lowered his head in a moment of consideration, then tugged on the guide ropes and told Zack, "Follow me."

They walked up half a block and the trader pulled the horses in front of an alleyway. "Now you just wait here with them. No sense in bringing on any unwanted commotion . . . Nothing ever in here but some old building materials."

In the cold and shadowed alley, Zack stood next to the one with the brown-and-white mane. "You're a hell-on good-looking piece, aren't you?" He stepped forward and ran the flat of his hand along the horse's side. Feeling the skin pull tight against the muscles until it wrapped around the bloat of the stomach. Then dragging his finger down the shank of her rear leg and along the center of her underbelly where the two sides met in the middle. Kneeling down, and resting his head against her intestine-grinding gut.

"There you are, you layabout." Zack looked up and saw the old man standing at the end of the alley. "I been walking up and down the goddamned street looking for you . . . Now let's get the hell out of this useless place."

Zack stayed down on his knees, still pressing his face against the horse.

His father started toward him, walking in a bowlegged limp that sounded as if it broke the ground with each step. "What're you gonna do, start humping that thing? Now get away from that creature."

It wasn't that Zack didn't want to move, but he couldn't move.

The old man bent over Zack and reached around and grabbed his son by the scruff of the neck. His fingers froze like a vise grip as he squeezed.

Zack bit on the inside of his lip so hard he was sure it must have been bleeding. Remembering that stone-white face of his mother looking up at him from her coffin. As though there was some kind of intentional warning left on her face before she went. The old man, her husband of twenty-one years, wouldn't even look at her. Said he didn't want to "catch nothing."

"One of these days you're going to learn to listen to your father. Like the senator did," he added, not as if he was giving good news, but more that he never was appreciated. He gave Zack's neck one last brutal twist, with a boot kick to the ankle, before he straightened up, hands held to his hips.

Zack slowly rose. His face was blushed red and his eyes were stinging with tears and dirt. The inside of his stomach felt as if it had flushed white, and he tasted the acids and bile working their way up his throat and into the back of his mouth where he just swallowed, and hoped they would stay down there for good so he could catch his breath.

"I thought you don't like horses no more, anyways," the old man said, looking away and grinding his jaw. "Unless you've gone lying to me like your mother always did."

Zack felt a strength pass through his body. It wasn't a deep strength, but something more electric that traveled the surface of his skin. He picked up a plank that was resting against the alley wall. He hated his father so much right now.

Zack Hargrove gripped the two-by-four and twisted to his right and swung with all his might into the horse's side. The mare initially burst out an alarmed cry, then fell silent with the beating. Zack swung repeatedly, slamming into the muscle until it collapsed into a soft mush. The old man in a high-pitched cheer stood behind him. And Zack took the plank and lifted it over his head and crashed it down on the nag's head, and the sound of the cracking sent the other horses scampering down the alley, trailed by the broken rope. Blood rained up purple-red. Zack hit the mare again and again and again until the legs of the brown-and-white beast gave in and the horse fell to its side in a quiet thump with a cloud of dust shrouding its carcass. Zack's eyes bugged out of a sweat-glazed face; his lips pulled back showing off a crooked grin. And his father laughed and doubled over at his waist giving his thighs a good strong slap. Zack lifted his right foot off the ground, leading with his heel, and stomped on the horse's face, then kicked and kicked and kicked with his toe until the horse's teeth were half broken and dripping in blood, and the eyes of the mare were swollen into yellow pus. Then Zack leaned back with all his strength and gave the mare a swift kick right in the gut, and when the horse didn't move or respond, Zack kicked again and again, each time more and more frustrated at the lack of reaction. Zack grunted in deep breaths that seemed to anchor long, thin hollow screams. And the old man laughed his wrinkled little head off and grabbed his son by the shoulder and said we'd better get out of here before the owner of this thing gets back and has us hanged. Don't think the senator can get us out of that. And Zack just scowled, an expression bound for permanence, and let his father lead him away, the bastard that he hated so much. Zack looked back down the alley and saw the horse lying on its side, running in blood, flies already buzzing around its eyes.

Fuck Annapolis.

The next day Zack Hargrove went and enlisted in the Union Army to fight the Confederate rebels. His eyes had turned so hard that some swore they had no color except solid black. Within two days he'd killed a man. Something he could never imagine stopping.

✥   ✥   ✥

The nothing lieutenant Simpson and Zack Hargrove jumped off a trainload of soldiers into the heart of Richmond. A town simmering in defeat, nervously twitching as it became overrun by its challengers. The two men wandered into the crowd of Northern cheer, pushed their way through without a word and settled themselves onto a porch set back from the folly. They dropped their legs over the porch's edge and rested their arms atop the rotted pine posts. Union soldiers ran shrieking up to the crowds, occasionally trying to engage the two soldiers on the porch, but only getting polite, worn nods back in return, whereby the celebrants maybe paused for a split second before tearing the grins back into their faces and whooping out to the open blue sky.

Simpson thought about linking arms in the celebration dance, but he was too tired. The war had taken every bit of spirit out of his body. He hung over the porch trying to soak in the cheer, saying it might revive him and send him back into the arms of his family with as much life as he had taken with him. He looked over at Zack, whose shoulders were pulled tight, nose lifted into a sneer. Zack's hands gripped the fence post so tight the tendons practically broke through the skin. "Hell, you might as well be a rebel soldier," Simpson commented.

"What the fuck is that supposed to mean?" Zack said, looking out over the crowd.

"You just don't look like you're much for the celebration, that's all."

"You don't exactly look the life of the bash, yourself," and Simpson admitted that was true, but he was just whipped, and that was where the similarities ended.

The crowd hushed itself. Soldiers and civilians alike pushed on each other's backs in a forward procession, all up on their toes, suddenly hushed, and squinting their eyes for clarity. Even Zack and Simpson stood to see what everybody was looking at. Zack shook his head what-the-hell, and a young soldier who probably hadn't seen more than a month of battle turned and looked up with his soft-skin smile. "It's Lincoln . . . It's the president."

Zack squeezed down tighter on his eyes, thin lines cracking out the sides, until they were fully focused. "Well, sonabitch," he said to Simpson, "if it ain't Lincoln himself, coming to set us all free." He turned and spit off the porch.

Simpson stretched his body forward, pushing his palms on the porch, trying to just make out a glimpse of the president. "Jesus," he said.

Zack blew a cloud of chilled air over his lips. "Nice of him to show up," he said. "Just in time."

Simpson continued craning his head from side to side. "Looks like he's talking, giving a speech," and some burst of life shot through his veins, and he turned to Zack and said, "Come on, let's see if we can get closer, close enough to hear him."

Zack shook his head but jumped off the porch to follow Simpson's hurried steps, only stopping once to huddle his hand over his mouth so he could light the last cigarette he'd been carrying since Beaufort.

Like the true veterans of battle that they were, they

maneuvered their way along the side of the greater mass, parting people out of the way with crafty hands and intuitive skill. Zack followed behind Simpson, occasionally lifting the butt from his mouth when the end got too spit soggy.

The crowd became too thick to overtake. Simpson came to a stop. "Let's stand over there." He pointed to a breath of space off to the right.

The two veterans stood on their toes and watched the jaws of the president moving up and down in rhythm with the flowing gestures of his long, thin arms. "Man, I wish I could hear what he was saying."

"Same crap as usual, I'd guess," Zack said, his attention drawn to a gray horse loosely tied to a post a few yards away. An old mare who sagged at the stomach and bent slightly at the knee. She would hold her head up in a moment of pride, then drop it in dead weight, slowly letting it fall until it just chewed and gnawed on blades of broken grass in rueful resignation to better days passed. Flies buzzed around her eyes.

"I bet Lincoln's thanking us for all we done."

"Probably talking about himself, like he fought the battles alone."

"Bullshit," Simpson said.

Zack gargled a cocksure laugh, then looked back at the old mare.

"Look," Simpson said, touching Zack's elbow, "look."

Zack looked up at the stage in time to see Lincoln bending down and leaning over the edge. "What the hell is he doing?"

Lincoln reached out and took the hands of a small black girl who was dancing around the front of the stage. A low cheer waved through the crowd.

"He's holding that Negro girl," Simpson reported in an excitement matched with disbelief.

"That's all he thinks about," Zack Hargrove said. And his breathing became heavier. "Been fighting this whole thing about the Negro, all about the nigger." Then he yelled out in a voice drowned by the rising cheers, "Fuck about us, Mr. Lincoln? Been out there busting our balls so as you can dance with a little slave girl."

And the crowd cheered louder. Even Simpson was banging his hands together and catcalling at the stage.

"I been spending these years fighting for your war, Mr. Lincoln, and all you do is thank the niggers," Zack screamed out for no one to hear. His throat felt torn and dragged, and he said to himself, *Mothafucker-this-ain't-right*, and he turned to each side in a stilted circle, not knowing what to do, feeling like the only thing he knew how to do was kill, and suddenly feeling so hopeless, and breathing out more air than he was taking in, and acting without thought by untying the ratty yellow rope from the pole and pulling himself up onto the mare all bareback, and forgetting that he'd never ridden before, but, feeling something strong like being driven by a great sexual power, he knocked the mare in the side with his heel and pushed along the edge of the crowd up toward the president in order to just be heard.

A few people noticed the tired soldier in tattered blue riding with his back hunched, and his hands twisted tightly into the mane of the beast. And when he got close enough he yelled out again that he didn't fight this war to be forgotten to the Negro, and when he realized nobody heard him, he kicked the gray mare harder in order to move closer to the president.

"You nigger-loving sonabitch," he yelled, and a few stragglers finally took notice.

Lincoln was bent over touching the hands and heads of all the children who had pushed to the edge of the stage.

"You sonabitch," he yelled again, and this time kicked the mare so hard that she screamed in pain and arched back, kicking her front feet impossibly high into the air, leaving Zack Hargrove to pull even tighter on her mane for balance.

The horse landed on her feet, wobbled on her legs stunned for a moment, then charged forward toward the president, driven by the beating of Zack's boots.

And Zack just screamed. A high, wailing scream like that of a soldier who runs blindly into a gray cloud of cannon smoke while the popping of bullets tears all around him. His arm stretched out, charging with an invisible sword. Closing his eyes and baying, feeling the sides of his mouth tear from his cheeks. Every ligament and vein ripping from his chest, and his heartbeat thundering and overtaking him until it's the only sound he hears.

He screamed a steady howl until a bullet knocked him off the old gray mare and felled him to the ground. And then he just lay there, the old knife scars on his calf shining like fresh fang marks. A worn old soldier, dead as the day.

The Idiot Brother

In this sad world of ours, sorrow comes to all; and, to the young, it comes with bitterest agony, because it takes them unawares.

—December 23, 1862

$$* \quad * \quad *$$

*J*esse and Thaddeus Arnaud were blood brothers from New Haven, Connecticut, who had come from the same set of parents, Jeremiah and Becka Arnaud. They had been born four years apart and brought into the world with two different sets of circumstances. Jesse was born first, as a strong healthy boy who was said to have fire in his eyes and gunpowder in his soul. He was a boy of average intelligence who sought to please without compromising his own inner sense of dignity. And he grew quickly, big and strong, with a farmer's back like his father's and hair the deep rust of his mother's. He worked in the open fields behind the family house helping his father raise corn, spending a fair portion of his youth scampering through the corn-shock alleys with undirected boyish energy and imagination, before coming back to the home to help tend to his brother.

God had played a cruel trick on Thaddeus Arnaud, at least that's what the doctor said; in fact, the doctor suggested they might just want to relieve the misery of the newborn right then and there before the damage got too far gone. There was something wrong with the second child. He had a big head with little slits for eyes in the shapes of almonds, no chin to speak of, and lips just thin enough to leave a mouth left for breathing. His nose looked like a mischievous God himself had pinched some skin between his fingers and pulled outward, and then there was his big forehead that pushed out from the middle and looked swelled at the eyebrows, causing Jeremiah Arnaud to ask the doctor if maybe that meant his second son had too much brain, and the doctor replied, "No, he's just a flat-out idiot."

Thaddeus never grew more than an inch over five feet. He walked with his legs falling from side to side and his arms hung down bent at the elbow, his hands curved up and in. He never learned to talk as such, but he could grunt out a few words to indicate food or outhouse and maybe repeat an occasional word that was said to him. Nobody really knew what he understood for sure, other than the orders he took from his father, who put him to work with the chore of feeding the horses on the family farm. "Now, get yourself out to that barn and feed them all good," Jeremiah would say at six in the morning in front of the rest of the family, rubbing his hands over the steam from a pot of boiling water.

"Feed," Thaddeus repeated back.

"Yeah, feed the horses," Jeremiah said, pantomiming

the act himself. And Becka would look at her feet, then look around the room.

"Feed," Thaddeus said, walking to the door.

Jeremiah poured himself a cup of coffee and looked over at his eldest, Jesse, who was pitching a forkful of eggs into his mouth, and commanded, "Jesse, get out there and help your brother feed the horses."

"But . . ."

"Don't be so selfish, boy."

Thaddeus repeated, "Feed," and Jesse put down his fork and grabbed his coat from the wall and walked out the door not even looking at his brother or back to his mother, who covertly tried to offer a drawn-mouth expression of sympathy.

Becka Arnaud quietly dropped two eggs in the iron frying pan, letting them spread out and sizzle until the edges were barely brown. She put a towel around her hand and reached over to grab the cast-iron handle to take the fryer off the stovetop. With one loping motion, she swung the pan onto the countertop and scraped an almost rusted spatula under the eggs to plate them up; one for her, the other for her husband. And she thought about Jesus, wondering how much He actually watched over her. All she had ever asked for was health and the health of her family, and He had gone and sent Thaddeus. Twelve years now past and the boy was slower than a turtle, and sometimes she had wanted to just tell Jesus to go ahead and take the boy, *I don't care anymore, he's yours, yank him*

up by the collar and right on through the gates, for what I care.
He's of no use to me. And she'd feel spite tremble up her
back and want to castigate Jesus: "Of course you don't care
about Thaddeus having been planted in me, after all your
father forsook you." But she never did anything more than
think it. Instead a light prayer would tremble off the ends
of her lips, and she would ask the dear Lord to watch over
her son, Jesse, for he was a boy who could mean something.

The two brothers walked into the barn single file, their
feet breaking the thin layer of ice that had frosted over the
soil. The barn smelled of old wood that was knotted and
graying, and it also stunk of horse shit and horse hair and
horse breath, and Jesse, with his hands deep in his coat
pockets, couldn't think of anywhere else he'd rather not be
right now. He was about to turn eighteen and he was a
mean-looking stud and the pretty girls smiled when they
looked at him and he got excited just thinking about it.
He looked back at his younger brother, who stood still for
no apparent reason, tongue thick as a cow's, licking all
around the outside of his mouth, then pushing back in and
caressing the open gums that lay between his two
remaining front teeth. Jesse looked at his brother, who
stared at the dirt floor like he was seeing and discovering it
for the first time, and Jesse, frustrated and cold, barked,
"Thaddeus, get your ass moving," and Thaddeus slowly
rolled his eyes up at his brother.

"I swear to God," Jesse said, "I'm not gonna live my

whole life being a caretaker to my idiot brother . . . You hear me? . . . Momma and Daddy should've put you to rest the minute you were born and saved us all the trouble . . . And you . . . Well, I don't know what-in-hell goes on inside that skull of yours, but if you're thinking that I'm gonna spend the rest of my life caring for you, then you're as good as wrong. So don't rely on me so much . . . You get it?"

Thaddeus stared blankly at his brother.

Jesse pointed his finger. " 'Cause you know what I'm gonna do? I'm gonna go and enlist myself in Lincoln's army and go off to fight the South, 'cause it's better than waiting around here and being your personal slave . . . I'm gonna join Lincoln's army is what I'm gonna do."

"Lincoln," Thaddeus slurred back.

"Damn right, Lincoln. He's thinking he's out there freeing the slaves, but truth of it is, he's freeing old Jesse Arnaud. So you got it right, Thaddeus: Lincoln . . . Lincoln. Lincoln. Lincoln."

"Lincoln." Thaddeus bent down and picked up a chip of ice and held it up to his squinting eye, trying to look through it, and groaning in frustration as the ice melted between his fingers and dripped off the tips. He held up his fingers one more time behind a squib of sun that snuck through a knot in the wood, but there was nothing to see, and he stamped his foot to the ground in a succession of bursts and called out pained and frustrated to his brother.

"Thaddeus," Jesse hushed back, "shut up, would you?"

Thaddeus kept stamping his feet and crying out, wounded.

Jesse sighed from the middle of his chest, hating his parents and God and anything else that had put him in this circumstance. He walked over to his little brother, repeating, "Calm down and knock it the hell off," and he stood behind Thaddeus and hugged his arms around his brother's body and jammed his knee into those squatty little legs so that they'd buckle. It usually worked for calming him. He pulled his own head to the side so he wouldn't get a concussion when Thaddeus threw his head back, and Jesse just held his idiot brother, who cried out and wiggled like a dying fish before eventually slowing down from exhaustion or just plain forgetting.

Jesse dropped his arms and looked around the barn. He watched as Thaddeus resumed his chores. Jesse thought about enlisting as soon as he could. Wine. Women. And war. No idiot brother.

✧   ✧   ✧

The winter wind bent the walls of the house, bringing low cries from the pine siding. Jeremiah and Becka Arnaud sat on their couch in front of a fire, each holding a book, their feet in front of the flames.

Jesse came down from his room, creaking the boards of

the middle stairs, and Jeremiah Arnaud, without even looking away from the flames, said out loud, "If it isn't my oldest son, Jesse. He ain't never been able to walk down those stairs without bending the boards."

Jesse walked along the walls until he was facing both his parents. He felt the heat on his face. And the sweat in his palms.

"What is it?" Jeremiah asked, looking into the fire.

"Well," Jesse said, and he stopped with the light spanking his face.

"Speak up, son."

"I wanna join the army." And Jesse thought his head might swell so much he'd float up and drift off away.

Jeremiah turned around to look his son square on, as though he hadn't heard right. "What?"

Jesse cleared his throat and tried to raise his voice. "I said I want to join up and go fight the rebels."

Becka stayed silent.

"You wanna tell me why?" Jeremiah leaned forward, his hands bracing the couch.

Jesse knew he couldn't say the real reason: that his brother was making him mad, and nothing was changing and he'd been starting to feel like he'd been raised to take care of his brother, and Christ, he'd die an early death without ever knowing anything but an idiot brother, and he was nearly eighteen now and he had other things on his mind, like girls and smelling new smells—anything other than horse shit. But he answered back, " 'Cause I want to help the president with his cause."

Becka Arnaud looked at her son for the liar that he was, but didn't say anything.

"So you wanna help out Lincoln, huh?" Jeremiah smirked. "What you wanna do, stand by his side and help him feed the horses?" His mouth drew serious. "Jesse, you don't know what you're doing. This isn't tending to your brother. This is blood and guts. I don't want you involved in that."

Jesse straightened his shoulders, ignoring his father's reason. "I got friends that are joining up, and just the other day me and a couple of guys passed Reverend Samuels and he said, 'There goes a group that could go off and be their own infantry unit and probably defeat those Southerners on their own,' and it made me think . . ."

"Well, Reverend Samuels doesn't . . ."

"So it's not like I'm scared or anything . . . I just know that if everyone else is doing it, then it must be sort of okay."

"What I know," Jeremiah said, "is that when I go into town on Tuesdays and I stand around at Macaby's General Store, and a whole bunch of us are there, and we're leaning back on bags of rice, and each day someone, whether Bickleton or Williams or Murphy or Cunningham, someone will come in and say he's been telegrammed that his boy has been killed dead or missing in the war. And each of us will fall to silence, unable to think what to say, each one thanking the good Lord that it wasn't our boy that was taken, and finally one of us will break the air and say something like, 'Yeah, that war sure is mean, but your boy died for the right cause,' and we'll start talking around in circles until we all eventually convince ourselves and whichever father it is that the boy was a hero and he died by Lincoln's side and, and . . . There's too many heroes in this war . . . And I don't ever wanna have anyone tell me my boy . . ."

"It's not like that," Jesse countered back.

"It's boys dying is what it is."

"Well, I'm still gonna enlist." Jesse looked away from his father's coal-tipped eyes until he caught his mother's stare. Her lips were drawn, and she looked at her one healthy son, who stood with the pride of a man's face in a trembling adolescent's body. She lifted her body, heavy and tired with the long day, and her voice drew out a long fog-blown sigh, as she spoke out in a tone just above a whisper. "Let him go." Her eyes washed over and her teeth cut into her bottom lip. "Let him go."

"Becka," Jeremiah said.

"If it's what . . . Well, God bless . . ." And she walked through the stare of Jesse and Jeremiah into the kitchen. She braced her hands against the counter and looked down at them, grayed in the moonlight. She said in a low whisper, "O Lord, you'll hear me now," and she stopped at the fear in her own voice.

Thaddeus lumbered into the living room and stood

between Jesse and Jeremiah. He pulled his eyes together like
he knew something wasn't right, then spotted something
shiny on the floor and reached down to pick it up. All
eyes on him. The fire sounded like it was breaking up
the chimney, and the wind cried at the house, and
everyone held perfectly still, as if the slightest breath
would be seen as some sign of betrayal. Thaddeus just
picked and picked and picked at the shiny object on the
floor, concentrating so deeply, unaware of anything else
in the world.

❖ ❖ ❖

Although the war seemed new to most folks, it had
actually been going on a year now. Down at Macaby's the
men would say things like it isn't gonna last, or it's
nothing but politics and Washington, or it'll peter out
when the point is made or the Capitol's done being built.
But the war wasn't fading or staying on the surface or
going anywhere except deeper and deeper down.

Jesse Arnaud stepped over a platform and onto a train
that would take him south. He had on the blue uniform
whose buttons still shined, the boots that still reflected, and
his shoulders were still pulled back with his head still held
proud. His mother reached out with both arms and
embraced her son. Feeling his heartbeat. Letting it pound
against her breast.

Jeremiah reached over and tried to find the strength to
slap Jesse's back.

Thaddeus stood behind them, looking up at the sky, watching for birds.

"Don't get too stubborn-headed, now," Jeremiah said quietly. "Just follow the orders like they tell you."

Jesse rolled his eyes. He was a soldier now, and he just wished the train would start moving.

"Are you gonna write to me?" Becka asked.

"Of course I will."

"Every day?"

"I'll do my best, ma'am."

The train whistle blew. And all along the platform there was a deep sigh and the sound of people lunging forward for a last farewell. Jeremiah grabbed Thaddeus around the upper arm and pulled him up to his brother. "Your brother's going off to be a soldier, now," he explained. "Gonna be a brave man and go fight for Mr. Lincoln."

Thaddeus stared for a moment, then his eyes wandered in circles until they went completely white.

"So say good-bye to your brother, Thaddeus."

Thaddeus dropped his head back and let it roll side to side.

"Go on, now," Jeremiah prodded.

"Lincoln," Thaddeus said, drooling and looking up at the clouds caking the sky.

Jeremiah's voice trembled as though it might break. "Jesse, you say good-bye to your brother," and the wheels started squeaking against the tracks. The smell of burning metal left an acid taste on the tongue. Jeremiah yelled out,

"Tell him good-bye," and Jesse pulled back, and Becka reached out with both hands as if it were the last chance and touched the tips of Jesse's fingers, and said through her tears, "My only son," and Jeremiah pleaded, "Just tell him good-bye," and the train rolled off in a cloud of white steam, and boys hung out the sides for one last wave or a kiss floating in the breeze, and Jesse Arnaud hid himself away, finding a seat, closing his eyes, feeling the breath coat his stomach, and feeling entirely lost, but entirely free.

The Arnaud family stood on the platform. Becka watched the train disappear from sight, her arms hugged around her blue dress, keenly aware of her ribs bellowing in and out. Jeremiah looked around for a bench because of the sudden pain to the small of his back, while Thaddeus bent over the edge of the platform studying the shine off the tracks. Seeing the way the light seemed to cut in at one point, then skid down the length of the rail.

"Thaddeus," his father beckoned.

Thaddeus didn't break his concentration.

"Thaddeus, come here," and the boy looked up at his mother. She stared at the shadows on the horizon, opening like dark arms. Thaddeus reached for her hand but she didn't notice. He bent his head forward and looked down at the tracks and grunted.

✤   ✤   ✤

The men of Macaby's gathered around the front of the store for the Tuesday bull session. There was Lyle

Bickleton. Henry Williams. Colin Murphy. Maurice Cunningham. Alexander Fitzgerald. Ralph Crispin. And Jeremiah Arnaud, who brought along his son to assist with the weekly selling of the corn.

All the men leaned on rice sacks, letting the hard cushions mold into seats. Thaddeus stood by the doorway and looked out at the day.

Ralph Crispin asked if there was any word about Jesse, and there was a faint light in his eye remembering the loss of his son, William.

"He was writing nearly every day," Jeremiah said, "but we haven't heard from him in a few months." And he looked down.

Alexander Fitzgerald said that's bound to happen in war. "Matter of fact, hadn't heard from Obie for nearly six months . . . Thought the worst . . . Then got a letter just the other day," and the men exclaimed pleasure at that news, each with something to say, except for Colin Murphy, who hadn't heard from his son for almost a year and lived a fine line between dreaded expectation and hope.

Jeremiah looked over at Thaddeus and started to say his name, but decided to just let him stand. "You know," he said to the men, "Jesse said in one of his letters that he met the president."

"Lincoln?" Henry Williams asked.

"Well, I hope it wasn't Jefferson Davis," Maurice Cunningham replied.

Jeremiah continued: "Jesse said he was big and tall and as powerful as the light of heaven. Said the troops were wearied and beaten down on a Saturday afternoon, sitting around a fire trying to keep their feet warm against the coals, and Lincoln comes riding up and gets off a horse . . ."

"Lincoln wasn't riding no horse," Alexander Fitzgerald said.

"Well, in the letter he was," Jeremiah sneered. "Anyway, the letter said Lincoln stopped and talked to every soldier, and Jesse asked him what it was like being president and Lincoln told him it was like fighting a million wars."

"If I'd been out there," Lyle Bickleton spoke up, "I would have asked him what he could do to bring my boy back the way he started. That's what I would've asked him."

The men fell quiet, each one shifting a little on their sacks.

"I'm sure he'll write," Henry Williams said to Jeremiah. "You know how boys are. Give them a taste of freedom and they hardly remember that they have parents anymore. You'll hear from him." To which the other men looked to the floor and grunted a reserved affirmation.

The clouds completely blanketed the sky to hide the sun, causing Thaddeus to stomp his foot and cry out an indistinguishable word.

"Thaddeus," Jeremiah called back, and Thaddeus stomped his foot again, and his father yelled back, "Stop."

"Now if that boy were fighting for the Union," Ralph Crispin eyeballed Thaddeus, "we'd probably have won this war ten times over."

The men laughed for a moment, then collapsed back into the pause of silence.

Thaddeus walked over to his father and stood before him with a blank expression. His eyes wandered to the side and his hands opened and closed into fists, as though just discovering them.

"Thaddeus knows who Lincoln is," Jeremiah said with pride, looking at the boy.

"You know Lincoln, Thaddeus? Big old ugly guy with the beard on his chin?" Henry Williams asked.

"Lincoln," Thaddeus said, and the men all smiled, especially Henry Williams, who had grabbed his lapels while pantomiming the president.

"Well, we'd better get going," Jeremiah said. "Gonna go check on the mail to see if there's any news from Jesse, then go back home and see how Becka's doing . . . And Thaddeus can feed the horses," to which the men sang back, *Oh, Thaddeus, you're gonna feed the horses, what a good man,* and Thaddeus just rolled his tongue over his lips, completely unaware of anything but the clouds.

The father and son walked slowly down Jefferson Street. With an unexpected mix of panic and purpose,

Thaddeus gripped his father's arm and tugged down. Jeremiah ignored him, but Thaddeus pulled harder, and after a short battle, Jeremiah stopped and blurted out, "What?"

Thaddeus stubbornly pulled to the side, breathing heavily through his nose. "Come on, Thaddeus," his father said impatiently, but the boy wouldn't relent. White spit gathered at the corners of his lips.

An eye-burning wind kicked up and the dust swirled in spinning tops and miniature tornadoes. Thaddeus continued his lumbering sidesteps, dragging his father until they eventually stood before the platform of the train depot, smelling the smoking coal and livestock off the massive Southern Midland parked at the station. A depot sign painted in red was beaten illegible by the seasons. It flapped with the wind.

"What's with you and this train station?"

The train gave three sharp whistles and began to pull away from the deck. The grinding metal off the tracks was so remarkable that the body could do nothing other than absorb the sound. And soon a flurry of people, mostly women, all walked away from the platform with their heads down, having waved off the next round of troops, each carrying an expression of sorrow that was masked by the optimistic hope that it would be somebody else's son and not theirs who would arrive back home draped in an American flag, carried back on the same

train that took them out. And this group walked slowly,
the motion of their legs seeming as dreamlike and steady
as the wheels of the train carrying them down the steps
and off the platform.

Thaddeus and his father kept moving forward through
more and more people trampling the dust, and it seemed
as though everyone was wearing brown or tan or some
related color, all walking in silence with bowed heads.

Once the platform finally emptied, the boy pulled him
up the steps to the precise spot where Jesse had boarded
the train some eight months back. Thaddeus knelt down
and touched his palm to the planks, running his hands
back and forth, feeling for something, while he stared out
at the tracks.

Jeremiah bent down next to his son and placed a warm
hand on the boy's back, but Thaddeus didn't seem to
notice. He was still too busy patting his hand along the
platform slats.

"Did you find it?" Jeremiah stood up, uncertain what
to do. "What you're looking for?"

Thaddeus cocked his head to the side, his gaze as lost as
dying stars.

"What is it you're looking for, son?"

Tears pooled in the corners of his helpless eyes. The
water then rolled down Thaddeus's cheeks in several thin
falls, gluing the dust to his face until it caked disturbingly
festive, like glitter.

The boy couldn't stop crying. His tears ran harder and the dust turned to mud. His chest heaved up and down while his hand grasped at the floor like a blind man lost.

Jeremiah reached out to him.

Thaddeus kept his head cocked, looking up impotently at his father.

So confused.

The Willie Grief

Dear Mary:

In this troubled world, we are never quite satisfied.

—APRIL 16, 1848

✳   ✳   ✳

Mary Todd Lincoln had just about taken all that she could take when Edwin Stanton chuckled at her assertion that the war had seemed like it would never end, and maybe there had already been enough dying to make the point. "There are some things that you needn't concern yourself with," Stanton admonished. Another Washington bureaucrat who knew nothing of the war besides what the maps and telegrams showed him, no doubt using it to bolster his credentials. And there he stood, in the president's office, a stout little pudge barely knee high to the lanky Mr. Lincoln, the two of them in comic disproportion.

Sometimes her husband could be so sterile. Since Willie's death he had hardly been able to look her in the eye. She couldn't recall him ever even saying Willie's name to her. As if to ensure that the subject was never broached, he began working through the night, crawling into bed under the dying light of a blown-out candle, and pulling back the covers with a cool draft that drifted over her legs like a nervous ghost. She wasn't easy to be around. She acknowledged that truth. Her days stretched long, and the nights were frightful with the knowledge that the first sprig of sunlight would reveal a new day, one more without Willie. The indulging pity wearing her down until there was nothing left other than a pleading cry to be noticed. Sometimes she wished her husband would just hold her. Squeeze the maniacal grief that possessed her. Taste her tears. Get really mad and scream out that he missed Willie like a sonabitch. They could struggle for breath together, writhing on the bed angry and sad, cursing the injustice that a man who is potentially more powerful than God cannot find peace in this world. Then maybe they could hold each other with the passion they had known in Springfield. She could tell him that Willie was still here, and if they held on long enough, he too would see the light that sometimes darted across the bedroom window and know that it was their son passing by, checking in to make sure that his mother's grief didn't fatally consume her. Instead her husband had turned scared. The fear made him cold. And by the true definition of a man, he swallowed back his emotions and threw himself into his work. As though it were the only truth.

Lincoln stepped aside from Stanton and looked down at his secretary. "Mr. Stanton," he said formally, "the first lady has been personally touched by this war in a way that you and I wouldn't understand." The office turned pallid as a passing cloud shadowed the sun from the window, reinforcing the dullness of the decor's stale antiquity.

Stanton prodded his fingers through the coarse gray bristles of his beard. His spectacles had fallen to the tip of his nose, highlighting its dented bulb and flared nostrils, and he peered his veiny blues over the tops of the frames. "Please pardon my neglect at remembering the loss of your brother."

"Sam Todd was a good man," Lincoln said. "And even if he died with a Confederate flag in his hand at Shiloh, he was still a man of principle." He reached for her hand, and held it in chivalrous mourning. "Mary's right. The war has dragged on too long. And it has bared its shame in the tearing apart of families like the Todds."

"My prayers," Stanton offered.

In her husband's hand she understood the commitment that made so many people believe in him, how the power of his fingers wrapped around her sweating palm in righteous honesty. But the death of her half brother had hardly stunned her. She couldn't remember the last time she had seen him, could barely remember what he looked like other than having the same almond eyes and symmetrically round face as all progeny of the Robert Todd seedling. There were fifteen brothers and sisters to complete the Todd set, each one as boring as the next. She hadn't liked most of them while growing up, and she had certainly lost all feeling for them when her husband had become president and they said the things they did,

proving that politics is indeed thicker than blood. Her
husband didn't understand that, and she hadn't bothered
to try to explain. It would be beyond his comprehension
that a sister wouldn't mourn the death of her brother. So
he felt compelled to comfort her, and that was okay. But
she didn't understand why he never did that when Willie
died. Even holding her hand as he did now would have
staved off a million miles of misery.

Mary's stomach started to turn light, and her hands
grew tingly and shaky. The grief over Willie's death was
washing through her, as it could randomly do. She saw the
familiar picture of her boy, pale and consumed with
disease, as he had looked desperately to her without a sense
of peace or calm, as the preachers would like to believe, but
with a gut-wrenching fear of feeling his life slipping away.
She felt the sick helplessness that she harbored at not
having the ability to stop Willie's suffering, or even comfort
him—a feeling that never went away, only sometimes
hibernated if she was lucky. She ran her tongue over her
cracked dry lips, and fought for air through her panting
nostrils. She dropped her husband's useless hand when the
sweat turned a clammy cold, and turned her head to
swallow, instantly nauseated by the must and mites that
inhabited the red velvet chairs of her husband's office.

Lincoln stepped away. His eyes fixed stiff and cold, as
though watching a concoction of clouds turn to storm.
He stepped closer to Stanton, nervously pushing the hand
that had just held hers into his pocket. His big yellow

teeth worked themselves into his bottom lip, gnawing and chewing, while his Adam's apple lumped in and out.

Stanton spoke in a voice of semi-authority to deliver the exit line. "Mr. President, we are expected at the State Department to review the battle reports."

Lincoln nodded too quickly, as though the patron saint of relief had just spoken, and added, "We shouldn't keep them waiting."

Mary focused her stare out the window behind her husband's desk, watching the sunlight wind its way down the wisteria vines in thin green streams, with some points just touching the edges of the shriveled brown buds with a teasing glow. The blood gathered in her stomach and welled into a fury that kicked and screamed to come out, but her exterior remained staid, padded by a thick layer of cultured gentility. "Then you better go," she said, followed by a long inhalation.

Stanton looked back, his head half bowed. "Once, again, Mary, my prayers."

"Save them for a just god," she muttered. Then she said it again as he walked out the door, so he could hear her loud and clear.

✣   ✣   ✣

Mary Todd Lincoln sat in the carriage riding backward on a slow, lonely trip up Seventh Street heading toward Campbell Hospital on the north end of town. The horses seemed bitterly restrained, barely moving, perhaps in protest at having to tug a carriage through Washington on what might have been the coldest day ever to have come sweeping down the Potomac. The sky was clear, with an icy blue edge to it. The boards of the sidewalk looked shiny and new pushed up against the empty streets. Brownstones stood tall and still, with curled whiskers of smoke winding out the chimneys, their windows frosted and steamed with hand-smeared peepholes wilting in condensation, behind which the illusion of ordinary life played itself out without tragedy.

When her grief overtook her, making it nearly impossible to move or sit still, she liked to go out to the military hospitals to visit the wounded boys. Talk to them. Maybe hold their hands. Try to feel the power of life fighting for a chance, instead of hopelessly expiring in shattered deliverance. Sometimes she took her boy Tad along and let his tiny little grip escort her through the wards as though he were a guide dog. Other times she needed to be alone, in order to not be weighted by the expectations of being Mother and having to monitor her expressions and emotions to prevent uncertainty or distress in the boy. The visits went better when she was alone. Without Tad by her side, the infirm rarely recognized her as the first lady. The anonymity liberated her to comfort from compassion and not from politics. For once she could just listen without having to indulge in her own misery.

With the road turned to ice, the carriage bumped over

frozen divots and shimmied an occasional slide from side to side. She closed her eyes and tried to imagine how the young debutante who had boarded at Shelby's and Madame Mentelle's studying French and dance, the belle of Lexington who was living proof of God's exquisite plan, had come to be this fragile shell of a woman whose soul was left pillaged by the deaths of two of her children. Her once-thick dark hair now appeared teased and light. The skin that had defined her proud jaw now pouched into little jowls, and her watery eyes were loosely set upon dark half-moon pillows. Her hands, once delicate and smooth as porcelain, were ragged and bent into odd positions, resting on a waistline that had expanded into a permanent reminder of her unhappiness.

✤   ✤   ✤

The wards of Campbell Hospital were long and narrow. They were separate buildings made of rough gray boards and built low to the ground, with a dining area in the middle, and surrounded by a sprawl of pale landscape textured in rotted tree trunks. Injured boys by the hundreds lined the interior of each ward with their cots evenly spaced. They stayed there until they recovered. Or went to the dead house next to the Negro quarters. These boys were lonely and scared, casualties from all over the map who had been sent to the military hospital because the field hospitals had run out of treatments. Most didn't know a soul. Delirious from pain. Stunned by the cold.

Starved by the rations. Only able to count on the goodwill of the nurses and women who took the time to touch their arms, or sing a mother's melody, or just tell them that they would be all right while the infections bore away their insides worse than any rebel bullet could ever do.

Mary Lincoln stepped down from the coach red-cheeked against the bitter cold, and told the driver to circle for an hour. She quickly tucked her hands under her overcoat when she felt the joints stiffen, feeling the cruel intentions of the elements.

She entered Ward 3 shamelessly aware of how free she felt from the confining burdens of being Mrs. Lincoln. Her step fell lighter as her shoes touched the plank floors, the sounds of the convalescent machine in full operation gracefully lifting her out of the silent bitterness of the bedroom walls. At home in this company of mangled strangers.

She had been here twice before, each time startled by the smell—the stench of rotting flesh, diarrhea, and sour mold. A thin streak of bile rose up her throat and stung the back of her tongue. She forced herself to swallow it back, and marched deeper into the ward. Powerless men lay side by side on green cots spaced no more than six inches apart, pails filled with blood-soaked towels set between them. Their warm breath, visible against the cold, rose above them like hovering souls. The uniform moans of pain and melancholia made a low vibrating hum, a basslike bottom against the frantic treble of the nurses barking orders back and forth across the cots, desperately trying to gather the attention of the doctors, who looked worn and exhausted by their idle attempts to heal and cure.

Mary carefully walked down the center aisle looking for someone who seemed in need of company. A hand latched on to the back of her black coat and tugged, startling her. She turned to see the desperate face of a woman about her age, skinny and tired, with dry eyes shifting in fear. "Are you a nurse?" the woman asked Mary. "Are you a nurse?"

"I'm not," Mary said. She looked at the woman's white-knuckle hold on her sleeve. "I'm sorry."

The woman dropped her hand, letting it dangle awkwardly before bringing it up to her neck, nervously scratching a red spot. "My boy is in so much pain . . . so much . . . I'm just looking for some help, is all. Just looking for some help."

Mary had to turn away. She didn't want to see a desperate mother holding on with the fruitless belief that her terminal son might make it. She couldn't bear to see the false hope or the wishing or the naked fear. That was not why she came here. Even as she walked briskly down the row, she could hear the woman repeating that her boy was in pain. Maybe she wanted Mary to turn around with the kindness of a stranger and grab both of her hands and look her in the eye and tell her not to worry. Mary just walked faster. She couldn't handle hearing that selfish self-pity for one more second.

At the last cot in the row, a boy lay flat on his back, his ghost-white face peering above an olive blanket cinched around his neck. A pillow pushed against the crown of his head. There must have been at least 150 boys warehoused in this ward, and for some reason this nondescript one caught her attention. Maybe it was the diffident expression on his face, gone beyond resignation and self-pity into a state of nothing other than existence. His hands were tucked in at his sides, while his teeth chattered from the cold. He shifted his eyes up to Mary and spoke in a confident whisper, "They say you lose ninety percent of your body heat from your head."

Mary Lincoln took that as an invitation. She asked if she might, and sat down in one of the visitor's chairs made from whittled pine and straw—gifts from some old man's rotary to help the cause. She self-consciously shifted her bottom from side to side to test it against her weight, then settled in. The boy rolled his eyes over to her, and kept a plain expression that was neither welcoming nor off-putting. He kept his stare fixed on her without moving an inch of his body. Maybe he was one of those boys who had been caught in the cannon fire and only survived from the waist up, with arms and legs severed from infection. She imagined the grotesque figure that would lie beneath that wool blanket, a chest and abdomen that might at first have the appearance of a strong healthy boy's, but made hideous by the wretchedly crude carvings of shrapnel and a hurried field doctor. And maybe at the bottom of the awkward and uneven torso, his penis hung nestled against his testicles, forever useless except to involuntarily wet the bed.

"That's why I keep the pillow on top of my head," he said. "Keeps me warm." He wrestled an arm out from under the covers and clumsily adjusted the pillow up over his forehead, just above his grimacing eyebrows, like a malformed bishop's crown.

"It is cold in here, isn't it?" she said, relieved to know that he indeed had arms.

"Like a witch's tit." He spoke again in that hard whisper, as though that was all that his lungs would allow. "Not one ounce of heat pumped into this joint. Stoves don't do a thing. Never even this kind of cold in Brooklyn."

Mary leaned in, almost seduced by the will of his struggle to talk, and the care he took in the choosing and eliminating of words in context with his shortened breath. "You're from New York?" she asked.

"No. Brooklyn." He tried to roll to the side to face her, arching his knee (thank God!) up for support, but instead rocked back again to his vulnerable position like a helpless beetle. His face turned a deep red as he struggled for breath, then all his features, maybe Irish or Scottish in physiognomy, contorted and contracted into one long grimace that quickly released itself. He rolled his eyes back over to her with a sigh.

"You are a long way from home, soldier."

"Go where they tell you to." The pain in his voice surrounded his words in a nearly visible warble.

"My name is Mary." She placed her hand on his chest. His shallow breaths felt oddly dry against her fingers. The pure simplicity of his life, with the only mission being to take in air, made her eyes begin to water. She began to swallow back every urge to cry, until she realized that she wasn't really sad. Just moved.

"You're not coming to sell me something, no religious speech, or anything? Fruitcakes come through that door like it's a free-for-all."

Mary smiled, and for once the smile felt genuine, not the mannered dilettante expression guided by protocol. "I'm just here to visit anybody who wants the company."

He looked her over again, then nodded. "I could use the company."

"And so could I."

They sat in the white noise of crippled screams and hollow cries. The nurses' shoes squeaking along the planks. Odd rhythms of metal clanging so disjointed that it had nearly become symphonic. The bitter timbre of hard, frozen fear.

The boy never stopped looking at Mary. His eyes were

sea green, deep as an untouched cove, brilliant against his pale skin. A tuft of red hair mussed out from the pillow, its luster dulled by lack of nutrition and oil. When he smiled to introduce himself, his teeth looked charred but straight. His name was Sean. "Sean Connely," he elaborated.

Mary told him it was a pleasure to make his proper acquaintance, and said the name sounded Irish.

"The name is," he spoke freely, despite his pained whisper, "but not the boy. Folks left Ireland before they were too old to leave."

"I'm sure they're good people," Mary said.

"Seamus and Moira Connely are their names. Two brothers. We all went to enlist. The folks were relieved of the responsibility. They can barely handle one another."

"I'm sure they are proud of you."

Sean turned his head a little more to the side. "Mary, could you do me a favor?"

"I don't know."

"If I get you the address, tell my parents that I'm doing okay? How I am."

"I can help you write a letter."

"I don't have that much to say."

"I will tell them I met with you," she said. "I can wire a telegram. I'll tell them where you are, what's been going on, and whatever else they want to know."

"They don't ask much. The caring scares them."

"I'll tell Moira and Seamus that I met with you."

Behind them the crazed mother came wandering down the aisle crying out, "Nurse, nurse! My boy needs a dusting of morphine. Nurse, nurse! Somebody help me. Him. An opium pill." Mary inhaled in contempt, disgusted at the woman's lack of humility and total disregard for everyone else who didn't want to hear it; then she exhaled, willing that woman to keep to her end of the ward.

"You hear all kinds of things in here," Sean said.

Mary nodded, embarrassed by her selfishness, and hoping it was not too transparent, because she really did feel calmness in being here with Sean. Something about the struggling will of the boy's voice inspired hope, and she wanted to just keep listening. "And what happened with you?" she asked. "How did you get here?"

"Don't really know. A battle in Virginia. Pure craziness all around, and I tripped over the leg of this clumsy pisser named Peters. Then a sound over my ear buzzing like a million-pound mosquito. Woke up here with a bullet cornered in my lung, and aimed right at my heart. Been out cold for five days."

"And that's why you don't—"

"If I move too sudden the bullet goes right into my heart." His voice was tighter, as though he could barely dislodge the words from his chest. "If I'm real unlucky, it'll push backward into my lung and drain me flat."

"What do the doctors say?"

"Hope that it works itself out."

One thing Mary hated about doctors was how they all walk around so high and mighty, like they hold the key and password to enter God's most exquisite creation, but when you really call upon them, when you need real help, they toss out some drugs and throw their hands up and use words like *hope* and *pray,* and tell you that some things are greater than man. "Maybe I can get someone here to look at you," she offered. "Not one of these washed-up army kinds, but a real doctor."

Sean didn't answer. His eyes didn't even brighten at the prospect. Maybe he didn't want to be a charity case, or maybe he just really didn't care at this point. Or perhaps he knew the real truth, the same one that kept Mary from continuing on: that even a real doctor wouldn't know shit about what to do except hope and pray.

"Is there anything I can do for you right now?" she asked.

He shook his head, causing the pillow to lose its place. "Maybe just sit for a few more minutes until the nurse gives me my morphine. Pain sneaks up on you and stabs you blind. Nurses here are psychic when it comes to needing morphine . . . Please wait. At least until the shit knocks me out."

Mary leaned forward and maternally edged the pillow back into place. She ran the back of her hand along his cheek, feeling the moist tenderness of his skin, cheeks too young to be roughened by whiskers, just the softness of the thin blond hairs he was born with. She might have broken down and cried right then, tortured by the fact that Willie was so much younger on his deathbed; instead she felt calmed and oddly reassured, as though some preserved precious moment was deliberately being shown to her.

She started to draw her hand away. Sean rolled his face over and trapped her fingers against his cheek. He didn't say anything. Just a sad childlike smile.

"It's okay," she told him.

The nurse appeared by the bed. She was tall and young, her amber hair twisted and layered into a bun that she pinned to the back of her head. The beauty of her face was hidden in exhaustion, with eyes that seemed like they could care but had instead been willed and trained to professionalism, knowing the caring could destroy her. She spoke tenderly, with a trace of southern laziness that punctuated the ends of her sentences. "Well, hello, Mr. Connely," she said. "How's the chest today?"

Sean peered up at her. "Like hell, Sharon."

She reached into her pocket and pulled out a syringe, the metal dulled in fingerprints, the tip of the needle fogged from the cold.

"I'll have the usual," he said.

Sharon smiled politely at the joke she had no doubt heard a thousand times over on her rounds. She glanced down at Mary's hand tucked under the boy's face, then looked over at her. "Are you a relative?" she asked in what appeared to be a tone of genuine interest.

"Just a friend." Mary smiled.

The needle caught the reflection of a lamp. It looked like a flame. "Thank goodness for boys like Mr. Connely here," Sharon said. "Wouldn't you say so?" A lightning scream from across the ward seemed to penetrate the whole room, then died just as quickly.

Mary looked down at Sean's pale face.

"Giving their hearts and souls so we can keep our dignity." She tapped the syringe twice to remove excess air. A chemical tear balled on the edge of the hypodermic.

Without moving his head, Sean offered his left arm. Sharon squinted one eye for aim, and slid the needle under his skin. She depressed the syringe's head with her thumb in a manner so mechanized that its precision seemed perfection. "Very good, now," she said. "You rest up, Mr. Connely, and I'll check back after a couple of hours. And, remember, no sitting up. You'll rip the stitches from your chest." Sharon smiled at Mary. "Nice meeting you. Pity the circumstance." She dropped the spent syringe into her pocket, then walked into the aisle under a dull yellow light that outlined her hipless figure. Gone to the next bed. As though she was never there.

Sean's eyes followed Sharon, then settled back on his visitor. "Used to get whiskey before the shot."

"Is it better now?" Mary stroked his shoulder with her free hand.

"Springwater driving through my veins," Sean narrated. "No cold anymore. I forget how hard it is to breathe. Just lay back and go to sleep. Lucky to get to forget."

Mary felt his cheeks flushing warmer. His eyelids seemed to be swelling, with his green irises in full bloom bathed in sleepy tears. "Glad you came by," he said in a whisper that was dropping into sleep. "I'll live a little stronger. Thanks for the comfort."

Mary nodded. "Thank you for the comfort." She watched his eyes close and felt his breathing lighten against her hand. She cautiously worked her palm out from under his cheek, although it appeared that now nothing would disturb him. She pulled the blanket up to his neck and fixed his pillow back into place. She thought about kissing him, but that felt too intimate and she wasn't really sure she had that right.

When Mary Lincoln stood up, the reality of the ward came rushing over her in a tumbling, jostling wave that nearly knocked her off her feet. The cries. The writhing. The rot. The reality that this was not going to end. That she would walk out that door and go back to the mansion, and mothers would still be screaming, and boys begging for anything to kill the pain, and doctors cutting and hacking and drugging and praying, and nurses and women staking their responsibility for comfort, and in every minute of every day knowing that the pain she has felt for Willie is being replayed over and over in wards like this throughout the country. She thinks of how embarrassed she is by her last name, and that maybe she'll just go by the name of Todd because she can't bear the thought of being associated with any of the responsibility for this suffering.

A nervous humming panicked over the top of her skin. Mary ran down the hall without looking at any of the patients. Past the screaming mother. Past the weary nurses. She slammed the door of her waiting coach and turned down the bolt until she was certain that it locked.

The horses trotted their way down Seventh Street back toward Pennsylvania Avenue. Washington still felt quiet, content to be quarantined from the terror and misery that breathed beyond its borders. Mary watched the frozen city float by through the window. She had the odd sensation of feeling better. Even when she felt an echo of her own grief wash over, she noticed that it didn't hurt as much. Mary closed her eyes and tried not to understand. Just let herself be taken along by the rhythm of the horses.

❖　❖　❖

She never got Sean Connely's parents' address that day. Nor did she ever go back to Campbell Hospital again. Her husband tried once or twice to get her the information, but nobody at the hospital could seem to produce that kind of detail.

The grief for Willie still washed over her.

Sometimes she thought of Sean.

Sometimes it made her feel better.

Sometimes it didn't.

$\mathcal{H}$is Stepmother's Sister

Towering genius distains a beaten path. It seeks regions hitherto unexplored.

—JANUARY 27, 1838

❋   ❋   ❋

Abraham Lincoln didn't go to his stepmother's sister's funeral. He stood in the middle of one of those shit-dry Indiana roads whose dusty clouds would become nondescript to his memory, and looked up once to the hill where the small crowd gathered around a six-foot hole in the ground, a black parson's coat, and an open Bible. He watched for a moment, holding a clear bottle of homemade whiskey that his father had not-so-secretly stored under the bed frame, the side where his mother had both slept and died some years ago.

His father's aching posture was perched right over the funeral hole. The half-familiar faces, ragged and terror-stricken, of those who came to funerals like a social outing, stood a pace back, heads routinely bowed, over that poor woman now wrapped snugly in a white cotton sheet in order to hold in the disease, with the pine top slats nailed down shut in a kingdom of fury to ward off the devil and the gophers. And goddamn she shouldn't have had to die so young. But the Lord has a plan, somebody had said. Well, fuck the plan, how about a doctor who knows about more than just praying? But they say that's part of Indiana living. Where the only thing you can count on is the change of seasons. You certainly can't count on love. Or the doctors.

He walked along the road some more, until a glance over his shoulder revealed a wave of empty, dry, brown meadows, where he eventually sat down. The haggard grass broke under him and formed an imprint of his long, dangling frame. He took the bottle of whiskey he'd been carrying and gripped the cork in the butt of his hand, wrestling it until the thing broke off halfway into the bottle. Abraham studied the stray piece floating just below the neck. Cruel fumes leaked out in a brutal medicinal odor that watered his eyes and singed his nostrils, yet somehow seduced his body into a sense of immediate longing and craving. And with that he took the first sip. A long thin stream that burned and bored its way down his throat and through his chest. His head exploding in a suicide of thoughts that would never allow him to even look back at his old Indiana home.

And under a dull, clouded sky, the young man came to understand the curse. To be born into a world of thick heads and iron muscles, where the real purpose to living is to work your body so goddamn much that you don't have the energy to hear or think your thoughts, and every available milligram of calorie is just enough to swallow your food and get to bed in order to rise again the next day. And such is the legacy of the Lincolns. Sonabitch slaves to themselves. And sometimes you want to know more. Sometimes you've really got a desire to learn about more than Jesus, suffering, and redemption. You want to think about things. Stop dwelling on the how and get to the why. And he told his stepmother about that one day, and she guessed it was okay, "but don't tell your father."

And the young Abe asked why not.

"Your father only makes time for Jesus and work."

"That sounds no different than the Negro slave."

"Just don't tell your father about these thoughts that you have."

Abe just looked at his stepmother seated on a stump, framed by the rickety gray boards that made their house, under a bleached yellow spotlight. A summer day so intense with heat, and she was wearing a black dress that started right below her chin and didn't stop until it touched the back of her heels. And she looked so impossibly tragic. Whereas she couldn't be more than twenty-eight years old, the wear on her face looked centuries old. And her eyes stayed close together, her brow in a permanent frown as if she were always trying to remember something. And before her stood her stepson, the innocence ringing hollow in his bones, and sometimes, he sensed, she couldn't bear to look him in the eye because she knew that this was where it ended. That outside the hymnals there was no such thing as hope. In spite of her brave posture, her thick shoulders squared off perfectly and her neck held stiff with her chin up, it was her heart that beat soft, and it made the stepson whom she taught to read at the young and tender age of eight so miserably sad to think of her that way. So much so that there were nights when he couldn't even sleep, his father snoring a laborer's song while his stepmother lay motionless, and Abe just looked up at the knots in the ceiling, the same ones night after night, and contemplated the impossibility of change.

There is no justice for the living.

And now her sister was dead.

He emptied the bottle with one last swig, then lay back into the grass, inhaling the sweet perfume of the breaking straw. The heat would certainly stay through the night. And with that he closed his eyes. And buried his stepmother's sister.

✦ ✦ ✦

Abraham Lincoln awoke the next morning to the squawk of an ugly flat bird that flapped its big black wings in spastic frenzy before building enough stamina to let itself catch the wind and glide over the countryside. Abe's head was dizzy from the alcohol still trapped in his veins. He stood carefully, his long, agile bones settling into the form of a man. He looked forward at the hills, the stalks bending with the wind. And below him an old dirt road narrowed until it spiked the horizon. There wasn't a Lincoln ever who knew for sure if anything lay beyond there.

Good-bye, old Thomas Lincoln.

You miserable fuck-up of a father and husband. Dumb as shit, and vicious in your ignorance.

And please don't be cruel to Sarah Bush Lincoln.

He walked forward into a dense Indiana sunlight mixed thick with yellow and orange, knowing that he might be walking into death itself. His legs moved fluidly, while his heart raced a million beats a second. A slow dry breath passed over his lips. And with each step the sun burned his eyes a little more, until thin tears peeked over his bony cheeks, and he didn't really know if he was crying from the rays or from the fear that built inside at the truth that he had no idea where he was going, what he was doing, and even more important, who he was besides the son to a dumb-as-shit farmer who hated his son for not being as dumb as he was.

And with that he kept walking.

Walking.

Walking.

Walking.

✧   ✧   ✧

In the kerosene-lit hallways of the Executive Mansion, with the sounds of carriage clocks ticking behind doors and alarms going off to signal somebody's change of shift, the president walks alone. The flickering wicks throw his shadow as a distorted ghost along the walls. And he thinks about that day when he left Indiana. He thinks about it often. How his bravest moment was really just tightly knit strands of fear. And when he thinks about it his eyes still burn, and his heart pounds a little deeper. Then, as with every other thought that crosses his mind, he inevitably starts to picture Willie. Picturing the almost consumptive glow on his face in the days before he passed, and when he starts to see the eyes, the helpless drifting blues, that is the point where he forgets he is the president and quickens his stride, his big heavy feet bending the boards of the floor, hurrying into his office where he can stick his leg as his own angel of mercy, and instantaneously forget about Willie with the first prick, the coolness of the morphine icing through the top of his thigh and racing over his legs until his head goes clear and there is nothing to see at all except the shadows of the branches sweeping in long brushes against the purple night windows.

He closes his eyes, resting his head against the high-back leather chair. Indiana back in his mind. The straw smell of the dehydrated hills. A mind that had gone cloudy from the numb of the alcohol. A boy orphaned to a new land. And so goddamned scared.

So scared.

When he thinks of that day he feels comfort. Because nothing has really changed.

Once the morphine finally reaches his head he starts to drift into sleep. Knowing that in the morning he'll wake up and walk away from tonight.

A Letter to President Lincoln from a Good Girl

It may seem strange that any men should dare to ask a just God's assistance in wringing their bread from the sweat of other men's faces.

—MARCH 4, 1865

※　　※　　※

O Mr. Lincoln, I'm just a someone from southern Pennsylvania who's been wasted away upon for her whole life.

I'm a woman who married when I was supposed to, tried to anchor my legs to a floor and believe in God and everything else I was told. I washed the vegetables, scrubbed the dirt out from between the stalks, and boiled them until they were just ripe for eating. And I sat down at the table and pressed my palms together and bowed my head, and prayed for the Lord to give me just enough strength to continue on.

O Mr. Lincoln, my husband, Ansel Williams, was nothing short of a bastard. He was so handsome and kind when I first met him. But as time passed, an anger brewed in his eyes, and his once tender hands turned to calloused gloves that would rip the robe from my body and grab the inside of my thigh and squeeze so hard that bruises appeared. Then he would shoot his hands up and grab my breasts, squeezing my nipples while he groaned over my ear that I was Daddy's little girl; and he'd spread my legs and force himself inside me, pushing and pushing and pushing until he was done, when he would slap me across the cheek with the back of his hand and tell me what a whore I was.

When your war came my husband went off to fight. The night before he left to join the Pennsylvania Regiment, Ansel put on a mean whiskey drunk. He staggered himself blind across our house holding his arms out for balance and knocking into everything in sight. I tried to help him but he said I was useless and in the way as he backhanded me to the floor. "You little . . . ," he said, and he pushed up my dress and grabbed the whiskey bottle and shoved it inside of me, twisting it around, side to side, scraping and tearing until I felt warm streams of blood crawling down my leg. It was like when I was fifteen, nearly fainting in a wagon ride in Harrisburg, where an older boy called Josiah had said he could make me feel good and reached his hand over my crotch and had tried to wiggle his fingers under the seam of my undergarments. I had let him leave them there because I was unsure of what I should do, then just scooted slowly away into the corner against a mattress of hay and dropped my head and said a prayer to Jesus, for he had always watched me up until then, and I asked Jesus please don't let my father find out because he lives his life in fear and I would do nothing to make him more fearful because I am a good girl. The anger in Ansel's strength brought forth a devil's howl, and he kept repeating *whore,*

whore, then said how he'd like to rape me with a gun, squeeze the trigger, and see the bullet come out the crown of my head.

He left the next morning to fight the Confederate Army. I hugged him good-bye, but I didn't look in his eyes. I didn't want to remember them. I was hoping he would never come back.

A few months later, a blond boy, no more than eighteen years old, who slurred his name, knocked on my door and said my husband had been killed at Shenandoah. Said a Confederate cannon had landed at his feet with an explosion so quick and so fierce that my husband had already been sunk down before he knew what happened. The boy confessed that Ansel was sonabitch and that his death was celebrated by some in his company, and then the boy looked away and said, "I'm sorry to have offended you, ma'am," and I said not to worry, "I would've shot the cannon myself if I had the chance." The boy looked at me with half a smile, not sure if I was kidding or not, then sat down on the sofa, his uniform buckling at the knees.

O Mr. Lincoln, I am not a whore like Ansel said, and I swear against my soul that it was an almost godly purity that washed through me like a warm bath. And Lord knows I can't explain it, but I reached my arms around that boy with the same ferocity of Ansel, except not with anger, but with passion. And with no shame I took down his pants and pulled the curtain of my dress above my waist. I made him go inside of me. All the while thinking about him telling me of Ansel's deserved demise.

My body started heaving and shaking like a celebration, and as the boy's legs stiffened, I whispered, "Tell me again what happened."

He could barely talk from breathing so hard. "Cannon got him."

"And what happened when the cannon got him?" I grabbed the behind of the young boy and pushed him even harder into me.

"Blew him to smithereens."

My thighs dripped when I asked him what he saw.

"I don't know if I can recall," he moaned.

I ran the tip of my tongue delicately around the inside of his ear, and when a chill ran over his back, I whispered for him to think harder.

He remembered seeing a leg hanging almost the whole way off at the knee. "Tendons," he said, "just like on a chicken bone, hanging and bloody."

And I asked if Ansel screamed, and the boy said Ansel was trying but the pain must have been so great that he couldn't make a full sound, only something that sounded like a slow noise.

"Make the noise. Go in and out of me and make the noise."

The boy stopped for a moment, his body uncertain. "Be a good boy," I whispered as an almost manic tribute to Ansel's way, "make the noise."

The soldier's knees buckled and we rolled off the couch and thudded to the floor, taking a few objects along the way. He stayed on top, then pulled his neck back to look at me. A drunken look was in his eyes; he could've pulled out, yanked his pants up high, anchored his suspenders to his shoulders, and, not even bothering to straighten his hair, walked straight out the door in a combination of triumph and shame.

O Mr. Lincoln, I must have had a devil inside me, because as soon as I saw the indecision in that boy's eyes I dug my nails deep into the flesh of his bottom and said, "Make the noise," then pushed him so hard that my shoulders knocked against the floor.

The boy groaned an imitation of Ansel's wound. A high falsetto sigh that sung from the throat and echoed through the hollows of the cheeks. The spirit flew from my body; I was beginning to feel beauty in Ansel's pain.

"And then . . . ?" I said.

"Then," he whispered, "he threw his body into a convulsion." The soldier arched his back up, then let it down with a long breath.

"On the battlefield?" I sighed.

"In a thick mist."

"And then . . . ?"

"Oh God," he cried out Ansel's last words, "please don't take . . . Oh God, you're such an ass . . . You're such a jackass, God."

With a louder version of the falsetto cry, my whole

body tensed and contracted into one single muscle, just balling up and waiting to give in. "And then what?" I called out.

"And then," the eighteen-year-old moaned, "he died with just a long sigh," and the boy moaned from the bottom of his gut, as he doubled in size then grabbed my hair as though he really could love me.

"Those were Ansel's sighs?"

The soldier screamed yes, and once I saw Ansel die in the horror he deserved, my body exploded, and lightning crept from the crown of my head and didn't stop until my toes had cramped.

He tried to kiss me but I turned away.

I went into my bedroom and sat on the end of the bed. I didn't come out until I knew he was gone.

❖   ❖   ❖

O Mr. Lincoln, I'm good girl from Pennsylvania who has been raised by fear and by God. And I believe in purity and the beauty that it brings. I will go to heaven, Mr. Lincoln, I will. Ansel Williams robbed my goodness and soul, and I did what I could to get it back. He died in your war, Mr. Lincoln, died. He was a cruel sonabitch who was hated by all, deceived his God, and broke his vows.

It was no dirty deed with that young boy, it was salvation, and I guess, Mr. Lincoln, that I have to wrestle with the shame of salvation. When I see you, Mr. Lincoln,

I see your eyes and I know you fight the same battle. It hurts so much and there is nothing but loneliness.

I'm not ashamed of what I've done, Mr. Lincoln. Although I admit I should be ashamed of celebrating the death of a man. But I won't make angels out of devils. I will bring the light back to my eyes. God bless you and your family, Mr. Lincoln.

The Ward

*The world will little note, nor long remember what we
say here, but it can never forget what they did here.*

—NOVEMBER 19, 1863

✳   ✳   ✳

The nurses and the ward keepers, they say Lincoln killed my son. Talked bad-mouth shit as if Lincoln himself had gone up and put my boy in a headlock then sliced the breath-life right out of him. Then they said Lincoln just laughed his bony ass off, like some kind of madman, or spook, or something. But I don't believe in that. I ain't got the time for that kind of talk. No sir. President's a good-hearted man. Just doing what's right. And I know he didn't ever feel anything but love and pride for my boy. He didn't kill my son, no way in hell is that the case. And I'm gonna tell him. Gonna go tell him face-to-face.

We got this big old dumb-ass warden here called Walter. Built like a tree with a tiny little head all fuzzed blond, and he's got himself an ass that sticks out halfway across the room, and he rolls the sleeves of his shirt up so tight that they cut deep into the flab of his skin. And Walter's always wearing white, and he's always got an expression like those Southern boys who sit and watch the stalks and wonder why they never see them growing. And

he props himself up against the wall all the time, holding
his hands behind him, and talking an awful lot without
ever saying much. He's always holding court about this and
that, and nobody ever really wants to listen because Walter's
dumber than shit, but he keeps on talking and talking and
we keep listening because, even though Walter's bite-ass
dumb, it gets so lonely in this ward with the only sounds
being the squeaking of a few wheelchairs or the incoherent
babble of someone passing by, and even Walter's
monologues start to seem interesting, or at least different.

The other day, I stopped this old geezer who's been
wandering these halls for the past twenty years, and I told
him what some of the nurses and other wardens had been
saying about Lincoln killing my son, told him how they
said that Lincoln's done cut the throats of every boy that's
died out on the battlefield. And I told him what they said,
and then I told him again.

The geezer looked at me for a moment. Then he
reached up and scratched the end of his chin. He looked
around the room, then back to me. "I don't know, Albert,"
he said to me. "I just can't see it. I mean, sure he's a tall
guy, but I don't see how he could actually be out there in
hand-to-hand combat, taking on the Southern boys as
well as his own. He just ain't got the strength, and even if
that beard did give him the strength of Samson, I can't see
him having the guts," he said. "No, it don't make sense to
me," and he turned from me and walked off shaking his
head, saying it didn't make sense, no, none at all.

I knew it wasn't true. And I sat down at the head of my cot and reached under the pillow and took out the letter that I had received almost a year ago telling me of my son's dying in the war. I unfolded the paper and it was starting to tear along the crease, right in the middle of the words, and it was yellow now, and it smelled like mold. I stared at the letter. It was addressed to me, Albert Marcus, and it started off *Dear Mr. Marcus,* and it regretted to inform me, and it still does regret to inform me, and it told me that Jack had been killed, and it really didn't say why or how, but just the fact that it had happened, and the president's name was typed all crooked at the bottom, but there wasn't a signature. And I held the letter like I sometimes do, and I remembered Jack was dead, and I remembered he wasn't going to come to this ward and visit me ever again, and I looked at the letter like I sometimes do, and I remembered Jack was dead, and I looked at the letter like I sometimes do, and I remembered Jack was dead.

"And over there"—I heard Walter's voice across the room—"over there, sitting on his bed, is a man hell-bent on the past. You see, we all gotta remember to walk forward, to just keep on moving. That's what Jesus did, just kept on moving. And along the way we learn to forgive ourselves, and when we forgive ourselves we forget. So Albert," he called out to me, "are you gonna learn to forget?"

I looked up at him.

"You gonna learn to forget, Albert Marcus?"

I saw the green in his eyes. And the colors of every

pupil of every man standing in the room. I felt flustered, and my toes started to wiggle, and I licked my lips, and it seemed so hard to breathe.

Walter didn't move an inch, leaning ass-back against his hands, and he looked out at me, and asked, "Well?"

And all I could do was look back at the letter like I sometimes do, and remember Jack was dead.

❖ ❖ ❖

About ten years back my wife, Natalie, died. Three years later Jack went to live with his aunt and I went to the sanitariums. Jack brought me here to Hamilton two years ago. A horse and carriage ride all the way up to 130th Street. Told me he'd visit every week, and I asked him why I had to stay, and he said the judge ordered it on account of my behavior, and I asked Jack what my behavior was, and Jack just laughed to himself, and said he couldn't believe I really didn't know. And he told me of the crying, the hours of endless crying, and the yelling and the screaming, and the shaking of my fist when nobody would believe that Natalie was following me everywhere I went. When Jack told me what I'd done, it did sound crazy, and I started to laugh like it was someone else, then I remember getting real quiet, and I said to him that if that is what happened then I did belong in the ward.

Jack did come to visit me once a week. "You're

looking too skinny," he told me on his second-to-the-last
visit.

"Ah shit, Jack," I said, "I just wear my clothes baggy
is all."

He laughed a little bit and he reached over and
touched my head. "They taking care of you okay?"

I told him they talk a lot of crap most of the time, but I
usually just sleep, because when I sleep I can be anywhere
I want and nothing seems to matter.

"The nurses tell me you've been screaming out loud
for Mother again."

"Oh, bullshit." I remember being a little sore. "That's
the kind of shit that's just nothing but impossible. Your
mother, even as a goddamn ghost, wouldn't step a chained
foot into this rat hole—Jesus Christ, she never even left
the Bronx. So you can tell that nurse she's full of the shit
she's stored in her belly."

Sitting on the edge of my bed, I remember feeling
frustrated, so I lay down and Jack sat on the edge of the
cot looking down on me. He had my jaw, long and
narrow, but he had his mother's thin lips and her eyes,
blue and sincere. And Jack always—even as a boy—had a
way of just staring while he thought of something to say.
His lips would kind of twitch and roll in, and his eyes
might flit to each side of the room, then he would always
reach across and touch his palm to me as if reaffirming
that he was still there and still caring.

Then Jack dropped his load about going into the war. Right on the end of my bed, on top of the olive wool blanket. Me on my back. "I don't got much of a choice," he said.

I stared up at the brown water stains on the ceiling and thought it looked like someone had pissed straight up in the air. "No one's making you go," I finally said. "You were talking the Fifty-something New York Voluntary Infantry, and you said *voluntary*. Voluntary . . . You remember saying *voluntary*? . . . Walter says there's been riots going on from boys who don't want to go . . . You don't have to volunteer . . . Leave it to the Germans and the Irish."

Jack shook his head, knowing what I meant, and looked down the row of empty metal-legged beds regimented in olive blankets. "It's what's got to be done," he stumbled. "Everything's being torn down and messed up . . . And, and . . . I volunteer because I have to . . . I have no excuse not to."

"Can't you tell them you have a crazy father?"

Jack laughed, as much as he could for having the red-blooded fear of a nineteen-year-old boy in his eyes. He started to talk, and his mouth actually moved without any sound or words, and he reached over with his hand and touched my cheek, and his palm was soaking wet and it pushed down against the stubble on my face and he pulled his hand away and wiped it on the blanket.

That night, after Jack left, Natalie appeared at the side

of my bed. She looked as pretty as she always had, and she leaned over and whispered into my ear. *We have to watch out for Jack,* she said. She apologized, as she always does, for letting the sickness take her, but that aside, Jack had to be watched. He was rushing out foolishly, unprepared for where he might land. And I told Natalie I would do my best, and she kissed me and said she thought about me often. I cried with my eyes closed.

Jack came by one time after that to show me his uniform. I couldn't bring myself to say I was impressed, even though I knew my silence was killing him. When he left, one of the real crazies that lives here saluted him, and Jack nodded his head, and tried his best to hold it up proud. But a father knows bullshit. I yelled, "So long, soldier," and the words echoed a million times against the walls.

That was the last time I saw Jack. And his mother.

✧　　✧　　✧

Lincoln was coming to give a speech in Central Park with the intention of drumming up enthusiasm for the ongoing war. I told Walter I was gonna go see him and take the letter and ask if he remembered Jack. I was gonna stand face-to-face with him, from one father to another, and tell him no one was responsible, and sure my boy was scared, with shit running down his legs, but that at least if you die while doing right, you ain't dying for nothing.

Walter's big face pasted over and he breathed heavy and just looked at me.

The ward was quiet with boredom. Just the fluttering of cards being shuffled and knuckles cracking and teeth grinding.

"And how d'you intend to get an audience with the president?" Walter asked me.

I looked to the floor. "Well," I said, pulling on my lip, "I guess I'd just go up and talk with him."

Walter asked if I thought the president would just let people come up and talk to him, and I said that if someone really had something to say they would be heard. That's what they say about him.

Now Walter's a dumbfuck who has never had a decent thought ever flow through the layers of fat in his head, but he was certain he had a few excerpts from his ward sermons that President Lincoln would want to hear. "I tell you what," Walter said to me, "I'll take you to see Lincoln, but I want to make sure I get to say a few of the things on my mind, too," and I nodded in placating agreement with the stupid look on his face.

That night the ward smelled rotten bad; weekly laundering wasn't until tomorrow. You could smell the sweat and semen rising out of everybody's sheets. Walter leaned his fat ass against the usual spot on the wall and let off his nightly sermon. He talked about confession being the salvation of the mind. He said the only way to rid the mind of its troubles was to say them out loud. I thought he was full of shit, but I listened anyway. I was *that* bored.

{ *Mr. Lincoln's Wars* }

* * *

Walter led me through the sanitarium gates out onto
130th, the new City College beaming across the street. He
was wearing a suit that looked like it had been made for
him twenty years ago. The bottom button of the coat
barely latched across his gut, looking like it might blow
any second; and when he turned to lead the way, his ass
pushed the seam in the seat so far out you could see the
cross-stitching. The suit was dark, with pinstripes running
down the length. The first time I'd seen him out of white.

I had on my regular baggy gray pants with the letter
folded and shoved deep in the front pocket. And I put on
an old black fishing sweater Natalie had knitted for me
when I used to go out on the harbor in the East River
during the cold season. It still smelled a little of fish, and
salt, and the rotted smell of old sea wood, and the yellow
smile of a young man who raised a son and kept a wife by
the skill of his trade.

I felt warm, and I felt safe.

A cold wind streamlined its way up the avenues and
sliced against my face. It was 5:00 A.M. again and I was
setting off in the harbor with my net and pole and bait in
hand, knowing that the day's end would bring me to
Fulton Fish Market, and then to my family.

"Have you ever seen him before?" Walter asked,
knocking me a couple of decades forward.

"Just in pictures," I said.

"Heard he's tall and skinny as a weed."

"I don't know," I said, and we just kept walking the epic march down Broadway, until we saw Central Park a few blocks ahead at 110th Street.

Walter trod a slight pace ahead of me in a gesture of authority, his ass falling to each side as he walked on the padded edges of his oval feet. Breathing in a high whistle, with a deep ring of sweat half-mooned under his arms.

We crossed into Central Park, bordered on the outskirts of the tremendous crowd. There was a low murmur, and the moist breathy warmth that comes when people are tightly huddled.

The park looked so green, and I thought about green, about the real green, and not that mint shit they used to paint the walls of the ward. And the new trees of the park breathed and there was life all around me. I realized how dead I'd been.

I turned to tell Walter we had to find the president now, that there was no time to waste, but Walter wasn't there.

"Walter," I called out, and somebody else said, "Walter," and coughed a deep stupid laugh.

I had already lost him.

Dumbfuck.

The sky was heavy with clouds and it looked like it could start raining with nothing more than a sneeze. Some muttonchopped drunk said he'd heard Lincoln was clear on the other side by the reservoir, and someone else said they just heard that Lincoln had stopped talking more than an hour ago around the Sheep Meadow, and by now was cozy in his train heading down the line back to Washington.

I pushed through the crowd for a while until my legs started to wear, and finally sat down against a tree stump, my eyes heavy as a moonless night. I dropped my head against the tree and kept an eye open for my dumbfuck caretaker. One eye open. Then that eye closed. Then I woke up to a light sprinkle of rain under the twilight.

The park was empty.

A creepy kind of quiet.

Sonabitch, I said to myself, looking around to find my bearings and figure out how in hell to get back to the sanitarium. And I cursed Walter about fifty times and just walked straight into a grove that turned green to black.

I walked over long and lean shadows, thinking about spirits, about a resting ground for spirits, and maybe I was walking across their boneyard, then the shadows stretched longer and nipped at my heels, and my steps became lighter and more careful, and I reached up and stroked my chin and it felt coarse and old like I could feel the gray aging the tips of my fingers. The wind picked up and I heard it whistling and I hoped it was the wind I heard and not the sounds of souls. And though I wanted to just scream out, my throat was a balled-up fist.

With my chin tucked into my chest, I pushed my hands into my trouser pockets, feeling the dull edges of the

letter. My fingers against it, the aged paper softly
wrinkled. And I kept walking into the zebra-striped night,
holding on to that paper like a soldier gripping the butt of
a gun.

I looked ahead and saw the outline of a man sitting on
a bench, alone under the bone branches of an ash tree. The
shadows were falling faster at my feet, and I moved as
quickly as I could toward that bench, thinking about
Walter's dumb-as-fuck saying about the devil's hound
licking at your heels.

The man on the bench was real. His breath smoked in
the air. I dropped down next to him with the last bit of
stumble I had.

The spirits couldn't catch me.

My head fell between my knees. I was out of breath
and unable to speak, so I stretched my arm out with a
handshake.

He gripped my hand with a mixture of power and
tenderness that seemed beyond human, and I cocked my
head and looked out the corner of my eye, somehow
knowing all along that I was gonna see Lincoln sitting by
my side.

The outline of his face looked just like I had seen in
pictures. Sloping forehead, pointed nose, and untamed
whiskers wrapping around to cover his strong jaw. His eyes
looked different, though. They were smaller and deeper
and further lost than I had imagined.

"Albert Marcus," I could barely say, introducing myself. And I continued to hold on to his hand.

"Abraham Lincoln," he said in a low, quiet tone that suggested the same exhaustion I was feeling.

We both sat there for a full minute. He was staring out into the night and I was looking at him. Seeing the way his head fell forward on a path with his slumping shoulders. He let go his grip, and my hand just kind of stayed frozen in the air, and he ran his fingers through his hair, and his hair stayed back for a moment, then fell forward to the same place, angled across his forehead. The president wrapped himself blanket warm with his own overcoat arms and just sat there, hugging his ribs.

"I didn't get to hear your speech." I finally spoke.

"A lot of people there," he said, just staring.

I tried to perk my voice up. "I know, I was there. It's just that everything got so confusing I didn't know my ass from my head. And sonabitch if I just ended up . . . ass from head."

Lincoln bit down on his bottom lip and started to grin, and he almost genuinely smiled. "Well, since you know which end is which now, I'll tell you that I spoke briefly and asked the people to be patient in the fighting of the war. That there is more involved than is realized by everyone. Like whether your children and my children shall enjoy the privileges we have enjoyed." Lincoln paused. "And that was really about it."

We both sat silently again. Staring out at the black blades of grass in the flat meadow ahead.

"Do you live here in New York, Albert?"

"I live uptown." I looked away. "In a sanitarium." I stole a glance to check his reaction, to see if he'd stiffen in fear or go overboard in pity for the infirm.

Shadows crept on up at my feet. The president reached over and touched my shoulder, and the touch felt like fire if fire could be cold, and I felt something from inside him go into me, and I got kind of nervous, and the shadows retreated, and it dawned on me, holy-mother-of-shit, Natalie, I'm sitting with Abraham Lincoln.

"Did you come just to see me?" he asked.

I reached into my pocket to pull out the letter. I had to stand partway up and was so nervous, I got flustered feeling around for it. "I came with this warden named Walter," I gabbed while getting the letter. "He doesn't really got a brain or even a heart, just a mouth that prattles on. And he took me here and then he went and . . ." I stopped when I found the telegram.

I shook the letter open and it unfolded into four squares, like a treasure map.

Lincoln looked at it, then over to me.

"You know this?" I asked. "You remember this?"

He tried to look at it in the blue dark night. His eyes squinted real tight, and he reached into his coat pocket for a pair of reading glasses.

"It's a letter from you," I explained as he put on his

wire-rims. He read the letter over my shoulder as I talked. "You wrote it to me about my son, Jack . . . New York Voluntary . . . Died somewhere on a battlefield in the Carolinas last October . . . You wrote to tell me . . . to tell me . . ."

Lincoln kept reading the letter even after I stopped talking. He looked away, then rubbed his palms back and forth over his legs.

"You know, at the ward, they—and I mean the nurses and all them other mental wonders—well, they're always trying to tell me that you're the one who killed Jack. That you actually went out and done it yourself." I kind of laughed. "Well, Mr. Lincoln, I tell them that they're full of—"

"It's all how you look at things." Lincoln cut me off, grinding his shoes and studying the ground. The burnt dry leaves scraped along the cement walkway, being pushed by the breeze.

"What I'm saying," I tried to explain, "is that I never wanted Jack to go, let's get that straight. I mean right or wrong, I never wanted him to go . . . But, be that as it may, when you go and fight for the good guys and the good guys are the right guys, well . . ."

"Allow me to tell you something," he asked more than he stated. He reached over and touched my elbow and his dark eyes looked into mine and, even from behind his lenses, his pupils were squeezing mine into knots.

I nodded for him to continue.

"I sleep in a room in the Executive Mansion, Albert.
I've got a huge feather bed that rises three feet off the floor.
It's a four-poster bed, with each post made from maple and
carved in delicate and intricate designs by the hands of
artisans. And when I wake in the mornings I see light
flattened against linen curtains that are embroidered at the
bottom. And I rise and breakfast is prepared for me along
with a cup of hot coffee. And just a matter of hours away
from me, boys are waking in the cold, if they've slept at all.
They are layered in clothes to stop the wind and winter, and
the leather in their boots is worn through to the socks. They
make coffee that is part dirt and part cinnamon, and they sip
it down like it's life itself while huddling around a fire
hoping to greet some warmth. Then those boys sit or march
or wait until the next battle. Then it drops on them like
flames from hell, and they are scorched and cry out in pain,
and fight without ever really knowing what they're fighting
for. And as the soldiers lie dying on the battlegrounds, I get
on a train, and I come to New York, and I tell all you
people to be patient while they're dying."

He crossed his legs, shaking his right foot back and
forth with the breeze. He removed his glasses, bent the
arms down one by one, and dropped them into his breast
pocket.

"I know I should write every letter personally," he
sighed. "I should know every boy that goes out there . . . I
should've known your son . . . I should know every father
that goes into a sanitarium after his boy dies."

I didn't correct him. Didn't tell him I was knock-dead crazy years before Jack got it. I didn't think he'd want to know his war took the only son of a crippled father.

"Tell me about your son," Lincoln said.

I closed my eyes and squeezed them real tight to bring Jack back to me. "He was big," I said. "Not an overstuffed ox like Walter, but just strong. Real strong."

I opened my eyes for a second and snuck a peek at the president. Hell if he didn't have his eyes shut down tight. "What kind of strong?" Lincoln asked. "Was he mountain strong? Or iron strong? Or rain-cloud strong?"

I closed my eyes again to see. "I think he was more the kind of strong of a tiny creek cutting its way through a steep hill."

I glanced at Lincoln again. His eyes were still locked and he was nodding his head and smiling. "Yes," he said in a tone of discovery, "yes, yes, I see it. I see the strength . . . And what else?"

"He was quiet," I remembered, "real quiet."

"Like a morning wind?"

"Gentle like that," I added. "And he was dedicated to anything and everything."

"I believe that, Albert, I believe that."

My eyes closed, and I kept seeing images of Jack rushing up to my brain then going away again. And I felt the shadows crawling up at me and washing over my legs, before I brushed them off like they were an army of picnic bugs.

"How'd he die, Albert?" Lincoln asked.

It was getting hard to speak, and my voice quivered. "I don't know, sir, I don't know. The letter didn't say . . . I guess he stumbled into the dark hollow somehow."

I heard Lincoln sigh a breath that spoke the warmth of sadness. And he asked me if I missed Jack.

"Every day," I said, "every day I have to remind myself that he isn't here. That he's not gonna walk into the ward to see me."

Lincoln drew the night air through his nose.

"I'm always reminding myself," I said. "Always."

"Me too," Lincoln said.

And those shadow spirits fell over us like a deeper swell of night, then lifted up and into the naked branches and out into the dark.

"Sometimes," Lincoln whispered, "I swear I see Willie. I'll be walking the streets and I'll see a boy's back running and chasing down a ball, and I'll say to myself, *By God, that's my son,* completely forgetting in that split second that Willie's dead. Then I'll remember and it seems like he's died all over again."

"I never see no one but the crazy-ass loons I room with," I said, leaving Natalie out of the equation.

Lincoln smiled for a moment, his eyes and cheeks showing off the lines of a thousand visions and nightmares. His lips slowly rolled into a frown. "Then again," he barely uttered, "I'll be sitting in my office, and it'll be deep in the middle of the night, and I'll have been working until the oil's almost gone, and Mary's long asleep, and there will be a flit of light. And I'll blink my eyes, then stretch them open wide to wake, and I'll see the light dash by again. Like a firefly. And . . . and I wonder to myself if it's—" He broke his words off.

A sharp wind blew over, but I was warm under my black sweater.

"Albert." Lincoln stared ahead. "Let me ask you something."

"Yes."

"Your boy died. You're in this sanitarium now, right?"

I nodded my head.

"Do you think you're crazy?"

"They tell me I am, so I guess I must be."

"But do you think you are?"

The question seemed to stir in my stomach. "I don't know." I bit down hard on my back teeth and squeezed my eyes to keep back tears. "I know I cry a lot. I know I miss my wife and my son a lot. And I know when it all builds up too much and crying isn't enough that I tend to scream. Just scream till the flesh is torn from the back of my throat."

"Is that crazy?" Lincoln asked.

"It sure feels like it sometimes."

Lincoln pushed his hands together, clasped his fingers like a prayer, and held them up to his chest. Leaning his body forward. "Can I tell you one more thing, Albert?"

I nodded my head.

"Sometimes I'm out by a battle site and I see all the boys that have died, and they're all rolled together and draped under a flat of canvas with the rain pelting it. At that moment, sometimes, I think to myself a deep evil thought: I imagine the parents of those boys getting the news, and the grief that will wash over and through them, and I'm glad of this thought, I treasure this thought, because then I know I'm not alone. There are flames burning all around me . . . and I catch myself thinking those thoughts and that's when I start to think . . . start to wonder . . ."

The clouds had faded from the sky, and there were a million tinkling lights, and they sat so still, suspended in the night, and one would catch fire and shoot off like a firework straight across the horizon. And I raised my hand up, sticking out my thumb, and I found the Big Dipper, and I traced down her tail and glided my thumb to the right until I saw the North Star shining the brightest light in the sky. I watched her burn for a moment, and I didn't feel as lost, and I recalled the same feeling as when I'd been out on the boat and the current had turned me around and night had fallen before I found my way back to port. There I was, drifting on a giant cradle of water where there was no beginning and no end. Feeling small, useless against the measure of a man's life. And I had looked up into the purple sky and saw a flaming beacon, and I cast an invisible line between me and her and started reeling in until I was back on land. My feet touched the soil, and I heaved a bag of fish over my shoulder all the way to Fulton, then walked home to my wife and son, believing I belonged in this world. "Sometimes," I said to Lincoln, "I guess you need to touch things, even if you can't feel them with your hand."

"What if you think you've gone crazy?"

"Crazy's only what someone calls crazy . . . Like you go up to Congress and start talking about that jumping light in your office and they're gonna think you're bone-up crazy . . . Me, I don't think twice about it."

Lincoln stood up abruptly. He wiped his hands against each other, then brushed them against his pant legs several times. He straightened his shoulders and pushed back his hair from his eyes. "We have to figure out how to get you back home, Albert." And I swear his voice changed from a scratch in the back of his throat to an echo from his chest.

"Well, if I know that dumbfuck Walter," I said, "he's probably still wandering around the park trying to find your speech."

Lincoln smiled. "Let me have someone escort you back," he offered.

"Can't argue with that."

And we walked to the edge of the park. Through the boneyard where the spirit shadows parted into a jagged reception line for us to pass through.

Two lonely fathers on a great big ball.

On to the Next Field

Reason, cold, calculating, unimpassioned reason,
must furnish all the materials for our future support
and defence.

—FEBRUARY 22, 1842

*T*he earth was gently upturned and the dirt was dry as corn flour, as if it had gone through a sifter. There were different shades of brown, the red of the clay, a coffee brown under the fresh pack, and a light tan dug deep from the earth by shovels and later kicked around by scrambling horses and the boots of desperate men. And scattered in the dirt were clumps of burnt yellow stalks that all seemed rooted together at their base, yet stood as individual and separate as the men that had trampled them. A light wind blew the stalks and they bent lazily in the breeze, while a white fog lifted from the earth, and it looked like smoke, but as pure as ghosts. The sky overhead was a ceiling of blue, and the sun hung in the corner like a lazy eye, just looking down on the field, trying to burn everything in sight.

Men laid out lonely on the field.

Holding themselves, rocking from side to side.

Crying out loud. Moaning vibrations. Praying to Jesus.

The battlefield after the fight.

"Tell it to Lincoln," someone called out, and another voice answered, "Yeah, sure," and the original voice said back, "No shit, he's gonna be here any minute, I just got the word . . . We're supposed to be at our best."

A sudden flurry of birds winged overhead, and they formed a long black thread, observing like voyeurs, gliding effortlessly, then shooting off with percussive wings and loud trumpet songs.

The day was cold despite the sun. Small fires burned along the battlefield. The survivors, the healthy ones, tended to the flames. They stoked them with dried branches and other combustible chips left from the destruction. Then there would be a scream as lonely as an echo in a canyon, but the healthy ones hardly noticed it anymore; and occasionally a medic would toss the end of an amputated leg or arm into the fire, and sparks would shoot up like a Fourth of July fest, flames climbing a little higher, and the oils in the fat of the skin would rise with the heat and gently coat the limb, then bubble and sizzle into a smell with an apple-like sweetness, before turning a deathly sour. And when the flames burned at their hottest, the healthy ones put the coffee on to boil.

A carriage pulled by a legion of horses dropped President Lincoln off at the foot of the battleground. He stepped down and stood for a moment. The stench wafting from the fires immediately turned his stomach. Lincoln closed his eyes, then opened them to see the same battlefield. His boot stuck to the ground for a moment, and he looked down to recognize the glue as caked blood.

This was his first stop on a short goodwill mission, something to lift the spirits of the boys in the fight. The war was dragging on and morale was falling, and soldiers complained up the chain of command, until Secretary of War Stanton had stood in the president's office insisting that the president take a train to Pennsylvania with him and Secretary of State Seward. "Give these troops something to believe in," Stanton had advised Lincoln. "Lord knows they need it, and so do you. We all need to remember to believe in what we're doing."

Now, here he stood on a lonely field outside of Harrisburg, where a purgatory of souls paced like expectant fathers, nervously impatient to find their destinies. Lincoln muttered to himself, "Oh my," and he turned around to face the open door of the presidential carriage while his face fell into a thousand pities, avoiding the gazes of Stanton and Seward, who slowly climbed down from the cab.

A three-striped sergeant had been assigned to escort the president. With his yellowed eyes worn well beyond his brief years, he walked with his chest puffed out and his arms stiff at his sides in the mechanical motion of a tin soldier. "Mr. President," he saluted, and clicked his heels together, freeing bits of dark mud. Barely acknowledging the members of the cabinet.

Lincoln didn't notice him. He was busy trying to recall the plans and strategies that he had authorized to bring this regiment to these grounds. Remembering the parched paper spread out across his desk as fingers followed the cartographer's trails, with Stanton's breath wheezing heavy and sour, and Henry Hallick and Ulysses Grant confirming the overall strategy and thanking the president for his courage and rational insight.

"Welcome, sir."

Lincoln looked up at him, and the eye contact made him nervous. Like Mary's day-to-day startled gaze ever since Willie's passing. Or the face in the mirror that made his legs go cold, helplessly aware of the tragedies, and unable to make the pain go away on its own for just a single, solitary moment.

The young sergeant spoke as though already anticipating Lincoln's concern. "We did have a rough one here, sir. We were outnumbered and we took it really bad." Then the officiousness in his voice fell. "We lost a lot, sir. A lot."

Lincoln turned around full port to face the field. "And it looks like we still are."

The sergeant breathed a nervous laugh, bit down on his lip, and kicked his heel into the dirt like a caged mare. "It's not good." He looked to the ground. "Not good."

Lincoln kept staring out at the field. A wind was picking up the smoke and carrying it as a low cloud layer. His eyes burned. The smell made him weak.

The sergeant introduced himself as Sergeant Wagner and said he had been ordered to take the president out among the troops.

"I don't think that will take long." Lincoln sighed.

Wagner stepped to the side in a gesture designed to guide the president. "I thought I'd show you the command tent first." And he pointed his finger north and said, "It's just over by those trees."

"There's boys between here and that tent."

Wagner fidgeted with his hands. "I know, sir, but . . ." and he pushed his hands into his pockets, then pulled them out again. "Or if you don't want to . . ."

Lincoln stepped forward. "What I prefer, Sergeant Wagner, is to walk around on my own. I'd appreciate it instead if you could brief the secretaries."

"Sir, I'd be honored to—"

"I need to digest this myself." And Lincoln walked off with a long slow stride.

"I don't know if it's a good idea, sir," Wagner called out. "I don't know if you should be walking out unprotected," and Lincoln kept walking, more than wide open, as he always needed to.

He walked past the fires where the healthy ones looked up, too weary and exhausted to talk. Lincoln looked at them unsure of what to say, then broke his stride and, linking his hands behind his back, simply said, "Good afternoon."

The healthy ones nodded their heads.

"Has it been rough?" Lincoln asked.

"Just piss and shit," one of the men said. The others shook their heads and tended to the fire. Pulling the boiling coffee off the red coals and back over to the gray ash to simmer.

A few yards ahead a boy writhed on his back, his uniform ripped around his legs. His arms hugged his sides, and he moaned a long constant sigh while trembling with a slight rock to each side. A field medic ran up to him, knelt down, and ran his hand along the boy's bloodied leg, then the medic jerked his head up and rushed over to another fallen soldier, leaving the boy alone again, blue eyes reaching out to the sky.

Lincoln stood over the boy, looking at the blood-drenched leg. The boy stopped moving when the long shadow fell across his body.

"What is this?" the boy asked.

Lincoln bent over and touched the soldier's shoulder. "Stay strong, son."

"Medic said he'd be back in minute," the boy warbled.

"Just hold your strength, son." Lincoln leaned over and eclipsed the sun.

The boy half smiled behind faded pink lips, as if he was witnessing a vision, and said, "Is that really you, Mr. President?"

"Hold on to your strength, son."

"Medic says I shouldn't die . . . says I have to lose my leg," and the boy broke into a grin to hold off the tears.

"I'm sorry."

"Can I call you Abe?" the soldier whispered upward.

"Call me whatever you need, son," Lincoln said, trying
not to notice the soaking of blood through the flannel,
and the hanging limb just below the knee.

"Abe, you remember the Jessups from Concord?"

"I can't say that name says anything to me."

"The Jessups," the boy whispered in an insisting tone.

Lincoln tilted his chin and rolled his eyes up for the
memory. "No," he said, "no."

"They run a boardinghouse in Concord . . . . You stayed
there years back when you were running for the Senate.
My aunt Betsy, she made corncakes, the best you ever had,
you said. That's what you said."

Lincoln closed his eyes and pursed his lips. "Oh, of
course I do . . . Of course . . . That was a long time ago,
now, wasn't it. But I do remember them, good folks . . .
You've got a blacksmith there, and your aunt, right? . . . If
I recall, hands just the size to shape a perfect corncake . . .
What's your name, son?"

"Delbert . . . Delbert Jackson . . . Betsy Jessup's my
aunt, blacksmith's her husband, Tom . . . Betsy's my daddy's
sister. She never stopped talking about you, Abe, never
stopped talking at all. Said you were kind, and that a kind
man in politics is a hard thing to find these days. Said she'd
seen it in your eyes, knew you'd always be something, and
when this war broke loose, my aunt Betsy said, 'You go
give what you got for Mr. Lincoln's war. He's done given

it all for you.' And I carry that thought with me every day . . . every day . . . what you done for me, and all."

The boy's eyes half closed as steam rose from the ground beneath him. He clamped down on his back teeth.

The president reached over to take the boy's hand. "Delbert," he began, "wars are cancers that eat away at the kindness of men," then he stopped himself. He was gripping the boy's shoulder so hard that his hand was shaking. Lincoln unclenched his grasp and tried to wipe the sting from his eyes. And there was Willie face-up in the coffin with his eyes drawn closed like he was sleeping, supposed to look like he was communing with angels; but truth be told that under the orange powder that was intended to look like flesh there was just the rotting carcass of the boy he'd loved to hold in his arms, and hum to the rhythm of his tiny heartbeat. He had sat beside that coffin for hours trying to see Willie. Instead only finding the shame of a father who couldn't protect his son.

Delbert floundered his hand out in a blind man's search. "Abe?"

The field doctor scampered over, his light blue clothes stained by a dark rectangle of dried blood. He greeted the president with a short nod of respectful recognition, and Lincoln backed away to let the medic proceed with his duty. He watched the medic hold a steady scissors and carefully clip up the remains of Delbert Jackson's pant leg. The doctor injected a syringe into the knee and massaged Delbert's ankle while looking over his shoulder. "Y'all got to accept that this could hurt a little bit," he said, and looked up at Lincoln as if in consultation and whispered, "It's just morphine, is all." And the medic picked up the bone saw, and looked down at Delbert, then back to Lincoln. "I'd suggest you look the other way. Both of you."

Delbert Jackson's eyes opened wide, then shut into thin lines. "Abe," he asked almost silently, "can you hold my hand?" and Lincoln, without thought, reached down and squeezed his wet palm against the boy's.

The saw ran back and forth against the flesh with no more sound than a serrated knife pushing through a cake. Then the medic broke a sweat and the saw's teeth started to chip away at the tibia in a loud forceful timbre.

"Your aunt's a good woman," Lincoln said, raising his voice over the surgery's violence. His eyes skirted side to side, and the battlefield blurred into a thousand thought dreams that spun him back through Kentucky and Illinois and places far away from his world of destruction. "She made some delicious corncakes, indeed. Just right," he said, breathing faster.

Delbert moaned, and his hand dropped and turned to a fist that pounded the earth, where tufts of dust billowed. His upper body convulsed, and his one good leg kicked out in reflex. Tears running down his face, tracing white against the flush in his cheeks.

"You've got to hold your strength," Lincoln almost yelled. "It's too damn dark on the other side."

And the saw snagged and vibrated as if it were a front-porch instrument, and Delbert cried out a long, almost melodious howl.

"You gotta hold on." Lincoln grabbed Delbert's hand again and squeezed with the strength of three lifetimes. "There are too many who are waiting for your body, they're sitting and waiting, and they're all around you, just hovering . . . And, and . . ."

Delbert shrieked from his gut, and Lincoln held on tighter.

The sawing stopped, and the doctor dropped the tool and backed away for a moment with a far-off look on his blood-dotted face, trying to catch his breath, his clothes freshly stained. He exhaled and with his bare hands reached down to pick up the severed limb as mundanely as he would regular firewood. He walked over to the open fire and threw it into the flames, where the healthy soldiers poked at it with a stick until the leg was lost in the coals. The scent was numbing.

"Just keep fighting them off," Lincoln whispered to Delbert.

Delbert Jackson's eyes showed nothing but white. His good leg twitched uncontrollably and his free hand dug a crevice in the dirt.

The doctor walked over with a red-tipped branding

iron in his right hand. "Just gonna hurt for a second," he
said routinely, as he pinned Delbert Jackson's thigh
between the biceps and forearm of his left arm; and he
held the branding iron against the exposed stump below
the knee with his right, trying to steady the leg against the
electrical brain wiring that tried to jerk the thigh away.

The skin and blood crackled under the searing smell.

"This is the way we gotta do these things out here,"
the medic spit out in a tone between apology and
justification. "Just do the best we can."

Lincoln nodded his head like a stranger to a new
language.

Delbert Jackson had long been passed out, but his body
jumped in convulsion and an occasional high-pitched wail
whistled over his lips.

The medic stood up. "That's about all we can get done
for him, now. Just leave him here for now, and hope that
that morphine doesn't wear off before he gets to a proper
hospital." He shrugged his shoulders and looked off at the
other boys lying across the field, and drew a hard sigh.

"He's going to live, isn't he?" Lincoln asked.

"He should survive."

Lincoln looked away. "Well, at least that's one battle
he's won."

"Sorry?" the medic asked.

"Nothing," Lincoln said. "Nothing."

The medic drifted off and Lincoln stood over the

passed-out body of Delbert Jackson. And just above the earth he felt a light vibration that traveled along invisible lines like telegram wires. He pushed his boots forward and walked with short careful steps as if not to trip over anything.

Lincoln traversed the field, stopping and kneeling down at the side of every boy and man who lay there. They all looked so helpless and confused, and blood dripped from their mouths, noses, ears, and eyes. Their faces all flushed red the same when they saw the president staring them deep in the eyes. And they all tried to smile, even though the stress might have pulled the wounds apart into deeper pains. He listened to their stories, and he touched their shoulders, and he spoke all the names, and he made each soldier salute a promise of strength.

Then the winds kicked up and all the individual smokestacks pushed into one and the field was a giant gray cloud. Hacking coughs broke through the fog as markers or indicators of the wounded.

Lincoln pushed through the smoke and back to the carriage. The horses were shifting out of boredom and hunger, tugging the carriage as if they were trying to uproot it.

Sergeant Wagner stood at attention at the side of the car, having already ushered Seward and Stanton into the coach. His eyes patrolled right to left as he watched the president return. "Sir," he greeted Lincoln.

"Sergeant Wagner," Lincoln said, "you've been a kind

host." He moved toward the carriage steps, anxious to take his seat, draw the curtain into total darkness, bury his face into his hands, and try to rub the visions from his eyes. He should've ordered some morphine from the medic.

"Sir." Wagner spoke in a plain voice. "Some of the men, the survivors, were kind of hoping to have a chance to shake your hand."

Lincoln stopped halfway up the steps. He turned around, nodding his head. "Of course, Sergeant Wagner," he said, "of course," and descended back down into the smoke.

Wagner barked out a command that was distinguishable only to military ears, and suddenly the surviving soldiers appeared from the borders of the field, almost melting out of the smoke. And they all appeared at once. Eighteen men. All calling off their names one by one.

Churchill. Smith. Johnson. Riles. Arnaud. Bamberg. Thompson. Jefferson. Williams. Mason. Porter. Smith. Smith. Harrison. James. Conners. Baker. Andrews.

Each man looked like a slightly different version of the others. They all showed deep, dark rings that surrounded bloodied and tearing eyes. Skin draped over their cheekbones with a complexion like flour paste. Barely at attention in tattered clothes that looked heavy. They watched the president with their lips a space apart, each man with his hand stretched out in the last strength of pride, fingers trembling.

Lincoln felt a vibration at his ankles, and recognized the nervous restlessness of the newly homeless souls, recognizing the way they hovered around the half-dead survivors like vultures, or flies, or even the greed of children over a probate lawyer.

"So these are the troops," Lincoln said.

"These are the brave soldiers," Wagner said.

And all across the battle site, groaning and hacking rose from under the smoke blanket, accompanied by the occasional moan or cry; and the whole area smelled like death, and the ground was stained by patches of blood and dead boys; and the air was filled with the combustion of body parts as the fires burned over the cremated ruins. And by tomorrow these survivors, eighteen of them, would break camp, pack their bags, await orders, and move on to the next site, where cannons and rifles would fill the air with fire; and each man could only look at every particular moment for what it was without the expectation of seeing the next hour, much less the next day.

A few of the boys spoke up, and one said he was originally from Kentucky, and another said that his girl lived outside of Washington and if the president ever saw her could he tell her hello, and the boy described her from her blond roots to her legs the color of maple branches. And the boy named Arnaud spoke out and he asked, "What's it like being president?" and all the men stopped and drew a breath waiting for the answer.

Lincoln looked deep into all their eyes with a stare that came from beyond him. "It's like fighting a thousand wars," he said.

The men fell quiet while the horses neighed and continued to trot in place. Lincoln looked away from the boys and he told them they needed to stay strong. Wagner saluted him, and Lincoln nodded his head and bent down and scooped up a handful of dirt and tossed it out at the battlefield.

He climbed into the carriage and sat down, his arms collapsing at his sides, facing the silence of his entourage. The rubber wheels of the wagon rolled off, bumping over the rocks and divots in the grooved road. Lincoln drew the curtain and closed his eyes. Even when he did finally fall asleep his dreams were nothing but solid black.

He should have asked the medic for a stick of morphine.

And the carriage rolled on.

On to the next field.

Crybaby Jack's Theory

The dogmas of the quiet past are inadequate to the stormy present. The occasion is piled high with difficulty, and we must rise—with the occasion. As our case is new, so we must think anew, and act anew. We must disentrall ourselves, and then we shall save our country.

—DECEMBER 1, 1862

☼   ☼   ☼

rybaby Jack had a theory and the theory
was thus: that Abraham Lincoln was a
prophet and a son of God. It didn't make a
monkey's ass of a difference that everybody
knew that Lincoln's father was a seed brain from Kentucky
named Thomas, and that the deceased president was
birthed by a woman so ordinary that the world made no
effort to keep her past her thirty-fourth birthday before
replacing her with a stand-in. That shit was common
knowledge. Part of the history.

Although Crybaby Jack never read much more than
the sum total of his bar tab, he did seem to be one of
those people who happened to know a little about a lot of
things. He knew the big picture, and usually threw in a
small detail as a knockout punch to maintain his place on
the pontificale court of the barroom. And one of the things
he had done some reading on was religions, and though he
couldn't tell a Deuteronomy from a Koran, he was learned
enough to understand that every major religion told the
same story of a common man who is exiled from his

people and is forced to wander the desert becoming a
seeker of truth that he is eventually able to bring back to
his people. And more often than not he's killed for it.

Sound familiar?

But the way Crybaby Jack saw it, Lincoln came down
from God's planet, and it was the earth that he wandered,
picking up and spreading truths, before being quickly
returned to his place of origin on the wings of a bullet
from a derringer. "And the fact is that he wasn't like you
and me. He had truth for brains. And thought with his
heart." That's how Crybaby Jack threw his knockout
punch on any conversation about Lincoln.

Ask him where he was on April the fourteenth of
eighteen hundred and sixty-five, and Crybaby Jack will
ask you for the specifics. He'll narrow you down to the
morning, afternoon, or evening, the hour and the minute.
And he'll tell you that time really started at about seven
o'clock in the morning on Good Friday when he pulled
on a pair of railroad boots and moved in a hobo's exit,
squeaking the wooden floorboards of the flat of a waitress
named Harriet. And God knows he was a shit for sneaking
out before she awoke, a streak of ghost-white flesh from
her back peeking through the sheets, the cream of her left
thigh exposed on the mattress edge. He was a shit when
he came in, but he was a drunk shit, and Harriet wasn't
exactly pure of mind herself, and maybe then, at that point
of the night, he didn't know that he would be leaving at
the break of day, up almost half the night with his head

pounding out nothing thoughts, wishing he could sleep
yet knowing the impossibility of it, with his iron courage
nearly reduced to a shivering piss stream at the very
thought of this slumbering Harriet actually rolling over
and clamping her arm around his chest in a manacle of
affection. So at the first feasible moment of dawn he was
gone. One of her bulging brown eyes drifting a sideways
open, the other smothered in a pillow, and she smiled like
he was just heading out for a leak, and he smiled back just
the same, an index finger across the stubble on his cheek,
and for how long can he hold this phony expression, he
ought to be in the goddamn theater, until her eye closed
in apparent contentment, and the overzealous air emptied
out his chest, and with that last aching floorboard he was
gone. A real piece of work, he was. A real piece of shit.

He didn't want to go back home. He had a mother
there way past seventy who sat in a rocking chair day and
night looking like she'd been buried alive. Her face a
misery gray, with a slack jaw leaving her mouth
permanently open enough for a view of the two or three
rotting teeth that were left, where the breath produced a
whistle only a dog could hear followed by occasional
punctuations of spit. And she always sat in moral judgment
of her son and his times. Prattling on about when
Washington was the kind of town that brought out the
good in a man, like her long-gone husband, Benjamin.
How he had worked the stables that housed the horses for
the processions of the members of the Senate. It was dirty

work, she'd say. (Lord knows the truth of his job was to make sure that there weren't any fecal remnants hanging out their asses or stuck to the tails.) But her husband knew that he was serving his country. Then she'd inevitably look at Crybaby Jack, and remind him that he was two years past forty and not even fit enough to serve the Union cause. That the mention of his bum name brought nothing but shame and guilt.

It was sonabitch cold that morning, and Crybaby Jack wandered down the Northwests, kicking at the frozen clumps, working his fingers against his palms to try to bring back the warmth. Maybe he should have stayed at Harriet's. Just have rolled over and kissed her top of the morning, trying to pretend that her soured liquor breath wasn't like a putrid sirocco that practically turned his eyes back inside his head. And they could have had breakfast, maybe eggs and rashers and coffee that tasted like it was dredged from the shores of the Potomac, while he scratched his sandpaper face and returned a longing smile. Then gone off to his mother's to announce his civilized and about-time union, followed by a dinner invitation and an ultimate plan to all live together as one fully functioning family unit. Jack, Harriet, and Mother.

Or he could just drive a stake straight through his heart.

Washington was quiet that morning. The final bout of winter had come recently, but not enough that it was in anybody's mind anymore. It had left behind this morning

chill, but once the sun took full command of the sky, the
ground began to loosen, and the leaves hung a little more
freely, and the bland stalks that had suffered for the past
four months bore buds that were likely to explode in a
brilliant cache of colors. Crybaby Jack remembered this
time of year well. It was when his father would have to
really wake up from the winter slumber that stayed him
though the cold season, and now truly get down to
business. Because spring brought the people out, and in
Washington whenever there are people out there is sure
enough a politician ready to dance among them. Which
meant that all those winter-gutted senators were going to
leap out of hibernation and jump straight into the saddle
of an old mare that could parade them past the public eye.
Such was the season when a young Crybaby Jack became
the unwilling apprentice of his father. Walking toward the
stables, a pace behind the nervously ticking Benjamin
Newman in an ill-fitting black suit that revealed angled
wrists and bony-ankled socks, babbling aloud as part
lesson to his young apprentice and part eccentricity about
how the winter can knot and nap a horse's mane and tail.
"It takes sawteeth, not brushes."

The young Jack lagged a pace behind, hoping that his
lack of interest would translate into a lack of ability.

"And they eat that moldy hay all season long and it
makes havoc with their insides. You know what I say when
I say insides?"

Jack knew.

"The whole darn business gets runny and sticky, and it's a real artistic craftsmanship that goes into cleaning them out and making them presentable. They do represent the United Sates of America, you know. Carrying our brightest minds. So what about today you take your own horse from start to finish? Find you a messy old beast that you can turn to a princess. Sounds good to me. What about you?".

Jack knew he didn't have a choice.

In the dull sheltered stables in the eastern corner of Washington, where damp knotted wood turned an effervescence of mold, and the hay had gone sour, and the piss had turned to rancid vinegar, Jack knelt down at the rear of a horse, its big long muscled legs poised for revenge, a bucket of water at his feet, and a ratty old gray towel that he used to pick at the wagging tail, watching little crusts of shit stick to his shoes, as other clumps disappeared under his fingernails. He didn't really hate his father, that would be too small; at that moment he detested everything about the world that he lived in, where picking three-month-old shit out of the ass of a horse was considered patriotism, where it made a man like his father indeed stupidly proud, and ignorance was the fuel that kept it turning. It was at this very moment, when a young Jack was fifteen years old and wringing the feces out of a horse's tail, that he thought that it was really going to take someone to come along and fix things. It wasn't gonna happen on its own. And throughout his life he thought about that. But try as he did, he could never really define the "it." Nor did he know what that someone could really do.

Springtime in Washington.

It makes the past seem like yesterday.

Crybaby Jack wandered up Vermont Avenue thinking he might call on his old pal Cy. Cy in fact was really named Harrison Nelson, and though he always carried himself well, with an authority in his swagger, the sloppiness of his lower lip routinely sagging under a bourbon weight betrayed the alliterative erudition of his name. It was Crybaby Jack who had christened Harrison "Cy." Harrison had been an early entrant into the war, hit the trail following Manassas, but his tenure was brief after a coastal battle in the Carolinas, when a rebel cannon launched its munitions in a dead aim at Harrison's battalion, knocking the life out of most of the boys and men, and scalping the left side of Harrison's face, eyeball and all. When he returned home it seemed that Jack was his only friend left. All the others had gone to war, or were old farts or young boys. Jack was there when the bandage was unwound off Harrison's head. "Cyclops," Crybaby Jack said in front of the doctor and the nurse. "You're the goddamn Cyclops risen from the sea."

"Who?"

"Another one-eyed war hero."

Crybaby Jack kicked along Vermont until he recognized the green door to Cy's brownstone. It was too goddamn early to be knocking on people's doors, but it wasn't like Cy never pounded the knockers in the middle of the night, half scaring Crybaby Jack's mom to kingdom come, having stumbled onto Jack's front porch as the last potential person to sop up the rest of the night at the last waking pubs.

Still, Jack rapped on the door with tentative knuckles.

He leaned his ear in, trying to discern activity. A one-eyed guy is not so stealthy as he makes his way down the hallway with absolutely no depth perspective. Especially at this hour of the morning.

But still nothing.

He pounded a little harder. This time it felt like he might be waking up the whole block. Make Cy look bad. But it wasn't like he'd never done the same to him.

The door finally opened like a tired eyelid. "Sonabitch you want?" Cy said in a parched voice. "Middle of the forsaken night."

"Maybe in Chinaland, but here in the Union states it's the top of a beautiful day," and in a strange way he meant it. "Maybe that bug eye of yours is getting the light and the dark mixed."

Cy pushed the door open a little wider, and immediately shaded his hand from the sun. He wasn't wearing his patch, and the skin around his dead eye puckered over a slit that disappeared into a pitch black that could take you from fascination to sickness in a matter of seconds. "If it's drinking that you're after, Jack . . . ," Cy began with a tone of protest.

"Just seeking the company of friendship is all."

"You're still messed up from the night before, aren't you?"

"I got a clear head."

"So why you come hanging around here looking for me?"

"Like I said, just seeking the company of good people . . . It's Good Friday, for God's sake."

"Shit, you've got a whiskey-smooth line drunk or sober." Cy shivered his shoulders. "Asinine cold out here for spring."

"Why don't you throw on something respectable and we'll go warm ourselves with a cup of chicory."

Cy stepped back into the doorway, a sunlight streak spotlighting his bad eye. "And what the hell would we talk about? Ten years going that we've known each other, and this might be the first time I've ever heard you claim to be sober . . . So, I repeat, what on earth could we talk about?"

"You can tell me some war stories."

"Not much to tell."

"Would you stop standing there like a two-bit whore arguing over the tip, and get some pants on, and let's go."

Cy nodded in concession, and said he'd just be a minute, but for Crybaby Jack to wait outside so he wouldn't wake the others who were flopping in the back bedrooms. He turned toward the hallway and walked away.

Jack craned his head around the door. "And don't forget to put on your eyepatch, for Christ's sake." He stepped back outside. "Goddamn trying to make me sick he is," he mumbled to himself. "Goddamn trying to make me sick."

❖   ❖   ❖

Crybaby Jack and Harrison Cy Nelson sat at the end of a knotted pine table inside the Eastern Branch Hotel on Ninth and Pennsylvania. The ghost of tobacco matted to the yellowed walls, with the decaying smell wafting down from the ceiling beams. The two of them together looked out of place in the daylight. Both tall and long, they sat stooped, as though dragging the night in a washed-out comet behind them. Each with one forearm braced to the table, and the free hand gripping the coffee for all life. And Cy said that he always honored a good cup of coffee because when he was holed up in the battlefields in South Carolina they made their coffee by grinding the dried berries with loose dirt and mixing it up in boiled water. "One would have figured Honest Abe to perk up the troops with the real shit, and not leave them to slug through with the gruel."

Crybaby Jack got a little nervous when people desecrated the president. He automatically felt inclined

to leap in to defend Mr. Lincoln from the blows of
cynicism. He could only imagine the plight of the
president sitting alone in that Executive Mansion cradling
the cracking America in his palms, with barely two weeks
gone by since the Confederate capital surrendered, and
everybody's running around with goddamned shit for
brains saying that Lincoln ought to do this, ought to do
that, there's even people who think that he oughtta line
up the whole population of the South and execute them
one by one until the thing is just a long-ago memory.
And everybody has got an opinion, the whole damn
country is one big opinion, and the one opinion that
Lincoln needs is in Secretary Seward, who is now encased
in bandages due to some carriage accident, but who the
hell believes it was really an accident, because half this
country has had the heart sucked out of them, leaving
them with only a string of raw nerves, so everybody
better watch their backs now. Especially Lincoln. Even
Jesus would have to watch his own back if he were
wandering this desert. And when you've grown up as the
heir to the Capitol Horse Ass Wipers Union, then you
know what it means to be hunted. Crybaby Jack turned a
flushed red at his vigilance for being the protector of
Lincoln's plight. But all he said to Cy was that Lincoln
had better watch his back.

"Over shitty coffee?" Cy smiled.

There was no smiling for Jack. "Over a country gone
mad."

"You ever seen those pictures that Matthew Brady took of him? . . . Of Lincoln?"

"Some in the newspapers."

Cy leaned in. "Well, truth be told that they all pretty much look the same to me, and mind you I have never seen the man in person, but that been said, there's one picture from a couple of years ago where he looks totally different. Got his hair brushed back and it's almost sticking up like a rooster crown looking ever the Kentucky boy that he is, but it's his eyes, it is . . . They look gone."

"What are you trying to say?" Jack's right heel started pounding rapid drumbeats against the sawdust floor.

"I'm trying to say that something's already got him . . . The whole damn thing had got to him . . . The pressure and all . . . And it turns out the person that he needs to be watching his back from is himself . . . 'Cause he's probably making himself go nuts."

Jack's throat started to stiffen. "If you're trying to say something then say it." He spoke in a modulated voice motored by rage. "Without all your theorizing."

"I'm suggesting that he might be mad."

Jack slammed his palm against the table with a force just enough to startle the waitress, and to spill the coffee over the edges into cloudy brown puddles. "Where do you get off . . . ? Just because you had to drink shit coffee . . . ?"

Cy started to back off. "It's probably just pressure . . ."

"Goddamn right it's pressure . . . Wouldn't you? And

either way, what in fuck does that have to do with him watching his back?"

"You're probably right."

"I know I'm right," and in that moment Crybaby Jack caught a premonition that his concern was turning to some legitimate action, and that Lincoln in fact might be in some true harm. The anger fell from his throat, and now it felt parched and scratchy, and his proud bravado turned to a restless helplessness. He looked up at Cy and said, "We've got to warn him."

"Of . . . ?"

"Imminent danger."

Cy folded his arms and retreated into a strategy of placation, based on his current assessment of Crybaby Jack's mental state. "All right." He drew out the words.

"All of this goddamned city is like a cannon waiting to blow, and swear to God I get a feeling it's coming today." Crybaby Jack gritted his jaw together and looked into the light flash that spilled through the opening at the front door. He had had these feelings before, with nothing ever coming true of them, other than when he foresaw his father's dying, but that wasn't much of a premonition as the man had been hacking up blood for forty days straight. It was just that no one expected him to expire in the stables with his cleaning finger in the ass of Senator Barrow's filly that had been requested for a gala event, and the sick as shit Benjamin Newman dutifully bulled his

TB'd skeleton right through the doctor's orders and down to the stables where . . . Truth be told, Jack didn't really have a premonitory vision of his father's end, it was more like upon hearing the news from his gray-skinned mother in the doorway of the family home while he held the leaning screen door, he wasn't surprised that his father had died, nor that he had died in the stables. How else could it have ended, really?

"What do you suggest we do?" Cy asked.

"Tell the president."

"He's gonna think you're a fucking nut."

"He's gonna think that *we're* fucking nuts."

"There's no *we're*. I'm not involved in this lunacy."

"Shit you aren't."

Cy stood up abruptly, knocking the table with his knee, and letting out a cathartic *shit,* as the coffees sloshed back and forth and over the brims of both of their mugs. He raised his hands in a surrendered defense, palms forward, head shaking continuously from side to side. "I'm not involved," he stammered. "You can't make me do anything, you crazy mother."

Crybaby Jack pushed his lower lip forward in consideration. "I'll go tell the police that you're the one. Tell them you're the one who is aching to kill Lincoln."

Cy sat back down. Again knocking the table and spilling the coffee. "Why are you doing this to me? I'm in bed, sweet dreams, warm covers. You come pounding on my door. Why? Why are you dragging me into this shit?"

"Because this is patriotism."

"Are you out of your goddamn mind?"

"We've all got to be patriots here in America. If that means wiping the ass of a congressman's horse, or trying to warn the president of a life-threatening situation . . ."

"But you don't know if anything is going to happen."

"It is."

"How do you know."

"I don't know."

11:32 A.M.

Crybaby Jack stood up and nodded *let's go* to Cy and led him by the elbow, stumbling one-eyed on the sawdust floor toward the blinding daylight.

Two patriots.

❖   ❖   ❖

In moments of righteousness all actions are possible. There is no malice of reason where pros and cons are balanced, nor possibilities examined and weighed in their virtue. It's these momentous bouts of unabashed action that has created both the world's most celebrated heroes and villains. Where each nuanced fiber of every conviction is turned loose against an unknowing and needy victim. Singular focus. Determination. The inability to hear anything other than the mantra in your head that commands you to follow this through. It is with that exact clarity of resolve that Crybaby Jack marched a hurried but troubled stride across the mismatched Washington streets toward the

Executive Mansion. He had a feeling. His feelings are sometimes right.

Cy Nelson dragged a full walking length behind. His languid pace recalled the debilitatingly horrid posture that overcame his joints and muscles once his evening bourbons and beers had rendered him useless. When he would stumble out the pub's door and into a balancing act to keep from spilling across the wood planks like a more tragic version of the invalid he was. Where getting home was its own act of courage, and the faster he seemed to walk, the slower he actually moved. But today Cy wasn't drunk; he was only carrying the rotted remnants of last night's drink, which for him was a normal state of being. Today his body moved slowly in silent protest. Things like this tended not to end well. Especially when Jack was at the helm.

Meanwhile, Crybaby Jack had turned around and stopped in waiting for his unwilling accomplice. The street was his own. Nobody out except the two of them. The crisp air wrapped around in a sense of purpose, the sun spilling through as an anxious zealot lighting his face and burning his eyes. It was these kinds of days when the city seemed alive. Where the reds and greens and oranges that defined the storefronts came bursting out at you. And the stately homes washed in white sat in regal glow, and the Capitol looked like a castle on the hill wearing its crown proudly, victorious marble epaulets decorating its sides. Today the beauty was a ruse. A beard for the tragic

potential. Crybaby Jack tapped his toes vigorously. He
didn't have time to wait for this one-eyed fool on his
morning-after-walk-it-off stroll. "Come on, lame ass," he
yelled. "Pick up the pace, soldier."

Cy pushed his stride a little harder. His bottom lip
trembled in disdain as he muttered utterances that were
not clear to Crybaby Jack, but whose intents nonetheless
rang loud and clear.

"Quit your neighing, you one-eyed jackass." He
clapped his hands three times, and yelled, "Come, come,
come" in rhythm. And as Cy got closer, Jack told him:
"Holy Christ, you've got to get outside more. Between
the bars and that cave of a room you live in, it's aging your
bones fast enough for you to be even too old for my
mother. She'd mash you between her gums and spit you
out for dinner."

Cy finally caught up, collapsed at the waist, palms
braced against his thighs. His breath wheezed like it was
cold metal scraping against his ribs. "One second," he
uttered, his eyes fixed downward.

"No time to waste." Jack grabbed his arm, at which
Cy instinctively shook the intruding hand loose.

"I'm not worn," Cy explained, "because of drink and
laziness. I'm worn because this is crazy. Wearing me out
trying to keep up with your madness. It's like my body is
just telling me no. No more. Pass out before you reach the
madman. No, Harrison, it tells me, kill yourself before he
kills you first. You're a madman, Jack. Mad. And it is only

goddamn foolishness that guides you, and then drags the likes of me around behind you. So it's not wear—it's exhaustion. Exhausted by your madness."

"Are you done?"

Cy pushed himself back to an upright posture. He ran the back of a hand along his forehead to mop the beads of sweat. "Yeah." He nodded. "Yeah, I'm done."

"Well then, let's go, for God's sake." And he marched ahead, leaving the reenergized, if not slightly more reticent, ex-soldier in the requisite full stride behind and lacking.

❖ ❖ ❖

As Crybaby Jack turned up Pennsylvania Avenue through Lafayette Park and saw the bone-colored Executive Mansion, he felt the immediacy in his stride become overwhelmed by reverence. The lawn sparkling in a deep green, and perfumes of early spring in fragrance from each broken blade of grass. And at the center of the lawn the Executive Mansion sat back almost passively, especially for being the largest house in the whole country. The windows dark in shadows. And if you didn't know better you'd think that it was empty. But this shit was real. And Jack stopped sudden in his tracks. Not waiting for lazy-ass Cy, but more like his body had been denied permission to take another step. Like Lincoln himself was peering mysteriously out the corner of some window with a shotgun full of rock salt and sneering to keep the hell off his lawn.

Cy ambled up in broken stride and stood in side-by-side admiration over the mansion. Each breath sounding like it was puncturing a lung. "So there it is," he said. "You're just gonna walk right up and knock on the door?"

Jack didn't respond.

"Can you imagine even really going in there?"

"My mother and father came here once on the invitation of a senator whose horse my father cared for."

"Bullshit."

"Visited President Andrew Jackson. He had that niece of his dead wife's sister as the hostess."

"Scandalous."

"My father said when she greeted them he thought she was one of Jackson's children, goddamn baby-faced thing. My mother said she looked like a good caretaker. The old man thought sure there was something going on between the two of them, at which point my mother told him he should be ashamed of himself, and he apologized like he always did, without meaning it."

"What did they say it was like?"

"Royalty. Sonabitch glamour in every room. And dancing like they were in some how-do-you-do French castle."

"I've known you how long, and I didn't even know. Wouldn't even guessed by looking at your mother, nor your dad as I remember him."

"Being an ass-wiper has its perks."

They watched two guards who stood at arms at the bottom of the front doorsteps. The two men were dressed in formal Union blues. Fresh-faced boys who were still contemplating manhood, who had yet to pull the triggers on their rifles, but the gravity issuing from their faces informed of not only their willingness to do so, but the pleasure they would actually take from firing their Winchesters in the call of national duty. They stood in solemn earnestness, occasionally exchanging a glance and a periodic word whose expression indicated idle chatter to combat the restless boredom of inactivity. They paced in a casual stride, yet their feet seemed solidly rooted to the marble steps of the Executive Mansion.

12:23 P.M.

Crybaby Jack heard a passerby declare that he was supposed to meet a colleague for lunch at 12:30, and he didn't think that he could make it in the next seven minutes.

"Now remind me what we're doing?" Cy asked.

"We've got to warn Lincoln that something big is going to happen today. He needs to be careful."

"And we know this because . . . ?"

"I feel it."

"Because Jack Newman *feels* it . . . Flip you for who gets the shit beat out of them first for telling that to those guards."

Crybaby Jack sucked in a deep breath before responding. Trying not to be bothered by this one-eyed

imbecile who has publicly declared himself as a wounded
patriot not out of national pride or conviction, but instead
to woo the sympathies and generosities of publicans and
patrons alike who can soothe their own guilt by buying
the tragically brave infirm one more round because it's the
least they can do. And this wretch of a soul, who probably
would have taken his eye out with a hot poker by his own
hand three years earlier had he foreseen the rewards,
doesn't know dick about patriotism or courage. Doesn't
know that things happen and change out of risk. Someone
has got to take the first step. And not because they think it
leads into a bar. Which is exactly what this half-brained
Cyclops thinks this is all about. Some little fucked-up
scavenger hunt across Washington where the grand prize is
a hoisted pint. And guess who's buying . . . ?

Jack elected not to answer. Instead he began a slow
walk up the path to the mansion's front. Not
contemplating how he would plead his case. That would
spill naturally.

So far, of no interest to the guards.

Walking alone. Until he stopped for one moment to
brush the dust off his pant legs. Then he heard the lame
taps of Cy trying to catch him. He felt relieved, and
desperately disappointed.

Standing before the immaculacy of the soldiers, the
creases in their uniforms halted in precision angles, razored
pleats and the gray like polished silver, Crybaby Jack and
Cy looked like two stiffs risen from the pauper's cemetery.

And they were keenly aware of it. Both the soldiers, and Jack and Cy. Maybe that explained why the soldiers' initial response of stiffening their posture and gripping their rifles such that you could hear metal jiggling was quickly replaced by knowing looks that said *your turn,* with forced-back juvenile smiles.

"Good day." Jack spoke in a tone that was wholly not his own, rather his father's humbled voice that was reserved for those whose importance he ranked far above his own.

The guard on the right nodded an acknowledgment. Up close, both of them looked strikingly similar. Brothers maybe? At the very least neighborhood boys who were derived of the same lineage, learning to smile and pronounce and gesture and desire the same.

"Jack Newman," he introduced himself. Not bothering to risk the humiliation, he didn't offer his hand.

The guard on the right smiled politely, and quickly averted his eyes forward. His co-worker stared straight onto Pennsylvania Avenue, willing himself not to become involved.

"And this here"—he motioned Cy to step forward— "is Cy . . . Harrison Nelson. A veteran from the battlefields of the Carolinas. Lost an eye for Lincoln's war. A real patriot, he is. Giving up his eye, he did."

The guard on the left couldn't help but look at Cy to survey the damage, at which Cy, accustomed to this sort of inquiry, lifted his black patch to reveal what would have looked like an innocently sleeping eyelid, but was instead made grotesque by the long, seared scar that looked like it had caught the end of a misaimed branding iron. He then smiled his broken rotted teeth that were just disgusting enough to churn a man's curiosity into the pit of his stomach.

"Anyway," Jack stepped in, not wanting to kill their chances at such an early stage. He should have prepped Cy to keep his mouth shut in more ways than one. To understand that his role, and his only role, was to be the disabled veteran. That was what was going to open the doors. Then Jack could take over. He tried to give Cy a nudging kick at the heel, but couldn't reach the rotted leather without looking obvious.

The guard they had been dealing with rolled his shoulders, and seemed to take a step closer without actually taking a step. "Gentlemen"—he spoke in an imperious tone well beyond his years—"please state your business."

"Such formality from a soldier to a veteran," Jack said, trying to loosen the ice.

No response from the guard, while his counterpart neatly slipped into the shadows.

"All right," Jack said, "I can see we're all about business here, so let's get down to business . . . Truth of it is . . . and this may sound crazy on first hearing . . . but the truth of it . . . and I speak the truth, bring me a Bible and I'd lay

my hand on it . . . but here is the absolute, God-fearing-
strike-me-dead truth: after young Harrison here took that
gunpowdered metal scrap to the eye, he started having a
different sort of vision—one that saw things far off in the
distance, and I'm not talking nearsightedness, but what I'm
saying is the future. Knowing things that were going to
happen before they started happening."

Cy looked over to him with the beginnings of protest,
but just the tilt of Jack's head was suggestion enough
for him to keep his sorry little mouth shut. The guard,
meanwhile, looked vaguely interested.

"Anyway, young Harrison here had a startling vision
last night. One which turned him to the street, running a
half-blind mile until he rattled my door at first dawn,
awakening me and my elderly mother, a widow to a great
patriot. It was at that moment when the young disabled
veteran told me what I am going to tell you now . . . He
said he saw great harm coming to the president today.
He saw immense danger."

The guard turned serious. "Are you saying that
President Lincoln's safety is being threatened?"

"The very reason I immediately marched Harrison
Nelson straight to the porch of the Executive Mansion."

At the last utterance, there was the unmistakable
metallic click of a Winchester rifle cocking, followed by a
cold steel hollow the size of a coin on the back of Jack's
neck. And there presented an eternal second of silence in

which there could be an ignited blast that sent his head tumbling across the front lawn. Upon the realization that he was still living (and that his pants were still dry), the world came back into focus for Jack. The guard they had been talking to had his rifle drawn on Cy, but in a casual manner, since Cy was obviously neither strong enough nor witted enough to be a threat. And it was the unknown guard from behind who was currently threatening the very placement of Jack Newman's head on his shoulders. Never trust those silent types.

The two guards barked a plan back and forth to each other to find support, eventually leaving the silent one behind to hold the prisoners captive, while the other guard rushed off to find said support.

"Why?" Cy whispered to Jack. "Why did you put it on me?"

"I thought certain they would understand," at which the guard ground the barrel of the rifle a little deeper into Jack's neck spine—his way of saying *shut up*.

❖ ❖ ❖

5:37 P.M.

"Pour me another one, and this time don't be so cheap with the bourbon. It's supposed to at least reach the bottom of the lip of the tumbler. And for God's sake, can't you see this man here was wounded in the fight for freedom? Your freedom. My freedom. Their freedom. Put a round on the house for God's sake. A man like my friend

Cy Nelson is the very sinew and soul of this nation—one that allows you to pour the drink, and me to drink it."

Back at the Eastern Branch Hotel, the bartender capitulated more than likely out of intolerance instead of patriotism. He said something like "Here you go," but filled Jack and Cy's glasses to the same level he had been filling them for the past hour, incurring a mild but not-appearing-to-seem-ungrateful scowl from Jack as he set the rocks glasses down beside the half-drunk pints.

After the success of his speech, Crybaby Jack sat in reticence. His cheekbone was beginning to swell from the *shut up and I mean it* rifle butt to his face prior to the following events. He and Cy had been marched off almost unnoticed to the basement of the War Room across Pennsylvania Avenue that smelled of cultivated mildew and terror born from boredom. They were interrogated for nearly an hour straight by a high-ranking military officer who never gave his name properly, but appeared to be called Smith. And perhaps interrogation is not the most appropriate word for this situation, because Smith did not ask a question (other than their names) for the better part of forty-five minutes. He talked about the growing crisis that the war brought on, the increased threats to President Lincoln, the pressures of a man in his position, and something about a warrant for the head of Abraham Lincoln etched into a wall in Beaufort, South Carolina, that he had seen while briefly surveying the troops. And he talked about what a great man Lincoln was, but he wasn't paid to honor his greatness, rather to protect it. "So finally"—he addressed his comments to Cy—"tell me, soldier, are either you or your partner here aiming to bring harm to the president?" To which Cy responded with an emphatic "Hell no."

"Any concrete belief that the president is in imminent danger?"

"No sir, it was just a feeling," Cy placated. Jack thought he might burst apart vein by vein trying to keep his mouth closed. This feeling was real.

"Well, I appreciate your patriotism, and I appreciate your sense of honor and duty, soldier. I am sure you were trying to do the right thing. You do however understand that the United States Army cannot jump based on your intuition? And maybe later you can explain that with a little more oomph to your partner here."

Cy nodded, and asked if they could go now. Smith sent them on their way and suggested they stay clear of the Executive Mansion for a while. No sense in arousing any suspicion, but leave your full names and addresses with the clerk because I swear by God if anything should happen to the president in the coming hours you both are gonna be the first thing I think of, and don't think I won't find you with a noose in my hand, but nothing to worry about since we're on the up-and-up, right?

As they got up to leave Jack felt a plea clinging to his

throat, *Please just listen, I know I'm right.* And he was right,
he was sure. His nerves twanged and snared, his bones beat
hollow, and his muscles pulled tight enough to break.
Something was going to happen. Sonabitch, he should
have just stayed with that bored-out-of-her-mind waitress
Harriet, and never crept out from her room and into the
crisp morning. Maybe then he never would have had the
premonition. Although it's not like he believed for one
second that his actions could possibly influence the
outcomes of the greater world at large (that was for his
aunt Ruth, who always took responsibility for every global
action, based on her careless sentences. "I never should
have said the word *rain* today," etc.), but just that maybe
had he continued the lies that constructed the fabric of his
life he never would have had a reason to imagine such a
rueful notion. And if, in fact, something did happen to
Lincoln, then so be it, at least he wouldn't have been a part
of it. Just another universal someone shocked and amazed
at the out-of-the-blueness. Should have climbed right back
into the sack with Harriet. Or going back further, he
probably should have stuck to wiping horses' asses as his
father undoubtedly dreamed of.

Jack ordered another round of drinks, buying Cy's, and
grunting a thank you for getting them out of the mess.

"You probably shouldn't have . . ."

"Just shut up and have your drinks and your thanks."
He hoisted his pint stronger and harder than the four
previous, with the hopes that the numbness would take

him out of his live body and into a run-of-the-mill average maniac who knows no other concern than how to pass the time between meals. Hoping that the pauses between the seconds of the clock where a gasp might be heard, and a terrible wail calling about a tragedy to the president, would instead be replaced by the void and numbing passage of a time idly spent.

10:37 P.M.

Jack couldn't even his finish his last drink. His face slumped hard and heavy into his palm. Cy was still next to him, his stare a goner out the window.

A man Jack had never seen before burst through the door all gray-faced, with a sick posture, and screamed the news. No one knew if Lincoln was dead or alive for sure. The gunman jumped from the balcony, and was being chased down. It was this detail that brought Cy's attention over to Jack—at least they wouldn't get the blame and the consequential noose. Jack didn't lift his head to acknowledge Cy or the news. His head buzzed an empty thought from the well of his brain to the edge of his scalp, while his stomach constricted into a ball that felt like it might bore its way out of his back.

"Sonabitch," Cy finally said, "you were . . ."

Crybaby Jack didn't wait for the end of the sentence. He pushed himself away from the bar, forgetting to pay the tab, and strode through the near-frozen pub out into the black night. A select smattering of stars twinkled the last of their dying lights. He could have been the only one in all of Washington. A strong breeze pushed along Pennsylvania Avenue, though the air seemed still, in mesmerized sheets. Jack glided with it, the weight of his soul carried on the back of a feather. And he would float until he found the door to the waitress named Harriet's flat, where he would kick off his railroad boots, climb into bed, wrap his big empty arms around her, feel the life of her skin warm him, and fall asleep and never wake up thinking about anything else.

The Sad and Familiar
Ballad of Captain Carson West

If destruction be our lot, we must ourselves be its
author and finisher.

—JANUARY 27, 1838

✳   ✳   ✳

Captain Carson West was busy throwing a mean sweaty hump into a Raleigh girl that was so fierce he almost forgot himself. They were on the north side of town in some abandoned lean-to slave quarters, where the gray slat boards bent out warped in every direction, throwing up splinters like a porcupine back, stinking of piss and ash and rotted apple cores, with the flickering kerosene light on the floor jaundicing the single room. The Raleigh girl looked part whore and part survivor. She called herself Polly or Patty, or something like that, but Carson West settled on Polly. He wasn't really paying too much attention at the time of their introduction, just thinking on how to get her away from his stink-drunk unit and alone beyond the worn tedium of zealous camaraderie. And now she lay facedown on some maggot-eaten quilt, with a thick mane of black hair that almost looked blue against her faded Celtic skin, her big white ass rolling like a relief map of the Appalachians, and Carson West stupidly on his knees in vainglorious pride.

✣   ✣   ✣

As the nineteen-year-old son of a Chicago newspaperman,
one whose editorials on Lincoln almost looked like the
administration had funded them, Carson West had conspired
to despise the status quo that his father's paper promoted.
Everything from art to politics was always called into a
wishful jeopardy, leaving only the maintenance of self and
family to value. Until he enlisted, Carson West spent most of
his days with Ezeriah Stankman, a pressman in the South
Side plant, who had traveled everywhere, had sat in the cafés
in Paris, and had actually touched the edges of the earth.
Through Ezeriah's stories and philosophies, Carson was able
to see a faint light beyond his breeding. He pumped Ezeriah
for his views on everything from slavery to religion. He spent
evenings at the after-work corner bars with Stankman and
all the other production stiffs, learning a language far saltier
and more descriptive than the proper nomenclature that the
nuns who taught him had prescribed. He sat studiously
poised while listening to Ezeriah pronounce Lincoln's war a
war on mediocrity and the constant resuscitation of a dying
system just because everyone knows it can breathe.

"I don't exactly follow," Carson said.

"It's ever since those Pilgrims landed in Massachusetts
bringing their religious dogma disguised as freedom.
Setting some type of moral certitude that justifies any
actions they decide they want to do. You want to fucking
oppress people, well then fucking go ahead, because we're

Pilgrims, we're the children and grandchildren of Pilgrims, we not only know morality, we are morality. Make slaves of them. Kill the goddamned Indians because we're Pilgrims and we've got the roasted turkey and yams to prove it. So say what you want about the politics and all that other Capitol Hill rhetoric—the fact is that this war is about breaking the stagnant morality that has oppressed everybody in America, except for the chosen."

"So," Carson concluded, "that's really what this war is about, right? Changing the status quo."

"And say a goddamned nightly prayer to Abraham Lincoln for having the balls to do it. Bless his heroic heart and everybody who marches with him."

Carson West enlisted in the Union Army the next day. He understood the passion. The fight for change. And his father, not thinking it half bad for the boy to gain the discipline that parochial school obviously couldn't instill, encouraged Carson to join, while calling on the Executive Branch to ensure that his son got a taste of reality but was still free from harm. Ezeriah Stankman advised him to stay away from guns and backwoods soldiers whose theories and philosophies were based on a free ticket for killing and violence. He told Carson that his role was to be part of the change, and that he needed at all costs to resist the primal temptation of *war for war's sake*.

Ulysses S. Grant himself had dispatched the order, and two weeks before Easter, Carson West had sewn on his captain's bars and joined William Tecumseh Sherman's army with the primary task of communicating logistics and battle reports back to Washington. And as promised from the lips of Grant to Carson's father, the boy would not be carrying weapons. The first day after Carson joined his regiment, Sherman, with that swirling blue crazy in his eyes, jacked a revolver from his side and tickled it against West's groin and told him it was him or them, so West better take the pistol and plan to use it if he needed to. West took the gun, the metal still a sweaty warm, and tucked it secretly into his waistband.

"How does that feel down there?" Sherman asked.

Carson shrugged. "Okay," he said.

"You got hands that look like they've never worn a blister before. You gonna be able to use that thing?"

"Probably just be taking notes more than anything else."

"You'll be doing what you can to win this war, and the shit that'll be creeping up on you, you won't know what to do with except shiver your blue blood until it turns red. Just pray that your instinct knows what in the hell it's doing . . . You ever shit in the woods before?"

"Sir?"

"You ever taken a shit on anything other than a nice commode?"

"Not that I recall."

"Well, you're gonna be shitting in all kinds of places you never dreamed about. In streams. Behind trees. Under the shelter of a mutilated corpse. Probably shit once or

twice in your pants and not even know it until later . . .
You're a smart one, right? Good schools. Went to good
schools, right? That's why you're in charge of the scribing
here. That right?"

"I just volunteered to help the cause." Carson chose
his words cautiously.

"You'll learn what really helps. Trust me . . . You'll
learn to love it later."

As a man, Sherman looked tired and worn, while that
sonabitch demeanor of his could turn hard on you and
make you feel like shit just for trying. Not much grace in
that bag of bones; in fact he was just one giant sack of balls.
And his army lived like animals, staying close to the ground.
In the mornings when they took the Confederate towns
to task, West would stand on the perimeter of the battles,
scribbling down notes in his head, waving his Sherman
pistol like he would know what to do with it and screaming
a primal fear that nearly imploded his diaphragm. The
men looked beat. They had murder in their eyes and fear on
their breath. Carson West watched in awe, finding himself
strangely unaffected by the morbid desperation. And
sometimes he had the urge to leap into the fray, gripping
a bayonet under white knuckles, maybe run into the blue
smoke that stunk of sulfur and flesh, and ram that blade into
the chest of a fallen soldier, crucify him soul and all to the
ground in the name of Abraham Lincoln. The temptation
would rise through him, his eyes growing harder and his
heartbeat daring him under a score of terror. But he always

managed to resist. To will the blood in his veins to ice, and
stand calmly and coolly to the side. Not fall by Sherman's
logic. Instead be ruled by reason.

By the time they crossed the Carolina border from
South to North, the war appeared to be running its course
following the surrender at Appomattox. Sherman told
them to hang tight. Said he'd be negotiating the end
himself in Durham after this Easter weekend, and soon
you won't have to look at these boys with contempt, but
rather with camaraderie, because we're bringing this
country back together again. He had talked like that the
whole way into North Carolina, and while they set up
camp at the Governor's Palace in Raleigh. But today, after
a relatively calm Good Friday, West noticed Sherman
wasn't talking too much. He wasn't prattling on in his
way about this and that and himself, and in fact for the
better part of the day the general sequestered himself in a
small room in the east wing of the building without even
a sliver of light coming from under the door. Sherman
showed himself once in the early evening, and told the
men to go out and do whatever they needed to do. Fuck.
Drink. And watch your back. Be careful though, not every
cracker south of the Mason-Dixon Line knows the war is
done with. Get all the crazy-ass out of your systems before
we go to Durham for the surrender. You have to be
poised. Filled with dignity. Representing President
Lincoln. And then he retreated into the shadows, abruptly

turning away from Captain West's request of the daily update for Washington, his face looking tragically hard.

Carson West followed the rest of his unit into downtown Raleigh, where they quickly dove into the watering holes. He was tired. His stomach was empty, and what he really wanted to do was sleep. But Polly came right up to him, and in the dark her eyes looked sweet. Her breath smelled sensually stale from beer. A wisp of her hair lashed his cheek. He wished the war had ended two weeks ago. She knew a spot, but it was across town, safe in case Sherman decided to burn the place to hell like he did everywhere else. He told her she didn't know what the fuck she was talking about. She laughed, and said she was laughing because she felt cavalier. She looked like she was crossing the enemy line on one last suicide mission. He told her she was full of shit, the war was for the most part over. "I guess I don't know the hell of it." She grinned in a way that made West feel stupid for not knowing what she was talking about. But she sure was confident about it. Polly turned away, her hair swatting his face again. Carson West went with her in stupid trust, half expecting her to lay a six-inch blade into his neck for the cause.

❖   ❖   ❖

"You said you're from Chicago?" Polly asked. They lay side by side on top of his uniform jacket, the shack feeling a million miles from anything that mattered, warm, like fresh spilled blood following the hump. His crumpled trousers and Sherman pistol in a wounded pile of passion by his head. She stared up at him long and hard. Eyes the blue of a thick sea.

"Why do you ask?"

"We left there in '49, my father and me."

"So you're from the North?" He smiled cleverly.

"We were only there for the building of the Illinois–Michigan canal. Got out as soon as we could."

"Where did you live?"

"Where do you think? Bridgeport. With all the other Irish slaving six-day-a-weekers who dug out that canal with their bare hands, paid off in cholera and any other worthy disease . . . Couldn't wait to get out of the filthy piss stench." Her words formed around a deeply hollow yet secure breath, then hung on her lips before turning heavy and dropping off with a tragic confidence, while her eyes expressed a worn agedness that lacked the benefits of wisdom.

There are distinct moments when all your education and erudition and proclivities for the recitation of facts are shattered like a clumsy sun that comes crashing down on the horizon. Where you come face-to-face with someone whose brain hasn't had half the training of yours, who can't spill facts and philosophies on cue, yet in the most simple and languid manner can understand and reduce the world to a simple sentence. You know you are so much smarter than she is, yet she can make you see yourself as a complete imbecile. Carson West felt suddenly exposed. The intense fear that he is just another rich boy as empty as the rest of them and that his convictions will probably only carry him long enough to don his father's suit and jack-off opinions, undoubtedly ending up constantly mistaken for the old man, bald head and all. It's like she's reading a newspaper headline across his forehead. That his deepest scar can't even compare to her barest surface wounds. And as he gazed at the whites of her thighs, he began to think that he could love her down to the smallest curse of breath in his lungs, but instead was confronted by his intense resentment of her insight.

"I'm just glad we got out of there before the big Lincoln nomination," Polly continued, as though bored by West's internal battle. "Holding the convention in a stupid wigwam at Lake and Market. Whole goddamned place was out of its mind . . . Of course, this whole goddamn country is out of its mind for that matter . . . Both sides oughtta just kill each other off and start over again."

West leaned over, trying to compose a singular thought that would establish his confidence and promote the depth of his emotional and intellectual prowess. "So you're not a big Lincoln fan," he said, instead sounding more stupidly juvenile, made obvious by that goddamn contrite look hanging on her face.

"Not that I really care, but I do think he got what was coming to him."

West shrugged. "I don't follow."

"You don't follow."

"I don't follow."

"Sonabitch, you don't know, do you?" And for one moment the wear of her face turned to a wide-eyed schoolgirl expression of novel wonder. Her bare shoulders still braced and hard.

West was really starting to get pissed off. Now she was mocking him as well. Where the hell did she get off, a stupid Southern whore with no real convictions to anything other than herself.

"I can't believe Sherman kept it from you. What does he want to do, keep you as mindless troops that just march along and along and along, and then kill without thought? . . . No truth is good truth."

"Hell are you talking about?" West sat up fully, his chest vibrating.

Polly looked him in the eyes, the wick lighting her irises red, with her thin lips drawn down sympathetically. "Lincoln is dead. Shot dead last night in Washington." And she held her empathetic expression for two heartbeats, before exploding into a hysterical laugh that not only mocked Carson West, but mocked the order of the world as well. "Dead," she managed to say one more time while gasping for a breath, with no intention of even civilly composing herself.

"But I saw Sherman today, and he didn't . . ."

"Dead."

He swallowed any trace of a word he might have thought to say, and his throat jammed so thick that he could barely breathe. He just wanted her to stop laughing. Stop laughing. At Abraham Lincoln. At him.

But she kept on like a banshee.

Captain Carson West reached to his side and grabbed the Sherman pistol, the cold weight of the Colt .44 filling his hand. With his trembling finger on the trigger, the whole goddamn war washed over him. And fuck if there wasn't a moment when he could've stopped himself from what he was about to do, those .44 triggers do pull slow, but he couldn't let go, and that sonabitch whore with her treasonous smile, and Christ almighty if there weren't enough dead already, every stinking town they went through, burnt to the ground, and don't spare the children because they'll just grow up to be rebels and carry this shit on, and to hell with the women as they're likely to just bear more of their kind, and burn the town to a crumbling cinder that breaks apart and disappears all quiet with the wind, and damn if the earth wasn't bleeding herself as he marched behind Sherman like a wild beast stalking the whole of the South, swallowing worms for protein and boiling bark for drink, and the whole stinking earth stinks of blood, all iron and mulch, and it could make you sick, not only seeing all the dying but being an accessory to it as well, a real mind fuck, where your brain shuts down to a low buzzing numb, and your nerves rise to the very edges of your skin all cold metal, and they just take over like instinct until you become a pallbearer to your own conscience, and this is what Ezeriah Stankman warned him to avoid, being swept into the frenzy until you aren't fighting for anything—just fighting and surviving; and where Ezeriah Stankman may know philosophy, he doesn't understand that this shit is deeper than that, this is your goddamned nerves running the show, and if they switched places Ezeriah Stankman would sure enough know the feeling that comes over you when you have to blow your brains out if you don't do it first to someone else, because you can fuck the ordinary, but when you fuck the ordinary it fucks you back, until you're just like the rest of them.

It was a hollow crack. A bit of flame and smoke peering out of the end of the Colt's barrel. A clean shot through the temple. Might not even notice it if you were lying on top of her. In fact, she still had the same dancing laugh in her eyes.

Carson West walked back to the Governor's Palace in a jacket stained with rebel blood, the entire surface of his body abuzz in raw emotion. He debated about whether he would tell Sherman. The general would either pat the young West on the back and just laugh that cruel tobacco-drenched howl, or spit at his feet and call him a stupid pussy.

The Necropsy

Every man is said to have his peculiar ambition.
Whether it be true or not, I can say for one that I
have no other so great as that of being truly
esteemed of my fellow men, by rendering myself
worthy of their esteem.

—MARCH 9, 1832

‑ ✳ ‑ ✳ ‑ ✳

O N E

John Wilkes Booth sat alone in an empty guest room at the Surratt boardinghouse on H Street in Washington. Light streamed in rather aimlessly through the half-drawn window, tossing out dusty rays that stabbed like daggers. He should have been rehearsing. He had an audition next week at Ford's Theater, and he still couldn't speak his lines without holding the script. His father would have called him lazy. Would have been half in the bag, barely able to utter even one of his own words, as he first chastised his son about lacking respect for the craft and then reminded the world that Junius Brutus Booth had been hands down the greatest Shakespearean player that America had ever known. He had the reviews to prove it, and his sons should not only feel proud, but be thankful that he paved the way for them, because all their talents combined didn't equal a fraction of Junius Brutus Booth's. Then it was likely that John's father would kill the rest of the bottle, and burst out the door into the Maryland night and not return for a week, having no clue where he had gone, or that he had even been gone. But one thing was certain: the man had been a brilliant actor. The problem was that whether he was onstage or not, Junius Booth rarely stopped acting; and in those moments when he did, there was nobody in the mirror, frightening the old man into a panic whose best remedy was a concoction of scotch and two-bit whores.

John would not end up like that. He may have gone into acting. Become bigger than anyone initially gave him credit for—hell, didn't he kill them as Hamlet in Richmond? But still there were bigger things at stake than the theater. Like the whole goddamn country about to become a fiefdom under that despotic maniac, Lincoln. Now that ugly freak had not only been reelected, but was also claiming victory over the Confederacy, and threatening to make a citizen of the Negro slave.

Mary Surratt knocked on the door before entering. Her dark hair intricately traversed the back of her head before being set into place with two black needles. Her skin looked eternally twenty, making it easy to forget that the boardinghouse owner had a son Booth's age whom he called a friend. Surratt sat down on the bed, her beige cotton dress bunching to the side, revealing a single cream-colored calf that disappeared into a brown sock. Her expression conveyed a cultivated sympathy, although she adopted a wretched tone as she spoke. "Did you hear about his speech last night?"

"I try not to listen to Lincoln anymore."

"He's taking back everything he'd been saying all along. Now he's talking about not even letting any Southern representatives back into Congress."

"Of course he isn't . . . He's just going to keep that whole half of the country imprisoned. They might get in the way of King Abe . . . That's the way he's operated all along, hasn't he? If you get in the way of his thrust for power, then it's off with your head. Be it friend or family. Goddamn Richard Plantagenet, he is. *Thou lump of foul deformity*." Booth was steaming now. Once he started in on the topic his entire sense of being filled with a dark hatred. His lips drew taut; the muscles surrounding his shoulder blades contracted and burned. He couldn't think about anything else. Certainly not rehearsing his lines.

Mary Surratt remained seated beside him, her calf still exposed, as she delicately ran her finger along her white skin at the edge of the sock, satisfying an imaginary itch. A flash of light exposed a momentary glimpse at the heart of her inner thigh. She stroked his hair, bunched in tight, dark locks, and tried to smile, but could not catch the piercing gaze of his deep black eyes.

Booth drummed his fingers on the mattress, completely consumed in the volume of his shallow breathing. Not even noticing the crisp spring air that blew through the open window to relieve the stale plainness of the room.

Surratt traced her index finger along his neckline,

lightly grazing each unkempt hair with the chewed tip of her nail. "Don't worry," she whispered, "we'll get Lincoln."

"Right," Booth snapped, causing her to withdraw her hand. "That's what everybody keeps saying, this great band of conspirators. *We're going to get Lincoln. We're going to get Lincoln.* That's what keeps being said. Gonna abduct him. Barter him to the South. But you know what? You know what, Mrs. Surratt?"

She shook her head, no.

"They have all gone pussy on me."

"John."

"It's a fact, Mrs. Surratt. Sam Arnold. Mike O'Laughlin. George Atzerodt. David Herold. Lewis Paine. Even your own son, John. All gone pussy. They might as well go sign up to work for Lincoln, because that's what they're doing by doing nothing."

"It's just the timing . . . They're all behind you."

"Every day he breathes this country dies a little more."

Mary Surratt placed both of her hands on Booth's shoulders, gently massaging, while simultaneously rolling him onto his stomach. She climbed up next to him, her exposed leg pressed against distressed denim, and tenderly squeezed his neck muscles. "Why don't you clear your head," she whispered. "Then you can make better sense of it."

Booth closed his eyes. "I'm not a killer, Mrs. Surratt,"

he said, losing himself in the gentleness of her palms. "I am not."

"I know."

"But I love my country so much . . . Why can't he just accept that this is a country founded by and for the white man . . . If anybody is racist, it's Lincoln. Racist against whites. I saw him speak. Heard it myself. Tried to say that God is on the side of the Union. God's will. Doesn't he know that slavery is God's will? A God-given blessing to us . . . I'm not a killer, Mrs. Surratt . . . but sometimes . . . It's like a mother's instinct."

She ran her gentle and unblistered hands under his shirt, and settled them on his bare back over his quick-rising lungs, feeling the passion of righteousness that beat from his heart.

Not another word was said.

Booth still couldn't clear his head.

✧ ✧ ✧

John Booth paced his room in the National Hotel holding a derringer. Sonabitch pistol didn't have a snout long enough to sniff shit in an outhouse. The trigger was so small he could barely get his finger around it. But this is what he had. Fuck all the elaborate kidnap plots and theatrical schemes; those pussies were all talk and bravado, but no action. It was all coming down to him. If this little piece-of-crap gun was what all the months of planning had reduced themselves down to, then Booth was ready to proceed. It might not be the perfect prop, but hell, neither was that bale-of-hay stage in Atlanta where he performed Shakespeare monologues. If you have it inside you, you can make anything work.

Tonight, Lincoln planned to attend *Our American Cousin* at Ford's Theater. It was said that Lincoln liked that kind of drivel, but for Booth, having to sit through any of that trite play was more of a concern than committing the actual act. Ford's Theater was a perfect setting for Booth, because he had night-and-day access to the whole house as if it were his own living room. Cast, crew, and management welcomed him in for the celebrity that he was, granting him full access to the theater, no questions asked, some older members hounding him for glory-days stories about his father. In fact, he had learned about Lincoln's evening plans from a Ford's actor named Henry Clay Moore, who betrayed the agenda not out of malice, but rather in the trust between two bitching co-workers. "They told us he's not even coming in until about halfway through the play. Can you believe it?" Moore said as they stood outside the hotel on Sixth Street in the shivering morning breeze, coffee breath steaming from their mouths.

"What is that about?" Booth wondered.

"Apparently he has some meetings that won't free him up until later."

"So he's just going to march in with his whole entourage mid-performance like that's okay? Like the goddamn emperor. Every head in the place will turn. How do they expect you to keep acting?"

"We're supposed to stop." Moore frowned.

"What?"

"Exactly . . . Just supposed to stop mid-line whenever he walks in, play 'Hail to the Chief' or some bullshit like that, let him get settled in, and then just get on with it."

"And somehow stay in character?"

Moore waved his hand in disgust. "Don't talk to me about it."

"This guy's lack of respect for everything never surprises me," Booth said.

"You should come to the show tonight, John. The play is shit, but it still moves. Plus you can see Lincoln. You should come."

"Yeah." Booth nodded. "I should."

It was immediately following that conversation that Booth walked straight back to room 228 in the National and pulled the derringer out from under the bed. Pacing the floor back and forth. A cold steel weight in his hand. Measuring himself to see if he actually had the balls to do it. Realizing that he had no choice, because being the harbinger of morality is not often accompanied by the luxury of personal preference.

Still, he was a Booth, and the Booths were known as

the greatest acting family in America. Everything a Booth did had to be seen as theater. Wasn't that what the old man said? A Booth did not just eat dinner at a restaurant, a Booth performed dinner for the other patrons and waiters. The rest of the world was just an audience, or so said Junius Brutus Booth, and to drop your guard for one moment could cost you your larger-than-life status. It wouldn't be enough for John to just shoot the president and run. This was a one-act. It required staging. Blocking. Scripting.

He rode down to Ford's Theater, the daylight nearly blinding his eyes, and jogged upstairs to the State Box, first standing directly behind the chair where Lincoln would sit, then walking forward and placing his hands on the balcony rail, looking out at the empty theater, where the voice of an occasional stagehand echoed from behind the quarter-parted curtain.

All he needed was one good line. A monologue would seem cavalier and grandstanding (not to mention reckless, given the circumstance), and silence would be as pedestrian as the common foot soldier's duty. Nothing as epic as Prince Hal's rallying speech before battle at Agincourt, yet no line as subtle as Caesar's dying accusation to Brutus. Booth did decide that it would make better theater to declare himself after firing the shot. He imagined the crack of the pistol fading, leaving a single pause of silence for him to exclaim his locution, before he hurled himself over the balcony in Romeo's passion with the first piercing scream, and disappeared into the panicked and discombobulated audience and out the rear exit.

The role of a lifetime.

"O villain, villain, smiling, damned villain!" Booth stood before the hall, his shoulders squared, right hand outstretched, trying a line from *Hamlet*. Rehearsing the terror in his eyes, with the glory puffing from his chest. But as the words fell from his lips, they didn't seem to work for the scene. Even the most amateur dramaturge would stage those lines to be directed at the victim prior to his demise. Delivering that line following the shooting risked losing the audience, causing them to ponder the juxtaposition of line and action.

Digging deeper into *Hamlet,* he sucked in a breath and bellowed out a great stage voice filled with irony and victory, *"How now, a rat? Dead for a ducat! Dead!"* The words crashed against the theater walls like an offering to Dionysus. Filled with rage and contempt, yet glorious in their resolve. Booth closed his eyes, imagined the house lights down, a candlelit arc in front of the stage, with his leg propped up on the box's rail as he declared his loathing for Lincoln in both action and verse. But it occurred to him that his act might be misconstrued as one of a lunatic Lincoln hater rather than as a patriotic gesture.

He wondered if Shakespeare was the right scribe for his drama. He didn't want any essence of tragedy to be associated with killing Lincoln. Booth wanted it to be seen as heroic, almost inspirational, something for the country to rally around. The words needed to be profound, yet stirring. A hard epiphany, to send the audience home stunned and reeling.

He backed away from the edge and slumped down in the presidential seat. Booth inhaled large breaths that bloated his stomach, then, as he exhaled, placed an open hand over his falling gut. His father had taught him this technique to "abandon your earthly self to your character," a backstage prep between an actor and his mirror, just before the crowd hushed itself with the rising curtain. And once he was delivered to the role of "John Wilkes Booth—Assassin," a closing line that was deftly American came over him. *Sic semper tyrannis.* "Thus always to tyrants"—the state motto of Virginia. How boldly prosaic and poetic at once. The words of the South rising from bitter dried ashes into a force strong enough to overcome autocracy and brutality and call back the genteel foundation on which this country was built. Lord and God, he hoped that Jefferson Davis was sequestered safely somewhere. Because after tonight the Confederate president could come out from hiding and take his rightful place over this United States. And Robert E. Lee too. Pull on those mud-caked battle boots to kick the shit out of any Northerner who thinks Lincoln is still there to back him up, and then send the niggers back to the farms with the Emancipation Proclamation and the Thirteenth Amendment as tissue to wipe their asses. By the end of this day, April 14, 1865, Northern days will be gone. Gone.

Sic semper tyrannis.

Booth left the theater and went back to the hotel, where he laid his head down on his pillow with a vain satisfaction and napped for two and a half hours. The most solid sleep he'd had in months.

When he awoke Booth immediately rounded up George Azerodt, Lewis Paine, and David Herold in Paine's room at the Herndon House, the rest of the gang having turned coward. The room was painted in a smoky yellow, with rusty nails sticking out all over the walls, framed by permanent dust outlines of where pictures once hung. A distracting squeak came from the room above that Booth attributed to a couple fucking, although Paine discounted it as just another fat guy on cheap wooden floors.

Booth closed the curtains with a swift gesture, then hovered over the men, rubbing his hands together as if he were trying to start a fire. A single ray of sunlight fell on his forehead. "It's over tonight," he addressed them. "At a quarter past ten we strike the final blow." Gesturing with his index finger, he gently touched each man's chest at the heart. "You," he started with Azerodt, "will be in charge of taking out Andrew Johnson. All you have to do is walk right into the Kirkland House with pistols blazing. It'll be the easiest hit of them all."

"I'm not doing any killing, John," Azerodt protested, the tremor in his whisper almost hiding his German accent. He ran his hands through his messy black hair, leaving it standing straight up, then took off his round spectacles, rubbed the lenses against his shirt, and placed them back on his face. Two thumbprints still on each lens.

"What the hell is that supposed to mean?"

"I signed up when we were making plans to kidnap Lincoln and take him to Richmond. Not go off killing people."

Booth looked at Paine and Herold, whose studious faces nodded automatically. "You hear this? . . . Can you believe this?"

"You don't understand, John," Azerodt tried to explain.

"I don't understand? . . . I don't understand? Well, what I will tell you, you dumb kraut, is that you don't understand a goddamn thing about freedom. It's not just handed to you. You don't just get on a boat, get off at the pier, and be granted freedom. Maybe they don't teach you about the history of this country back there in Berlin, but every bit of freedom that you enjoy here has been won in a tooth-and-nail fight. If you don't care about that, then I can't make you. But if you do, and you just aren't up to the task, then fuck you and go back to Germany. Because, George, posterity will judge you as a hero. You want to go through your life oppressed by this Northern fiefdom, then go ahead. But don't give me any bullshit about not wanting to kill. Tens of thousands of men have killed and died every day fighting for this cause. They're still doing it in North Carolina. You're just a soldier, George. A fucking foot soldier who has infiltrated Washington. You're not doing anything less moral than what those boys in North Carolina are doing as we speak. So are you part of the plan? I don't have time to waste."

Azerodt nodded in acquiescence. "Okay," he said. "Just tell me what to do."

Booth turned his attention to Paine. "Lewis," he said.

Paine looked at him carefully. The perfectly round head of a country boy set upon a body the size of an ox. He was new to Washington, had come here just to work with Booth's rebellion after a mutual friend informed him of someone who actually had the balls to make a difference.

"Lewis," Booth said, "you're taking out Seward."

"Yes, sir."

"I don't care how you do it. Slice his neck, a bullet through the heart, a pillow over the head. Whatever you need to do. What I know is that he arrives home promptly at six P.M. and sits for dinner with his wife. After that he takes a brief digestive stroll around his neighborhood. The rest I leave up to you."

"John," Paine replied with a dramatic furrow between his joined eyebrows that looked like a dress sock glued to his forehead. "I don't know Washington at all. I don't think I'd be able to find his house in a million years."

"Mr. Herold." Booth looked to the last of the conscripts.

"Sir," he replied. His voice had the warble of a young girl. His green Scottish eyes looked bright and alert, in spite of the unusual age lines that plastered his youthful face.

"Your task is to guide Lewis to the secretary of state's house, and to make sure that sonabitch Seward doesn't live to see morning . . . Are we all clear?"

Booth adjourned the meeting by saying that the next time they met, America would be rightfully restored. Now all he had to do was go back to his room and change. Maybe have a quick cup of coffee. Splash some water on his face. Shave the stubble from his chin, and brush his mustache. Maybe lay back in bed and picture Mrs. Surratt naked and diddle his mickey for a few minutes. Then kill the president.

⊹ ⊹ ⊹

Sonabitch stage jitters creep up on you out of the blue. One minute you're lazy in confidence, peeking through the curtains to read the audience and to see how full the house is, then the next minute you can barely remember your name or how your knees work, and the juices in your stomach start to rise with a bitter taste, and everything around you smells metallic, while your forehead breaks into a flop sweat that could fill the basin of Niagara.

Booth went back to Surratt's house because the hotel walls felt like they were closing in on him. He paced a track back and forth in the empty guest room. It was nearly 7:00 P.M., and night was just beginning to fall, leaving a purplish hue to color his window. He wore his usual black trousers and matching jacket. His worn soles trod lightly upon the pine floors. Bottom teeth unconsciously wearing grooves into his upper lip. The derringer was tucked into his coat pocket, a single .44 bullet loaded in its tiny chamber. It was like all of goddamned time just stopped, refusing to budge another second, allowing Booth to run the impending scene over and over again in his head.

He would park his horse at Ford's somewhere during the first act of the play. He would make the rounds, ensure a comfortable presence with the house staff, then slip up to the balcony, part the red velvet curtain of the State Box with his left hand, draw the pistol with his right, press the barrel against Lincoln's skull, and pop the trigger. Then he would stand on the balcony rail, deliver his line, leap into the orchestra seats, and run to the exit. The staging seemed almost too simple.

But the more Booth played the scene in his head, the more he pondered the details. Would Lincoln scream? Would blood splatter back at Booth? And God knows he didn't want to be wearing Lincoln's brains all over his chest and only black jacket. One thing he knew for sure was that he didn't want to see the eyes of Lincoln or his traitor wife. "A good actor," Junius Booth had lectured his son, "knows that it is all about the eyes. All human sincerity comes from the truth inside those *windows of the soul.* You can tell a good actor by the conviction in his eyes, and if it's real the audience is left with no other choice than to become totally sympathetic with the character, evil or good." Booth knew one thing for sure, if he looked into either of their eyes he would never be able to pull the trigger. And if he saw them following the shooting, wrenched in terror and disbelief, his conscience would eat him from the inside out. He just had to stick to his steps, and remember that he was assassinating a system, not a human being.

Mary Surratt peeked around the open door, and despite her gentle knock Booth jumped, obviously startled. "You okay?" she asked. "Thought I heard you up here."

"Fine," he said, rubbing his eyes.

"It's after seven, and if you haven't eaten supper, I made a good one. Pheasant. Sweet potatoes."

"I'll be leaving pretty quickly, Mrs. Surratt."

"You've got to eat, John. All men need to eat."

"I've got a lot on my mind. I don't think I could even hold anything down."

"It's not an opening night for you, is it?" And as she spoke those words the obvious rattled the walls, and when Booth looked away, she asked, "Are you going to do it tonight?"

"It's best for you if you don't know what I do."

"But . . ."

"All you need to know is that I sometimes stay in your boardinghouse."

"I know that you're a patriot, John. I'm not afraid to say that."

"Well, you can't say crap with a noose around your neck."

Mary Surratt backed herself up to the wall. A hint of moonlight polishing her toes. "How are you going to do it?" she asked.

Mrs. Surratt didn't need to know anything in detail. No matter what happened, and until Lee's troops could remobilize out of their surrender, Lincoln's Washington posse would be combing the streets over the next few days with death warrants in hand, looking for anybody even remotely connected to Booth. She was a kind woman who had become caught in the fervor of all the young men surrounding her, and even if she did believe it with all her heart, she did not need to be part of it. Did not need to risk dying for the cause.

"You're gonna save us, aren't you, John?"

"It's not what you're thinking, Mrs. Surratt. Tonight is just about theater. Nothing else."

"Then come down for supper before your business," she said, honoring the lie.

He shook his head no.

"It's pheasant. With sweet potatoes."

The dining area was down a steep set of stairs into a

basement that served as both kitchen and sleeping quarters for the owner. The two of them sat end to end at a handcrafted table that Mary Surratt claimed had made the journey from England with her family to America. The pheasant lay in perfectly arranged slices on a fine piece of china, with sprigs of rosemary crowning the top of the dish and a long carving knife at its side. Beside it sat the sweet potatoes, whose perfume filled the room despite the skin looking sick and diseased. One thin white candle stood in the center of the table, the flame rising high and still.

Booth pushed the slices of bird around on his plate in a polite attempt to show gratitude for the meal. His stomach was sick from nervousness, and the thought of chewing brought a sickly taste to the back of his throat. His foot tapped rapidly under the table. He knew Mrs. Surratt was dying to know more. But he resolved not to say a word about tonight's plan, though he wanted to spill it out and purge himself in a litany of righteousness about his right to take a man's life quid pro quo for the betterment of all, anything to humanize the way he felt right now. But now he had crossed the line, and stood alone on his side of the border, just waiting for his cue to enter stage right, where he would rise up high and not even notice the jitters falling away.

"Do you like the bird?" she asked. "Not too gamy, I hope."

"Bird is fine, Mrs. Surratt."

"It's chilly out tonight, John. Better take a coat. Seems like spring gets colder every year."

He patted his coat pocket and felt the bulge of the gun. The tiny pistol seemed bigger.

"I do like a nip in the air, I must confess," she continued. "Keeps the skin feeling fresh." Mary Surratt placed her utensils on the edge of her plate and gently pushed it to the side. She backed her chair away from the table with a slight screech on the floor, and walked over beside Booth.

"Nothing like a Washington spring," he added.

She knelt down and rested her head on his lap, tracing her fingertips along his inner thigh as he instinctively opened his legs wider. "Shall I leave a light burning for you this evening?"

"Don't waste the wax." He dropped his fork and placed his hands on the table at attention.

"John," she whispered. She looked up, desperate and secretive, her hand just below his crotch. "Can I just ask you one question?"

"No." With a gentle force, he pushed her head aside and stood up. "I need to go now, Mrs. Surratt." He patted his coat pocket for assurance. "I need to go . . . I appreciate the dinner and everything else, but . . ." He leaned over and grabbed the carving knife from the serving tray, slid it under his coat, and secured it in his belt. Never know what kind of swashbuckling it might take to get home by the evening's end. "I'm just going for some business at the theater, Mrs. Surratt. Nothing more than some business."

Booth backed away from the table, and paused for a moment when he caught his reflection in a mirror across the room. He inhaled a deep breath, held it for a long second with his palm on his gut, then let it go. His footsteps sounded heavier as they creaked up the stairs.

"Break a leg," Mary Surratt called up, still on her knees in a prayer posture. "And don't go pussy on us."

Booth didn't respond. At the top of the stairs he closed his eyes and drew in one more breath, then walked out into the chilled Washington night. Each step sounded more sure than the previous one.

❖   ❖   ❖

The first act of *Our American Cousin* was bona fide shit. Lincoln wasn't here yet, and another act of this candy-ass amateur hour would likely lead Booth to turn the gun on himself. These forget-your-troubles farces were enough to kill the integrity of any serious actor, and Booth hoped that he, like his father, would have the sense to retire from acting before succumbing to an over-the-hill career of this trash.

He moved cautiously through the empty lobby as the audience waited for the second act to start, beginning to feel unsure of himself. Sonabitch jitters crawling out again. He felt pale, and it seemed impossible to take a full breath. Maybe he was in over his head. He was really only an actor with some opinions. And what if he misjudged the whole thing? Suppose those dumbfuck remnants of his gang didn't follow through on their assignments, and ratted him out. Or if it turned out that killing Lincoln would mean nothing to the rebel cause other than the taking of one more life. He reached down into his pocket and molded his hand around the derringer, desperately trying to remember his one-line speech.

"Mr. Booth, how are you?" Ed Spangler, one of the old stagehands, approached him with an outstretched arm. "Laura Keene's really sharp tonight, don't you think? She's got the audience in the palm of her hand." His face crinkled into a ball as he smiled, his eyes showing off specks of blue that still carried his European past. "But Hawk is hamming it up too much as usual."

Booth smiled politely. "That's how it is sometimes in the theater."

"And you would know, sir." Spangler smiled with reverence. "Heard from one of the builders that you were down here today practicing some lines."

"Yeah." Booth nodded. "Sometimes you need the echo of the hall to hear how something will work."

"Your father used to do that, you know."

"Mr. Spangler, there is nothing about my father that I don't know."

"Goddamn, I bet that's true." He smiled. "Your father

always was a walking piece of self-promotion. Writing his autobiography out loud since the day he set foot on the stage."

Booth leaned back against the wall, his head feeling light.

"You okay there, Mr. Booth? You look a little green, if you don't mind my saying."

"A little under the weather. That's all."

"Well, if you're thinking about going home, I would recommend that you stay around for a little while longer. Word has it that Laura Keene is dropping some lines in especially for Lincoln . . . You know Lincoln is coming tonight? You know that, don't you?"

"Heard something to that effect."

"They're really gonna ham it up for him. You wouldn't miss seeing his reaction, now, would you?"

"Maybe I'll just go next door for a drink until Lincoln gets here. They say whiskey and water is a miracle cure."

"You are your father's son."

"Would you mind holding my horse out back, Mr. Spangler? In case the whiskey doesn't work, and I just need to run on home."

Spangler nodded. "For Junius Booth's son, anything."

"I appreciate it."

"Don't stay at the tavern too long," Spangler called back over his shoulder. "You don't want to miss Lincoln."

Booth nearly slumped to the floor. His intestines felt like they were in slipknots. The pressure was nearly killing him. And if all the shit talk was true—that he was really nothing on this earth other than the son of Junius Booth—then he wondered how the old man would have handled this situation. Old Junius strutting around with so much self-pride bloating from within that he would probably give away the plan to the first person who would give him attention. Or drink himself shitless until he woke up twelve hours later in the bed of some cheap whore only to find Lincoln had been sound asleep in his own room for hours.

❖   ❖   ❖

John Wilkes Booth sat in the tavern next to Ford's Theater nursing a whiskey and water. The bartender knew the actor by reputation, but was kind enough not to bring undue attention to the celebrity seated before him. It was nice to be in the tavern without the usual contingent of theater people engaged in their clever banter and superstitious horror stories, eventually finding their way to him, and only striking up conversation in order to ask for some form of assistance in furthering their careers. This rare silence was calming, helping him to corral his belief in himself through solitude, whereby disappeared the demon jitters. Booth rubbed his hands along the smooth veneer of the mahogany, then looked up to see his anxiously confident face in between the dirty black veins of the bar mirror.

Thank God for whiskey. His father at least got one thing right.

A second man walked into the tavern. He was tall and wide, wearing a suit that had been clearly tailored to fit the unusually proportioned angles of his physique. He had groomed hair that parted to the side, the gray flowing in even distribution along the trim above his ears. He walked with a slight swagger, his shoulders thrown back and proud, before stopping to survey the place as if he were the proprietor. He stood before the bar, removed a handkerchief from his vest pocket, and using it to cover his hand, pulled out a stool for himself next to Booth. His mouth was not visible below the mustache growth, but one would have imagined that a scowl was being carefully hidden under there.

"Scotch, please," he ordered the bartender. "Your top-shelf single malt. Nothing that even knows the meaning of 'well.'" There was refinement in his voice, Booth noted, yet somehow a disingenuous erudition.

The man took the drink without acknowledging the bartender, and with the first sip, closed his eyes in a dramatic rumination of savor and sophistication. He sighed with delight, and looked over at Booth, and what John expected to see as the twinkling blues of the pampered were instead flat and gray. "My word," the man said, "if it isn't the acclaimed John W. Booth."

Booth nodded.

"I recently saw your Richard in Baltimore. And I must say I was . . . well, entertained."

"I'm surprised you saw it," Booth said. "It was a short run."

"Not surprising. The direction was steeped in laziness and carelessness."

Jesus Christ. Is this the ghost of Junius Booth come down to haunt his son? To step in with one more piece of advice and maxim on craft and what should have been, and next time will be. One last jab before his youngest finally upstages him.

"I felt like I was at the audition," the man continued. "That same overdramatic style of reading that is intended to show commitment and passion, but instead only displays the bare ass of the painfully amateur."

It was like his father had come back to life in the form of this jackass, except smothered in a cologne that watered the eyes. "I don't believe we've met," Booth said without offering his hand.

"Barryman Handley," the man said, focusing his attention back to his scotch. He lifted the glass and admired the glow before swallowing the last of it. "And we have met." He coughed out the remaining fumes. "You were just a boy."

Booth shook his head. "I don't recall." He motioned the bartender for another round.

"I'm now the theater critic for the Baltimore *Sun*. Theater has been my beat, if you will, for nearly forty years. I knew your father extremely well. A great admirer of his."

"Barryman Handley. I know your name. What are you doing here?"

"In this tavern, the same as you, my boy—getting away from that pedestrian nonsense they hope to pass off as art."

"You're reviewing that crap? *Cousin's* been reviving for at least five years."

"Yes." He sighed. "Someone told our editor that tonight's extravaganza would be specially tailored for the president. So here I am."

"Sitting in a tavern."

"Sitting in a tavern."

They sipped their drinks simultaneously. Booth began to feel more at ease. He gripped the derringer in his pocket and found it strong and almost sensual. "Anyway"—he looked up at Handley—"you said we'd met when I was a boy."

"Met once, yes. Your father was doing the Scottish play, his King Macbeth fearfully breathtaking, and you had come down to the theater with your brothers. I don't imagine that you were more than five years old then."

"I don't remember."

"That's okay, because I do . . . I was waiting for your father by the stage door to go get some drinks and women—in that exact order, I might add—when you came up and starting talking to me. 'Did you see my dad?' you asked. And I told you that he had been majestic, and the puzzled look on your face told me that you didn't know what that meant. Then you said that you were going to be an actor. Just like your father. And that you too would be majestic. When Junius came out, you ran up to him and grabbed his arm, but he shook you away and told you that a professional does not shed his character just because the curtain has dropped. He directed you to his dressing room for cigarettes, at which point he and I expediently vacated the theater."

"Oh, the good old days." Booth smiled.

Barryman Handley's mustache rose slightly, suggesting some trace of humor. "I have followed your career now and then out of curiosity, so I guess I know a little bit about you."

"And . . ."

Handley threw back the last of his second glass. "You are no Junius Booth. But I expect you know that. But what you lack against the purity of talent that your father possessed, I do think that you have captured in passion. A bit clumsy at times, yes. Rough around the edges. But your belief in your characters should be honored and well noted. And of course I would be in derelict in my assessment if I did not recognize that times and styles have changed, and that the nearly pure form of acting that your father mastered is now seen as passé by many younger people in my profession, and the cruder style that has become your métier is much more widely accepted. I suppose that is a comment on our times." He smiled to himself. "I hope I haven't offended you, but it's not intended to be a direct personal assault. There isn't an actor in this country who can even begin to compare his talents with those of the late Junius Brutus Booth. Not even his own flesh and blood." He finally offered his hand. "No offense, I hope."

The junior Booth shook Barryman Handley's hand, and rose from his stool. "I think Act III should be starting soon. Isn't that what we both came here for?" He reached back to adjust the knife handle that was cutting into his side. "No offense taken," he added. In fact he now felt stronger and more confident. This was a new generation, where passion outweighed finesse.

As he walked out the door, part of him wished he had instead nuzzled the nose of the derringer into the side of his father's temple and blown his brains out years before. It would have made John's life easier for sure, and then maybe he wouldn't have cared so much about these sonsabitches like Barryman Handley or Abraham Lincoln who thought that their word was the only word. Junius Booth was long buried with maggots eating out his eyes, but people still believed in the legend he created for himself. Before pulling the trigger, John would have explained long and hard in plain English, without the veil of iambic pentameter, or cleverly witty metaphors, about what true tragedy is, and how destructive ambition really can be, and its parasitic residue that trickles down through the generations. Of course his father never would have understood. No doubt he would have just orated in the character of Junius Brutus Booth while the bullet shredded his brain.

John returned to the theater with a nervous confidence, and grabbed the handrail to climb the stairs to the balcony. He passed Ed Spangler, who reported that Booth's horse was fine and ready to go whenever he gave him the word. Then Spangler pointed to the red velvet curtain. "He's in there. Right there. Can you believe it?"

"Do you know the time, Ed?"

"A little after ten, I'd guess."

A tremendous wave of laughter rocked the theater. Booth stared into the curtain until the red blurred into a thick fog. He reached his hand into his pocket and clutched the pistol. And he hoped his father was looking down now, because John Wilkes Booth was finally going to show that overstuffed carcass of ego what true talent really was.

T W O

Lincoln's body left Petersen's house on Tenth Street at nine o'clock. Quietly lifted out of the room he had died in across the street from Ford's Theater, draped with an American flag, he was carried by a hearse down G Street, then to the Executive Mansion. The crowds were thick with those who had awakened to the news, but there was not much to be seen through the fortress of Rucker's cavalry that surrounded the driving wagon. Patches of clouds daubed the sky, with a meddlesome sun prying its way through in a contrast of streaming gold rays and a gritty metallic sheen.

Washington stiffened in a permanently held inhalation that rendered speech impossible. Still eyes watched the procession roll by. The little bit of life the viewers felt they had left in them dissipated. The percussive rhythm of the horseshoes rose from the street to fill the morning with a dirge that did not seem ceremonial nor intended, but rather oddly familiar. And in a strange and almost devilish contrast, that Saturday morning held a freshness to it, carrying the same sweet fragrance that follows an overnight rain.

❖   ❖   ❖

Orville Browning sat in the back of the hearse. His palm rested on top of the casket where Lincoln's hands were at rest.

A friend to Lincoln, Browning had been summoned to Petersen's house in the middle of the night at the request of the first lady. When he had arrived she was gone, already incapacitated by shock and hysteria, and ordered back to the mansion by Edwin Stanton for sedation and rest. At Petersen's, Browning had sat down at his friend's side, whose lanky frame lay diagonally across the bed, and had taken his hand from under the woolly green blanket, where a trace of warmth still shimmied the surface, and gripped tightly. "Jesus Christ," he had said, looking into Lincoln's eyes, watery and gone, staring fixed into the ceiling. "What the hell have they done to you?"

Dr. Stone, whom Browning had recognized from Washington events, knelt down on the opposite side and placed his thumb on Lincoln's dangling wrist, closing his eyes and counting pulse beats. He looked up at Browning and said, "A weaker man would have been dead hours ago."

Browning shook his head and looked back at his friend, whose complexion was graying as a thin drool streamed from the side of his mouth. "Who did this to him, Dr. Stone?"

"All I heard was that it was one of the actors. Jumped off the stage yelling, and ran out the back."

The last bit of piss from Lincoln's bladder released on the bed, trickling an occasional droplet at Dr. Stone's feet. Browning held on to Lincoln's hand tighter. "It's not time yet, Abe," he said, then looked at Dr. Stone for confirmation.

"A weaker man would have been dead hours ago," Stone repeated, then placed his stethoscope against the president's chest.

Throughout the rest of the evening candles sizzled in flutters as they slowly burned down, filling the room with

a waxy scent, while members of Lincoln's cabinet filed in
and out to mourn and gawk, followed by nearly every
doctor in the Capitol area. Browning held his hand
throughout. Later he required the assistance of Dr. Stone
to release him from Lincoln's rigor mortis grip.

        ❖   ❖   ❖

The hearse turned in formation with the cavalry escort,
and Orville Browning looked up to see the Executive
Mansion ahead. Chalky white. Alone at the end of
Pennsylvania Avenue. He hoped that they would never
reach their destination. That they could maybe just circle
Washington for the rest of his life, and into the next.

Browning was in good shape for a man in his late
fifties. His hair thinned at the crown of his head, and
washed into a heavy black with rough locks that fell over
his ears. His chest still protruded further than his stomach,
not an easy feat for a man of his age. He was originally a
Kentucky boy, and his friendship with Lincoln had gone
back further than either of them cared to remember.
Somehow they managed to stay friends in the face of
contrasting politics. In the Senate and the House,
Browning had publicly confronted the president on several
occasions, especially over emancipation in Missouri. And
since going into his Washington law practice in '63,
private citizen Browning also made public his objections
to Lincoln's administration and the softness of his policies.

"You're pissed off at me because I won't just give you

what you want," Lincoln had told him while they sat together in the Red Room at the mansion. Lincoln removed the top of an ornate glass decanter and poured each of them a smooth, syrupy single malt. He then held the decanter up to an oil lamp, where the light sparkled through the crystal. He looked at Browning and laughed. "Would you ever have believed that two Kentucky boys who had never known anything but the kerosene taste of moonshine would be drinking from this? I'm told it was a gift from the French government. From the Louis the Fourteenth collection. All the way from Versailles into the blistered hands of a couple of Midwest yokels. Who would ever think?"

Browning laughed along, as the thought had occurred to him fairly regularly about how he ended up where he was, especially from where he came from. He didn't like to think about that kind of stuff too often, it could play tricks on your mind. Start causing you to think about things as you never would have thought about them before. Turning desperation into ambition.

"I mean look at us," Lincoln continued. "We cared about two things when we were kids: getting the hell out of where we were, and getting girls. Jump ahead thirty years, and we're down each other's throats on public policy, and you're turning cold because I won't nominate you to the Supreme Court. Goddamn, you're Orville Browning from Kentucky. I know who you really are and what you're really about. And now you're bent out of

shape because you can't get a Supreme Court
nomination?"

"I'm not bent out of shape."

"It's all politics, Orville. You know me the same as I
know you. President. Shit. If we were in the barnyard
playing, making up our own country and universe, you
know I would make you leader. But it's politics now. And
that's bigger than everything—especially you and me. And
guess what, Orville? It's just reducing us back down to the
yokels that we are."

"I'm not mad at you, Abe."

"Well, you sure made a show out of not campaigning
for me."

"But I did vote for you . . . Cast one for the Lincoln
and Johnson ticket . . . You don't really listen to what I say
about you in public, do you? No point in that."

"That tells me you must understand exactly what I'm
trying to say to you."

They finished off the decanter, both sprawled in the
parlor chairs, angled in slightly toward each other. The
room had warmed to a maternal comfort level that made
it seem impossible to consider leaving. For Browning, his
head felt pleasantly heavy, and his sense of place thankfully
skewed. It seemed like he usually felt better when he
forgot about Washington and politics and determination.
It was the fine line between his Kentucky past and the
ambitious future where he truly felt at peace. Only

Abraham Lincoln managed to be able to get him there. Abraham Lincoln and a bottle of scotch.

"You know"—Lincoln looked up at Browning—"I think I might be dying."

"What are you talking about?"

"Talking about dying."

Browning still slumped in his chair. He raised his hand in a lazy point of order. "Now what makes you think you're dying, Abraham? Could it be that shit they call dinner around here?"

"I'm serious, Orville."

Browning straightened himself, and leaned forward. He should have known to take this seriously. Between the war and Willie's passing, death was not a subject that his friend just threw around. "What's going on?"

"I can't sleep at night."

"Think of the pressure that you're under."

"No, it's not that. I know that kind of not-sleep. This is . . ."

"This is what?"

"It's not even like the not-sleep when Willie died." And his eyes welled when his lost son's name fell from his lips. He looked away from Browning, darting his eyes to the floor, then back at Orville, and to the floor again.

"Abe . . ."

"I lay awake all night, Orville. And all these disjointed fragments of my past start weaving in and out. Some

nothing conversation with my stepmother on a barrel in
Indiana. Flirting in a Massachusetts general store. Events
that were so inconsequential now come to life in vivid
details. I can smell the shit from my father's outhouse. Or
taste the sweat off Ann Rutledge's neck. I swear to God,
Orville, my life is unraveling before me in a very
purposeful manner."

"Well, that's not dying, Abe."

"I think the only thing that has kept me going is the
separation of all these different versions of me. Through
the war, through Willie, through the rest of the crap. I've
been dissected into a million different me's that have just
left their shadow as President Lincoln. But now they're all
trying to come back together. Like they want to connect
for one final time."

"You're not sick, are you?"

"No more than the usual."

"People just don't die for no reason."

"I'm not sure of that."

Browning leaned back and sipped the remnants from
his tumbler. "Have you talked about this with Mary?"

Lincoln lowered his eyes in disbelief. "If I mentioned
half of this to Mother, they would need to cut a lobe out
of her brain just for having listened to me."

Browning smiled and held his glass out for a toast. He
knew Mary Todd Lincoln well, and knew her predilection
for form, and the necessity of keeping an even-keel

consistency for the maintenance of her otherwise nervous composure. Sometimes fighting a civil war must have seemed easy to Lincoln. "How is Mary holding up?"

"Troubled."

"All the hardships?"

"All the everything. Woman spends money all day and all night on stuff she doesn't even know what it is. That's all she does. Her sister came north to visit and console her, but instead spent most of her time telling me what a cocksucker I was for having a war that took her husband and brothers. So I finally got her to spend time with Mary. Make her feel better about herself. Take her back to the glory days of the Todd family. All they did was go out and spend more money. I tell you, Orville, it's a good thing I'm president, because otherwise I'd probably be shackled up in some debtor's prison."

"You know she loves you, Abraham."

"All I can do is turn my back and leave her in her vitriol, then hole myself up in the dark waiting for the night to end. Swear by God that Willie was a miracle. How a boy like him could be so happy and filled with life coming from parents like us is nothing short of a miracle."

"Your tenacity amazes me."

"I've tried drugs," Lincoln confessed. "Morphine sometimes helps."

"I thought that's for pain."

"It just makes me forget about things for a while. Fills

my head with a cloud that just kind of drifts away, towing my body along in a hum. But it doesn't help with the sleep."

"Abraham, I don't think that you're giving yourself credit for all the shit you've been through—especially recently."

Lincoln shook his head no. "I know the difference. I can double a dose of morphine in the day when the pressure starts to back up and the whole chore is too overwhelming, and it takes me down then lets me back out at a point where I can set myself to work again. I know how to take the passion out of my life. But this is different, Orville. I'm telling you. It's not just psycholog-ical wear. This is something bigger."

"Abraham . . ."

"I thought about seeing one of Mary's psychics . . . The truth of it is that I don't need any bill-by-the-hour mystics. I can already see what's happening."

"And what is happening?"

"This is me on my way to dying. Organizing the papers, and getting the deeds in order. On my way to die."

✧ ✧ ✧

Orville Browning heard those words play over and over in his head as the hearse came to a stop at the Executive Mansion. He stepped down off the back, keeping a hand on the temporary casket, and quickly offered his assistance in carrying it up the stairs to the guest room. Once there he assumed that he would help open the top, loop his arms around Lincoln's legs, and on the count of three lift the body out and onto the makeshift table that would support Lincoln's body as the surgeons' blades rummaged it for information.

Although Browning intended to sit throughout the entire autopsy, the weight of the casket on his shoulder brought on a strange sensation of impatience. Instead he wished he were heading down to the residence to shoot the shit with his friend who happened to be the sonabitch president of the United States who wouldn't nominate him to the Supreme Court.

THREE

Mary Todd Lincoln lay collapsed on a plush red velvet chair in the residence. Her legs opened wide, blue cotton dress falling between her thighs. Her head was tossed back, and her fingers gripped the arms of the chair. The doctor's injection had nearly shut her down, though her eyes held steadfast in panic-stricken attention, waiting for her husband's body to arrive. Then she would know, for sure, that he was actually dead.

In a voice shrill with horror, she called for her eldest son, Robert. Someone had said he had returned to the

Executive Mansion an hour ago. She shrieked again, to no response. She was all alone. Nearly paralyzed in this pathetic chair. Treated like crap. Like she was nothing more than Abraham Lincoln's nigger.

"Robert," she called out again.

This time the words didn't echo. They seemed to hit flat against the colonial puke-green wall, and then slither down and die away. She just needed to know that Tad was okay. That someone was tending to him. But they talked to her like she was nuts, a mental defective who needed to be quarantined and "dealt with." It was that jackass Stanton. Probably in concert with the bullshitting, nothing-for-morals vice president, Andrew Johnson. Keep Mary out. Get her the hell away from here. Well, fuck them all. She was still his wife.

That was what she should have told Stanton. Right there in Petersen's house. It was her husband, for God's sake, who had been dying. And Stanton was up there practically with a baton in hand orchestrating the whole thing as a political event. She had just wanted a lock of her husband's hair. At one point she had even gone up to Stanton, and swallowing her pride, begged for just a lock. "Please, Edwin," she stammered in humiliation. "Please."

Stanton had been too busy being big shit, and barely acknowledged her other than with an irritated roll of the eyes.

"I'm begging you, Edwin. He's my husband." Tears and snot had nearly clogged her throat.

"He's the president of the United States, Mary."
Stanton spoke in a correcting tone. "We don't have time
for this nonsense now."

"Please."

Stanton pointed his stubby finger toward the doorway.
"Wait out there in the parlor, Mary. It'll be easier."

She walked alone through the doorway into the parlor,
the echoes of his bullshit sincerity hammering her
eardrums. Her body fell into a blue striped love seat, and
she dropped her head against the mahogany trim, staring
into the broken veins that ran through the plaster ceiling.
She tried closing her eyes, but the intense burning nearly
made her scream out with the last bit of hoarseness left.
Her fingernails dug into the upholstery and picked at a
loosened snag in the material. She worked it back and
forth, and side to side. Sonabitch Stanton. He has no right.
And when the strand snapped in her fingers, she leapt up
with a strength that wasn't her own, pushed right through
the doorway into the makeshift infirmary, and glared
through the flickering candlelight at the round secretary.

Stanton broke off conversation with one of the baby-
faced doctors, and his face turned a deep, ugly purple. He
marched over to Mary, and within earshot of the dead
president's body, he whispered with a gunpowder blast,
"Goddamn it, Mary, don't push. Not right now."

Her eyes felt so hard they could explode, and her fingers
tightened into a fist. She leaned in closer, her lips nearly
touching his lobeless ear. "Don't toy with me, little man."

Stanton gripped her upper arm and gently pulled her into the doorway. Half in the shadows. "Let me tell you something, Mary. And don't think I'm cold or unsympathetic, because you know that Abe and I have been more than about politics, and I do sincerely and honestly have pity and compassion for the shock you must be in tonight. But let's get one thing clear, Mary: at this very moment this is not Abe Lincoln, husband of Mary, father of beloved children who left this earth too soon, and may he rest in peace. This is the balance of this country at stake. Every goddamn face that you see coming in here is not to pay respects, but another politician making up his mind about which way he is going to go now that the door is left wide open. So Mary, right now . . . and I will offer you my apologies in advance . . . right now and for the next few days, this is politics. Pure, simple politics. And I can't have you going crazy on me."

"Edwin."

"Understand? . . . You can not go crazy on this."

"I'll bet both you and Johnson were certain when you had my husband murdered. Certain that you two boobs would be running the country. And don't think I won't tell Johnson to his face, that goddamn coward."

Stanton's full weight fell to his front foot as he tried to budge Mary into the parlor.

"My husband made you what you were. Took you from a playground sissy to one of the most powerful men in the world. And you do this to him. You and Johnson probably killed Willie, too. Am I next? The last bit of brain behind the Lincoln presidency."

"All right, Mary, that's enough." He had managed to knock her from her position, pushing her back in clumsy steps into the parlor, before letting her collapse to the love seat. "Now just sit there and wait." Stanton turned around and left.

In the quiet of the room, her breathing sounded like a hurricane wind. She looked around the room, sparsely decorated, with only the couch she sat on and a simple desk holding a single white candle whose flame seemed to pull up to the ceiling. The walls had been painted in a dark slate, creating a cavelike atmosphere. Mary's heart beat so loudly that she looked to see if the couch was vibrating. She wanted to take Johnson to task. She didn't know if she would publicly accuse him, or just whisper in his ear that she knew the truth, and that his days were numbered. But either way, that traitor would pay. She dropped her face into her palms. Her cheeks were wet. She wasn't sure if it was tears or sweat. All she knew was that she felt cold as hell.

She closed her eyes hoping to find some peace, but all she saw was the spark from the killer's pistol, and her husband's head practically exploding on her. She almost felt relieved when two soldiers pushed through the door with the force of thunderstorm and made the scene go away. One of them spoke. "Mrs. Lincoln, I have orders to escort you back to the Executive Mansion."

"Orders?"

"That is right, Mrs. Lincoln."

"On whose orders?"

"Secretary Stanton's, Mrs. Lincoln."

She shook her head. It figured. "What about Orville Browning? Is he here?"

"That's not information that we have, Mrs. Lincoln." The soldier took her arm in intended compassion, but she shook him off and stood on her own.

"I would like to see Orville if he is here. I need his help."

The soldier looked at her apologetically. "I am under orders, ma'am."

"Let's go then," she conceded, knowing she couldn't beat the Union Army. "But first, all I really want : . . all I've really wanted all along is a lock of my husband's hair."

"Mrs. Lincoln, our orders are not to let you pass through that room. We are to escort you back to the Executive Mansion in a safe and orderly fashion." It was with those words that she went unwillingly with two strange soldiers on the evening of her husband's death into a carriage that drove her to the mansion, where a doctor she had never seen before was standing, ready aim fire, with a needle in hand that pricked deep into her vein and rendered her unconscious until she finally awoke in the solarium calling for her son.

"Robert."

She looked up and saw a porter named Stewart peek

through the doorway, his glassy eyes melting against his coal-black face. He tried to dart away when the first lady caught him, but instead froze in indecision, his white coat shining in the candlelight.

"What is it that you want, Stewart?" she sneered. "Sent here to make sure that I'm still in my place?"

"Not the case, ma'am." Words straining to come from him. He then swallowed and gritted his teeth, his leathery skin breaking into streams of wrinkles that showed an aged but kindly face.

"Then was it that you're after?"

"Thought I heard you calling after someone."

"No one will tell me anything, Stewart."

"I heard the horses coming up Pennsylvania, and . . ." He daubed his palms against his eyes, and said, "Excuse me, I should leave you be."

"How can you hear the horses coming up the street?"

"Silence. The crowd outside turned silent. And I could hear the hoofbeats stronger than my own heart."

The air drained from Mary's chest, and her throat swelled to a thick ball. She closed her eyes at the moment of falling apart, and upon drawing a long soothing breath, opened them in contrived dignity. Being first lady had ingrained that instinct. She patted her hair into place, the texture feeling sticky and disheveled, and considered that those political lackeys almost got away with it, and nearly kept her from her husband in his last resting moment on earth. "Stewart," she commanded, "please come help me up."

"Ma'am is sure?"

"I need to greet my husband." She modulated her voice with every ounce of self-control. "It is my duty to be waiting for him on arrival."

"It's a sad day, ma'am. Real sad." A tear traced along his nose. He didn't bother to conceal it.

"We don't want to keep the president waiting."

Mary reached her arms out without offering her weight, and Stewart, a man double her years and half her weight, hoisted her up until her body collapsed against his, sending them back in a three-step dance before regaining balance. She draped an arm around his waist while grasping his hand for guidance. The warmth of Stewart's palm was comforting.

"Someone should get Tad," she said as they began the journey down the hallway, whose rich reds had once been comforting but which now felt cavernous and comatose. Her sense of home was already being siphoned out of the corridor. "Someone should get Taddie. He should say good night to his father . . . Robert."

The hallway to the northwest side seemed endless, passing under the watchful eyes of dreary canvases whose stares seemed to follow every step and nuance. As they got closer to the main entrance, the swell of faces began to thicken, each looking away from her as she passed. Her dragging legs turned to a limp, and she began a somber stride with her own strength, though still holding on to Stewart's hand. She felt nauseated and hungry at the same time, and the mansion's air brewed thick and stale. "Somebody open a goddamn window," she said below her breath.

"Ma'am?"

Mary stopped in front of an open office where a desk sat neatly ordered in the darkness. She then had Stewart take her into the room, where she asked him to locate a pair of scissors from the desk. "I don't know if it's right for me to be rummaging through the belongings of someone else."

"It's for the president. For Mr. Lincoln."

A procession stood at languid arms inside the entrance to the mansion. Heads bowed, without a whisper. Staff and cabinet members alike, side by side, waited to watch their chief be carried into his home for the last time, while a shadow figure of Mary Todd Lincoln shuffled down the hall with one hand in the grip of an old black porter and the other holding a pilfered pair of silver-handled scissors intended to shear a lock of her beloved's hair.

✢   ✢   ✢

Orville Browning was the first person Mary saw when the hearse arrived. His firm stature was hopelessly stooped as he ceremoniously held a piece of the casket to help escort it through the mansion and up the stairs where the body would be prepared.

"Orville," Mary cried out. "Orville."

Browning kept his head down, keeping pace with the other bearers.

Mary ran up to his side, scissors still in hand, and kept pace with him. "Orville," she said, "look at me."

He shook his head. "I can't Mary. It's too . . . I can't."

"They kicked me out. Kicked me out. Not even the decency to let me be with him when he . . ."

"Let's talk later, Mary."

"It was Stanton," she said, hoping to expose the secretary. They moved down the hallway toward the side stairs, the soles of their shoes squeaking against the floor. "It was all Stanton. Pushing me out. Evasive and deliberate. I think he's behind all this. I think he's the culprit. Stanton. Orville Stanton."

"Mary," he hushed.

"Promise me you'll get Stanton. Promise me."

Browning followed the lead up the narrow staircase. Mary Lincoln squeezed her body between the dark oak banister and the unfinished pine coffin. Her lips a breath away from Browning's ear, repeating her plea to get Stanton.

At the top of the stairwell, General Rucker commanded the bearers to stop, as he awaited further orders as to the specific room to take the body to. The men still held the coffin on their shoulders. Even their breathing was silent.

"You know what I wanted, Orville? All I wanted."

"Please, Mary. Later." He hushed her, looking around to see if anybody was watching.

"A lock of his hair. A simple lock." At which she lifted

the scissors in an attack position and began stabbing the
casket at randomly wild intervals. Her face was oddly calm
with purpose. Fresh pine chips splintered out against the
walls, while the soldiers around her turned their cowardly
heads away.

General Rucker marched over to Mary, grabbed her
wrist, and twisted with a gentle force that was enough to
cause the scissors to fall. He kicked them down the
stairwell and turned her away from the casket. Rucker
took one of his men off coffin duty and ordered him to
remove Mary from the premises. "The rest of you just
move this thing into the first available room. Let's get out
of this hallway."

Browning walked with the casket without looking
back. "A lock of hair, Orville. It's the least you can do . . .
least you can do for a widow," she called. The word *widow*
echoed down the hollow hall.

⁕ ⁕ ⁕

The casket was shimmied through the doorway into the
guest room. Mary and the soldier were left alone in the
hall. She felt dizzy looking at the blue fleur-de-lis pattern
on the wallpaper, and the endless rows of uniformed doors
that reminded her of a residence hotel for indigents. A
window at the end of the corridor captured enough
sunlight to cast a yellow haze over the walls. Her
wheezing breath finally slowed down, and she let herself
collapse in exhaustion into the soldier's arms, feeling

comfort in his corporeal warmth, as though she had finally found the familial solace of Robert. "Ma'am should go downstairs and wait," the soldier advised in a monotone order, his voice flat as a Nebraskan's, drawing his head back in obvious discomfort.

"Everybody keeps telling me I need to be somewhere else," she said almost hypnotically. "I think I'm keeping half the Union Army in business." She tried to rest her head on his shoulder.

He pushed her body upright, until she stood on her own. "I am just following orders, ma'am. Now where may I escort you?"

Mary felt her chest tighten. Her head glazed in confusion, and for a moment she thought that she would throw up all over this soldier's blues. And he stood there so sure and proud, a pimply little face whose nose hadn't even fully formed yet, with patches of fur he'd call sideburns, so certain that the words of a superior gave him the God-given right to circumvent any of the natural laws of the universe, and at the very least, of social decorum.

"Now, please, ma'am." He gripped the flesh of her upper arm.

"I am Mrs. Lincoln to you. The first lady of the United States of America." She whipped her forearm, causing him to withdraw his grip.

The soldier looked down at his gleaming boots.

Mary stepped forward, smelling his sour breath. "So

now I will tell you what I need from you in the service of your country."

"Mrs. Lincoln?"

"I need you to find Elizabeth Keckley."

The soldier maintained a constant nervous nod.

"You can ask any staff in the residence, and they will direct you to her. You just tell them that you are on orders of the first lady, Mrs. Abraham Lincoln . . . Now please go," she shooed.

The soldier disappeared down the steps, his feet drumming a rapid exit, repeating Elizabeth Keckley's name over and over to commit it to memory. She hoped that he didn't waste time. She didn't know how long she could stay angry. If the anger subsided for any more than a heartbeat, she knew she would fall apart, break down into a thousand shattered shards that could never be mended. Her fury was all that was holding her together. Probably all that was keeping her alive. She needed Elizabeth Keckley to get her through this hell. Imagine that, a black seamstress randomly employed by the Lincolns, and it turns out that she's the only person who understands the first lady, who knows exactly how to get Mary back to that place where she can manage herself. Something her own husband couldn't even do.

Mary backed up against the wall and let herself slump to the floor. She wrapped her arms around her bent knees and curled into a ball. How could he do this to her? After all the bullshit trials they went through, losing elections,

the humiliation of his country manners, two children
gone, living in the dump in Springfield, and then he
finally gets it right to become president of the United
States and the whole country falls apart. Finally, their
dreams come together. The war ends. None of those
newspaper cartoons portraying him as some overgrown
freakish oaf, instead as a tall, proud hero. Nobody doubts
her husband, and she finally gets treated like royalty. She
had finally risen out of the black hole of Willie's death
and opened her eyes to see a brighter hue of sunlight
falling on her. And even Abraham looked at her
differently. He didn't shift his stare when she walked into
the room, or pick up papers and exit with little more than
a grunt. In fact, it was only two nights ago when they had
lain in bed and Abraham rolled over to kiss her good
night, and as their lips actually melted together, he pushed
his hand up under her nightgown and rested his palm on
her breast, whispering, "Mother, you have never looked
sexier than you do these days." Didn't she deserve this? All
these years later, didn't she have this coming? But now he's
screwed it up by getting himself shot just when things
were good. Now what is she supposed to do? She
certainly isn't leaving the Executive Mansion. She worked
too hard to get here, and who cares what Andrew Johnson
will think, this is her home and she intends to stay. After
all, she is the one who turned the place from a sterile
federal building into a tastefully elegant home.

Why the hell did Abraham have to go get shot?

Mary's thoughts froze in place. Out the corner of her eye she saw a flit of light flash across the center of the hall, and then seemingly disappear. She closed her eyes for a second, squeezing tightly to clean her mental palate. When she opened them again, the hall was empty, save for the familiar shadows. She sighed a breath of relief. Willie had come back to see her several times after he died, often in the form of a floating light, hovering over the foot of her bed when she slept alone. She had figured that his intention was to provide comfort, to remind her that he was still with her, but evidently nobody told Willie that a ghost spirit that just lingers is nearly terrifying. Like being under the vigilant eyes of a stalker who has no other agenda than to observe. She never said as much, but Mary was relieved when the ghost light finally left. She was finally free to mourn alone.

The light flitted again. This time with a more jerky flash in its instant of visibility.

Mary leaned forward. "Mr. Lincoln, is that you?"

She waited for a response. Imagining that maybe two quick flits would signal yes. Of course responsiveness was never her husband's best suit; often he dragged out a ridiculous interval of time to answer her questions, and usually only after she asked them twice more, each time the irritability exponentially rising in her tone. So she wasn't surprised that she did not see a light immediately following her question.

"Mr. Lincoln," she tried again, this time with more force, "I said, is that you?"

A light did flash, albeit only once, but nevertheless caused a stir in Mary Todd Lincoln that registered on a coordinate somewhere between fear, surprise, and pure expectation.

"I knew you wouldn't leave me alone with this, Mr. Lincoln. I knew I could count on you to see me through. After all that we'd been through, Abraham, each day I still woke up and felt thankful that we were still alive. How can I do that anymore? Maybe for Taddie. You know Robert doesn't need me, in fact he looks at me with a distance in his eye. Maybe for Taddie. But I knew you wouldn't leave me alone with this. You're not that cold."

The hallway darkened. Voices rose from the bottom of the stairwell, and the door to the guest room opened momentarily, then was slammed shut. The shadows filled in until they were nonexistent, and the passage was monotoned into one muted chalk light.

"Please don't go, Mr. Lincoln."

Mary reached her arms out, flailing her hands as though feeling for the density of the light.

"I need you, Abraham. I need you."

The room turned darker, and Mary figured it was just like him to go away when she needed him most. Sonabitch had made an art form out of turning from her in times of need. Taking one tiny step in with those overgrown feet of his, just enough to maintain the bare-bones level of intimacy, and then spinning high heel when the passion started and she needed him to be something other than a pair of elephant ears.

"That's okay." She spoke into the empty hall. "I'd be more shocked if you stuck around and listened."

A stampede tremored the stairwell, and Surgeon General Barnes came stamping by with an entourage of half-familiar faces, passing her without notice, then disappearing into the guest room, their words inaudible under loud whispers. Mary balled her face until the ugly anger squeezed out of every wrinkle, and shook her fist at them. Sonabitch bureaucrats just marching to the beat, not even for one second considering the humanness behind their president, and the fact that he had a family left grieving and about to lose their minds. The only thing that those sorry bastards care about is making sure the forms are signed and the copies initialed in triplicate. She had half a mind to get up off the floor, walk straight over to the guest room, and without even knocking, kick in the damn door and get that lock of hair. Of course those mindless civil servants would probably not even notice, what with their heads buried in the regulations, ensuring that all policies and procedures were adhered to so they could rest assured that they would get their salary-increase percentage at annual-review time. If only that lackey Rucker hadn't kicked her scissors down the stairs.

She started to push herself up from the wall, figuring she would go in anyway, when she saw the streak of light again. She let herself drop to the floor and tried to focus her eyes, but each squint seemed to send a pang of nausea straight to her gut.

"Now what, Mr. Lincoln?" She closed her eyes in disdain. "Are you afraid that Mary is going to do something crazy? Going to humiliate you?"

She opened her eyes, still unable to focus on the hall. It blurred into a big red haze, with the paintings on the wall like little blue smudges. What the hell kind of drugs did they give her? Probably Stanton trying to get her out of the picture too.

"Well, I don't know if you're still there, Mr. Lincoln, but if you are you don't have to worry. Because it's just like always, I'll bury all of my instincts and emotions to make certain that all views look favorably upon you. Don't you worry, Mr. President Abraham Lincoln, our secret hell is safe with me. Now you go on and do whatever it is that you need to do. I'll just stay here . . . I'll be fine . . . Don't you worry."

She remained slumped on the floor with rag-doll limbs, sadness beginning to penetrate her twisted stomach. She tried to think about how much she hated her father. Her stepmother. That tribe of siblings and half siblings that made up her supposed family. And she wanted to rile herself into a fury about how maddening her husband had been, how little he had paid her the attention that she deserved. Anything to bring a thick wave of anger that would flush away the sorrow. Good God, she had no idea how long she could hold on.

Mary heard tentative footsteps treading the stairs. They clumsily stopped before reaching the top. She recognized the voice of the boy soldier as he commanded in a whisper, "Now you wait here. Don't move now. Hear?" Then with his infantrymen's stealth, he craned his head around the wood frame corner and caught the eye of the first lady.

"So you decided to return." Mary looked up from the carpet, trying to use his tardy presence to summon back her rage.

He straightened his neck, then grabbed the banister and pulled himself up into the hall.

Mary didn't bother to move. She just rolled her eyes up to him as acknowledgment. Dark irises piercing from the corners. Her stale breath blowing out her nose.

"Mrs. Lincoln, ma'am," he started.

"Yes, soldier."

"My name is Carter, Mrs. Lincoln, ma'am. Carter."

Mary still hadn't moved her gaze. "I don't need to know your name."

"My apologies." Carter stepped forward. He leaned his trim lanky body over so that the first lady could hear his lowered voice. "I've got a woman waiting around the corner who is claiming to be Elizabeth Keckley."

"Well, then, let's stop talking and get her up here." She lifted her head and bellowed out, "Elizabeth!"

Carter raised his hand as if to block her voice. "I'm not sure that she is really who she says she is."

"And why is that?"

"She's a negra." His voice was barely a trace of a whisper. "Everybody is saying she's called Elizabeth, and she answers to the name of Elizabeth, but she is a negra. A seamstress negra. I'm wondering if there is a mix-up, or if she's just storying."

"Please just go." She waved. "Elizabeth! . . . On your way, soldier. You're a credit to your country, and you are honored for serving at the pleasure of the president, and all the rest. Now, off. Off."

As the soldier Carter gladly disappeared down the steps, Elizabeth Keckley entered the hallway. She stood tall and lean, and looked eight feet tall before the stairwell. Her white cotton dress fell straight and shapeless, rising slightly over her hips and then dropping to just an inch above the floor. She had a light almond complexion, and she wore her hair sheared close to the scalp. Her eyes were big, with airy whites surrounding dark, narrow irises, and her mouth drew evenly across her face in helpless honesty. She held her hands at her stomach, tapping her fingers against one another. "Oh, Mrs. Lincoln," she said, her eyes beginning to well.

Mary looked up and caught her stare, for one moment in this miserable life feeling like there truly was deliverance. "My Elizabeth is here," she said. With those words all the assumptions of Stanton, Johnson, and the rest disappeared into the warmth of salvation. "You are always here for me."

Elizabeth hurried over to Mary and knelt down beside her. She put her arms around her employer, who nuzzled her swollen wet face into Elizabeth's breasts. "I don't know what to say, Mrs. Lincoln."

"You don't have to say anything."

"It's a shame what they done to that man. What they done to you and the boys."

Mary squeezed Elizabeth's arm, as though all the strength she had in life was in her right hand. "You're not going to leave me, are you, Elizabeth? You'll always stay here with me, right? I don't want to be desperate anymore. I don't want to be desperate. I wish I were black like you. I want to feel freed. No more desperation."

"Mrs. Lincoln," Elizabeth said with some authority, "let's go downstairs. It's more quiet. More private."

"I just wanted a lock of his hair."

Elizabeth stood up and reached for Mary's hand.

"I just wanted a lock of his hair is all. I'm not crazy, running the halls like some kind of lunatic. I just wanted his hair. Maybe put it in a box. Or a locket. Somewhere that I could touch it every once in a while. Just feel him a little bit on occasion. That's all I wanted."

Elizabeth lifted her by the hand until the first lady stood on her feet, one hand braced against the wall.

Mary felt light, as if her body weight had given itself up for air, and her feet didn't feel like they fully touched the carpet. The walls blurred hazily, but it didn't really matter to her right now. She held on to Elizabeth's hand for guidance, and took small floating steps toward the stairs.

"Don't you let them drug me," Mary ordered.

"Mrs. Lincoln doesn't have to worry about that."

"They already drugged me once last night."

They stood motionless at the top of the stairwell. Mary looked down at the dark oak banister that slid all the way to the bottom, and tentatively gripped it, drawing in all her strength.

Elizabeth held her upper arm as they took the first step down into the shadowed stairwell. "Last night was last night . . . Easy does it now."

Mary smiled almost girlishly. "These steps are steep, aren't they?"

"Now hold on to that rail too, Mrs. Lincoln. Not just me. With these steps you're needing all the support."

"Elizabeth," Mary said, as she gingerly felt her foot forward for the next stair.

"Mrs. Lincoln?"

"Will you sew me a nice dress for the funeral? Something elegant and stately. Maybe cut with some display of pride, yet falling in a flow of sorrow."

"I'll sew you whatever you need."

"Maybe cotton. Flat black cotton."

They took another step down.

"Or possibly silk."

Mary nearly missed the next step, and had a momentary loss of balance before regaining it with the assistance of the rail and Elizabeth's forearm.

"I told you to keep focused and hold on tight. You're almost back to your room. A little sleep is always good for the just."

"And maybe Taddie and Robert can match me. You can sew clothes for the boys, can't you?"

"You just tell me what you need."

The light at the bottom of the hallway had a different shine. It carried the same brightness, but was somehow more diffused, making it softer, though less reachable. The voices of the president's staff had all but disappeared, leaving a creepy hollowness to the mansion. In fact, the whole place smelled stale and forgotten.

They stopped just before the last step. Mary turned to Elizabeth, a bit confused, her face hanging like a heavy mask, as though each and every pore refused to let the air in. "I need to rest," she said.

"We'll get you to your bed. There's no evil that's gonna touch you there."

"And you won't leave?"

"I'll keep you free from harm."

Mary squeezed Elizabeth's arm tightly. "That step looks steeper."

"Don't you worry, Mrs. Lincoln, I'm helping you down."

Mary Todd Lincoln let her right foot slowly slip off the edge of the riser. She turned to Elizabeth Keckley. "When I wake up we'll go buy the material for my dress. Then we'll buy the fabric for the boys' clothes. I know just the stores to go to. We'll buy everything we need . . . Just don't let me sleep too late . . . I won't rest until we get it."

FOUR

Abraham Lincoln's body lay on a board covered in sheets and soaked towels in the guest room. Nine men were present to oversee the necropsy, nine men whose names would not withstand history's fickle memory. Barnes. Stone. Taft. Crane. Notson. Rucker. Browning. Woodward. Curtis. Each standing in place as though the staging at Ford's Theater had extended itself to the northwest corner of the Executive Mansion.

His body was naked, a chest seemingly ordinary other than the lack of a heartbeat. And his face still had color, although nearly a nauseous green, as though it hadn't thoroughly made up its mind to die. While his dignity should have seemed parched and soiled, he somehow looked stronger. Like the carved musculature of Grecian marble gods, except with beard whiskers stiffened by brown blood, and his coal-black hair sticking ratty and matted to the back of his head where the bullet had entered.

The room held a brilliant silence. Dr. Barnes, the

surgeon general, was busy clearing the antique furnishings off an eighteenth-century end table that he would convert into a desk to detail the procedure for his final report as the chief prosecutor. As he moved the better half of a pair of matching lamps, kerosene wobbled in the glass bowl, the flame stretching and wrapping its way around the interior of the stained-glass shade, causing a diamondlike rain to fall over the room in reds and blues. In haste and frustration, the old white-haired doctor handed the lamp to an assistant surgeon general, Crane, and pulled the oaken table closer to the head of the cadaver. With the final pull, the table legs gripped the floor momentarily, then yelped a furious cry across the hardwood planks, bringing all mortal action to a halt, as each man unconsciously glanced at the dead president to see if the screech had awakened him.

On assignment from the surgeon general, Drs. Woodward and Curtis prepared themselves for the actual cutting. Dr. Curtis had not slept since hearing of the president's shooting. He had paced the upstairs awaiting news from the surgeon general's office on the status and condition of Lincoln. At about four in the morning he had laid his dressing clothes out, expecting that all the assistant surgeon generals would be called into action. At seven-thirty he entered a dispatched coach, a cinnamon roll beside him on the seat, and rode into the Washington morning, the windows of the houses stained by the rays of daylight's orange. He leaned back, his shoulders relaxing

into the plush upholstery, and watched the grieved mill
the streets, heads held low, walking toward the mansion or
just standing still. Curtis had recently turned fifty-six, and
ever since that birthday he had found himself possessed of a
new degree of exhaustion. His spine had become a little
harder to keep upright, causing his shoulders to roll
forward slightly; his breath took a few extra minutes to
catch from just climbing the stairs to the second-floor
bedroom, and his eyes that had once been vibrant and blue
now appeared duller, and it was harder for him to focus
them. Somehow this new tired version of himself had
made his work increasingly more difficult. His stamina
had not been affected as much as his ability to maintain a
fully dedicated concentration to the "importance" of
being a doctor. A week ago Edward Curtis had learned
that he was going to become a grandfather. He told his
wife that he felt old enough to be one. Then he asked if
that meant he could retire. When he gripped the handrail
going up the staircase to the guest room, he had wished he
were retired.

Curtis laid his surgical instruments out one by one on
a china serving tray that someone had found in a cabinet
in the next room. Steel scalpels, forceps, and scissors lined
in a row, their dull finish still managing a reflection.
Woodward pulled out a small bone saw from his bag and
placed it above the scalpels. Both men looked over to their
superior, Dr. Barnes, who still adjusted the table, then

wiped the dust with the sleeve of his rumpled black suit jacket. His head shook mechanically in disbelief, while a chant of inaudibles passed his lips.

Dr. Curtis broke the silence with a whisper that despite its slightness seemed to hammer the room. "When would you like us to begin, sir?" he asked of his superior, Barnes.

Barnes appeared not to take notice. With his makeshift desk finally in place, he became engrossed in digging blank pages from his satchel, inspecting them, and discarding them for no apparent reason. Meticulously folding each unwanted page in half, and then halving that again, and placing it back in his bag. His jagged and tired fingers shaking with every fold. "I just need something to take notes on," he finally replied, then returned to his task. "One that doesn't seem such a goddamn shambles."

Curtis and Woodward continued their preparation, carefully repositioning their tools, placing the skull chisel next to the saw, and laying out the heavy twine suture beside the Hagedorn needle that would eventually sew the president back together again.

Drs. Stone and Crane combined to assume the role of *Diener,* eschewing their usual leading roles in order to provide assistance to the more senior surgeons. They measured Lincoln's bloodied skull at fifty-eight centimeters, then drew a tape the length of his seventy-six-and-a-quarter-inch body. Stone gripped the president's wrist, and planting his full weight squat into the floor, pulled with all his strength to break the rigor mortis and extend Lincoln's arm for a full and accurate measurement. The arm still would not extend, so Stone tried to whip it like an old piece of jump rope, and then yanked again, causing the cadaver to lift slightly off the table and land with a thud.

"Don't worry about the measurement," Barnes said, still fussing with his papers. "We'll just guess at that."

"Yeah," Stone said, "it didn't feel right doing that to the president, and all."

Curtis just swallowed. He thought he might be sick at any moment.

"Body-back goes under the head first?" Crane asked Curtis.

"Sure," Curtis nodded. "As good a place to start as any."

Positioned at Lincoln's head, Stone drew in a long breath and cupped his hands under the great man's neck. He bent his knees for strength and pulled up as Dr. Crane slid a wooden block under Lincoln's neck, thus elevating the head for the ease of the procedure.

Curtis looked down at the soft pouches beneath Lincoln's eyes that had settled into a thousand distinctive canyons when he had smiled, now appearing molded thick and stiff like a synthetic from a craftsman's hand. A metal taste washed through the back of his throat. He felt kind of faint.

"Okay." Barnes spoke from behind his new desk. "It seems as though we're in order. I suppose we shall begin the procedure now."

Woodward was the first to respond. "Following the brain removal, will we be conducting a full autopsy, sir?"

Barnes loosed a deep sigh and stroked his chin in consideration. His lips mumbled concerns, and finally he looked up at Curtis. "What do you think?"

Truth be told, all Curtis was thinking about was how to leave the room. He had performed these types of procedures a million times over, but somehow the sacrilege of cutting into Abraham Lincoln seemed not only sickeningly overwhelming, but sinful.

"I look to your experience," Barnes added.

"Just get the bullet." Curtis offered what he thought would be the quickest solution. It was probably not the most medically sound answer, and certainly not the most thorough, but given the circumstances it seemed like all he could recommend. "There is nothing we need to get from the trunk. We know what happened."

"So we'll leave the dissection for the morticians?"

"That is my recommendation, Dr. Barnes, sir."

Barnes drummed his hands on the nightstand table, and coughed for attention. "Okay, men," he began. "With the situation as it stands I concur with Dr. Curtis. We will just be excising the brain to locate the bullet. However, in the name of medical science and research, I think we would all be professionally derelict if we did not utilize this unfortunate situation to further pursue knowledge of the human brain. President Lincoln lies before us as one of the great thinkers of our times. It would be morally shameful for us as medical practitioners not to study his brain to further understand the complex working of that organ. But given the delicacy of this situation I would like to make certain that we are all in agreement on this course."

"I'd bet the weight exceeds eighteen hundred grams," Stone commented.

"Ridiculous," Woodward countered. "Brain weight is brain weight. Nobody's intelligence is proportional to the weight of their brain."

"Would you care to wager on that?" Crane entered the conversation.

"Three-to-one odds," Woodward offered, proudly confident.

"Let's make that five-to-one, cash on the barrelhead."

"All right, gentlemen," Barnes interrupted. "I see how easily scientific discourse gives way to pedestrian ramblings."

Curtis pulled on a pair of gloves. He closed his eyes in anticipation and tried to visualize the entire procedure. He opened them immediately when the breath emptied from his chest.

Curtis and Woodward stood over Lincoln's head, his great big eyes only half closed, exhibiting an almost monsterlike quality.

Woodward turned to Curtis, his narrow brow drawn in a combination of concern and bravado. A good cutter in his own right, Woodward's broad shoulders and strong jaw had always been useful in giving the impression of strength and authority. He and Ed Curtis had worked some tough cases together in the past, considering each other colleagues of equal merit, although because of the almost ten-year deficit of Woodward's age they had never even entertained the notion of a social relationship. "All right," he asked, "how do you want to work this?"

Curtis swallowed, then shrugged. "It doesn't really matter," he said. "Doesn't really matter."

"I don't mind doing the cutting," Woodward offered. "I'm fine with it."

Curtis nodded. "Okay then."

"But if you want to do the cutting, that's fine too. You are senior to me."

"No, you go ahead. I'll just assist."

Woodward took the scalpel and carefully placed its razor edge behind Lincoln's left ear. "Can you hold that tuft of hair back?" he asked of Curtis.

Curtis reached over and took the president's hair, and pulled up, uncomfortably aware of the resistance from the scalp. Woodward grunted as he dug the blade in, his face balling as he pushed down, his arm shaking. He burst out a breath, and said, "There, I finally touched skull." Curtis looked down and saw the cherry-red blood soaking his gloves. A little bit had splashed on his forearm, and he noted how sadly warm it still felt, coming from a man who had been shot nearly twelve hours ago, and dead for three.

"Okay," Woodward narrated to himself. "Next step." He sliced upward, leaning full strength into the cut, and drew an incision that arced over the crown of the head, and ended up perfectly symmetrical behind the right ear.

Blood drenched the rug. With every step, their feet squished as if they wore wet galoshes. Curtis wondered who would have to clean this up, if some sad short-straw servant would end up on hands and knees scrubbing until the stains were gone. For him, this procedure couldn't go fast enough.

Woodward began to show signs of discomfort. After he had laid down the scalpel, he braced his hands against the edge of the table and leaned forward, drawing in breath, as if for strength. Then he lifted himself up and looked to Dr. Curtis with an expression of newfound camaraderie, and said he supposed that it was time to continue. "We can't keep the great ones waiting." His useless attempt at alleviation fell stupid and heavy.

"One moment, gentlemen." Surgeon General Barnes looked up from his rapid note taking. He turned to the gallery of onlookers and warned them of what they were about to witness. "I know that some of you are physicians, and have experienced the bluntness of how we are about to treat the human body, but for those of you who have not had this experience, I offer, with some encouragement,

a moment for you to exit." He looked specifically at
Orville Browning and General Rucker. "There is no
shame in leaving."

The six remaining men, some seated and some standing,
all nodded in acknowledgment. And they all stayed put.

"So be it," Barnes said. "Then let's continue."

Woodward proceeded to dig his fingers into the
incision and grip the bottom of the flesh at the skull. He
anchored his body to the floor and began pulling up in
the manner of ripping out a carpet, trying to draw the
scalp over the president's face. He tugged again, causing a
slight ripping sound, and then let go. "I can't get it by
myself." He turned to Curtis. "It's like it's nailed down."

Curtis responded by burrowing his fingers deep into
the incision. The skin that had hardened at the surface was
jellied below. His hands tingled as he gave Lincoln's scalp a
slight squeeze, and a rail of blood oozed from the seam.
Meanwhile Woodward had shifted position, and was
standing more to the front of the body. Together they
pulled. Curtis felt the ripping of the scalp tear through his
own body limb by limb, as he focused on the dull white
back wall.

"Okay," Woodward grunted. "We got it." He fell
back with the satisfied lapse of exhaustion that follows
accomplishment. "That was a tough one." He sighed,
looking over at Barnes.

A flap of spotty white pus in random relief mounds,

trailed by rich blood, hung down as a veil over Lincoln's face. Only the edge of his beard whiskers protruded, barely touching the ends of the hair on his head now thrown forward and laid underneath. And in that moment it felt like every conviction and doctrine that Curtis had ever believed in was suddenly without meaning.

Woodward moved behind the table and peeled back the rear flap of the scalp, gently tucking it under the nape of the neck. Where once had rested the last vestige of this American hero, now lay a common, run-of-the-mill, medical-school-skeleton skull. No different from the rotting bones piled high in the pauper's grave. Its ordinariness was its most jolting feature.

Woodward reached over the table to pick up the bone saw. "I sure wish there was more light in here." He spoke to no one in particular. "Do we have a kerosene lantern, or at least can we pull back the drapes a little?"

Orville Browning, who was the sole representative of Lincoln's personal life, pushed one of the drapes to the side, allowing an alarmingly brilliant light to pierce the room. "I can see if there is a lantern in one of the other rooms," he offered, but Woodward didn't respond, and nobody else in the room seemed to show much concern, so Browning fumbled his way back to his seat, not taking his eyes off the surgeon's table.

Curtis watched Woodward lift the saw above Lincoln's skull and lower it about halfway before stopping. His forehead glistened with sweat, and the stench of nervousness rose from under his collar. "I can't do it, Ed." He turned to Curtis. "I can't do it."

The two men switched positions. Woodward clasped both his hands around Lincoln's head as a brace as Curtis, a professional without choice, laid the edge of the saw on the dead man's scalp and let it rest there, drawing in the stamina to begin. He positioned his feet about eight inches apart, and bent his knees slightly for balance. With his forearms, he applied mild pressure to the saw with a gentle thrust, making sure that it wouldn't slip off the curvature of the skull. Then he threw all his weight onto his back foot, and following one long breath, leaned forward and pressed the teeth of the saw against the bone, filing back and forth in short rhythmic motions, the loose scalp jiggling slightly over Lincoln's face.

The sawing noise was soft, and eerily tender, the rhythm almost lulling the room with its low vibration.

Bone dust sprayed over Curtis's hands before they turned moist from marrow. Without missing a beat, he leaned forward and blew down, causing the residuum to dissipate upward and momentarily sparkle in the sunlight.

He moved in slow steps around the head as he worked, cutting fine lines, and only pausing for the slightest second to make sure that he was not cutting into the gray matter. Curtis felt himself part artist, part orchestral conductor, even tapping his foot in time with the cutting. So absorbed that for once in this lousy day he forgot he was anything but a craftsman with surgery as his trade.

By the time he had crept around to the right side of the head, he gave the saw one last quick filing motion, then leaned over and blew. A cloud of dust rose out of Lincoln's head. "Voilà," he said to himself.

"Are you okay for the rest?" Woodward asked.

"I'm fine," Curtis responded. Somehow it seemed fascinating to him, and perhaps even a testament to his professionalism, that once he had brought himself to begin his work, his anxiety and sickness and reverent rigidity had disappeared. "I'm ready to finish the procedure, Dr. Woodward. If you would just hand me the skull chisel, then we'll get off the calvarium and get to that brain."

He leaned in closely and began working the chisel through the scores he had made with the bone saw, carefully rocking the blade back and forth to loosen the bone and finish breaking open the skull. His breath was heavy. He could feel the warmth against the top of Lincoln's skullcap, steamy and moist. When he reached the last edge of his etching, he ratcheted the chisel in deeper and pulled back on it like a lever, loosing a vacuum noise whose pop just about startled everyone out of their seats, along with a rancid odor that only a proud surgeon could find sweet.

Curtis lifted the calvarium off and handed it to Woodward, noting to Barnes that the skullcap felt dense and indistinguishable. He peered down into the open top of the president's head at the exposed dura, its cauliflower ridges moist and shiny, with thin little lines running through it, looking stupidly useless, with no sense of posterity or awe. "Surgeon General Barnes," he said with clinical protocol, "I have reached the brain."

Dr. Woodward then handed him a scalpel to finish the excision, himself glancing quickly at the compacted source of reason and intellect.

Curtis hunched over the open head, his front teeth studiously cutting into his bottom lip, and with flowing ease split the spinal cord in half and swiped away the dural reflections. He reached into the skull cavity that he had so delicately and ornately crafted and lifted out the brain.

"Locate the bullet before you string it up in the jar of phenol," Barnes ordered, licking the tip of his pen. "Who knows, the phenol alone could probably disintegrate the lead in a minute."

Dr. Curtis stood with Abraham Lincoln's slippery brain balanced in his fingers. He pushed it into the sunlight trying to trace the bullet's point of entry in order to locate its exact lodging. The other doctors gathered around in curiosity, most peering for a brief moment before resigning themselves to the clinical ordinariness of gray matter.

"How does it feel?" Stone asked. "Heavier than you'd expect?"

Curtis shook his head. "It feels like a brain. A strong brain." At which point the early anxiety started to rise in him again, tingling his fingers and drying his mouth. The mind that had written the Emancipation Proclamation and the Gettysburg Address and led the War Between the States was literally in his hands. And maybe the somnambulist actions of this seasoned medical practitioner had failed to take note of the importance of the occasion while under the intoxication of the beauty of surgery, but now the man who stood as Edward Curtis with Lincoln's brain felt suddenly out of place. Like some kind of ritualistic monger who held the organs of a sacrificed leader on a thick wooden pole before a ceremonial bonfire. A position that might make others feel stronger had rendered him weak and almost helpless.

His hands started to shiver. He suddenly felt incapable of any medical judgment or decision. The cerebellum glowed in the brilliance of the sun ray.

"Do you see the actual location of the bullet?" Barnes queried.

Curtis answered no, and then hoped that maybe he could just hand the thing off to Woodward or one of those ambitious braggarts prattling on about the weight, and run straight to his house and back into bed, and not get out until the whole event passed into a memory with insufficient details. He knew if something didn't happen soon he was likely to hurl that brain across the floor in disgust with himself, watching it break into a dozen fleshy chunks.

"I need to excuse myself," he said to Barnes. "Just for a moment, sir."

Barnes waved him on without looking up. "Dr. Woodward, you can take over." He grumbled to Curtis, "When you return you can help with the forensics. We need your expertise. And watch out for the first lady out there. She looked ready to crack when I walked through."

As Curtis passed Lincoln's brain to Woodward, a little ping, barely audible, hit the toe of his shoe, and then rolled onto the damp rug. He looked down to see the fractured nose of the bullet. So little and harmless-looking. So nondescript it was almost laughable. And he thought that at any moment he was going to become violently ill.

Curtis let himself out of the bedroom door and moved past an expressionless guard standing at arms. The reds of the hallway fostered an overwhelming heaviness that betrayed the intended warmth. Curtis felt he needed some air. Something to keep him from fainting, and perhaps restore his rationality and help him work clearly again. But every exit was heavily guarded, and he realized that going outside would not be enlightening to any degree.

He walked the hallway until it gave out to a descending stairwell, then leaned against the patterned wall, putting his hands to his face. His palms felt cold.

"I am sorry to interrupt, but I've been asked to keep the hallway clear."

Curtis dropped his hands, almost chagrined at his

vulnerability. The soldier guarding the hall was a young Negro man. He stood before the doctor accentuating the proud blues of his uniform with rigid shoulders and deliberate fingers. His face was a deep black, and his eyes burned red, as if they hurt. His expression was apologetic, yet he maintained a degree of officiousness.

Curtis nodded that he understood.

"I need to keep the hall clear for the doctors. The surgeon general and his staff."

"I'm one of them, an assistant surgeon general . . . Just on a breather . . . Here to perform the autopsy." And those words had such an otherworldly ring to them that Curtis had no idea if they actually came from his mouth.

"He's really in that room?" the guard whispered, having given up the official for the fraternal.

"His body is."

"Sonabitch if the world don't get stranger every day."

"Do you have a smoke, son?"

"Stopped after I fought my last battle."

Curtis looked up with a sad smile, glad for the conversation. "Did you see action?"

"Fifty-fourth Regiment of Massachusetts Volunteers, sir."

"Your ranks got hit hard, didn't they?"

"Never did see so much misery as I saw at Fort Wagner."

"South Carolina?"

"South Carolina, sir . . . That's right, South Carolina."

"It's a mean world out there."

"That it can be. Sure enough mean as a devil."

Curtis paused in thought, and then offered his hand. "Edward Curtis," he introduced himself.

"George D. Washington."

"That's truly your name, soldier?"

"Swear to it. And that's why the *D* remains." He shook Curtis's hand with a firm grip that eschewed deference, his assuredness in his confident posture.

Curtis never remembered shaking the hand of a black man, and was momentarily surprised to feel a smooth hand as gentle as his, and not the dried leather that he had imagined. He had only known blacks as porters or laborers, people who were fixtures and atmosphere for the world that he inhabited. In fact, Curtis couldn't even remember wishing them a *good day* or a *happy holidays* even once. It wasn't out of malice or intent. It just never occurred to him. Yet now here he stood, thankful for the mere presence of this young Negro man. Lucky to have someone to talk with in order to keep him from facing his work. "Let me ask you, Mr. Washington . . ."

"George D."

"All right, George D., are you glad you fought? Glad you did what you did?"

"Sure enough beat the alternative."

Curtis nodded in agreement, partially embarrassed by the obviousness of his question.

"You know a man like Lincoln don't come along very

often. Not too often when a man such as he was would
look out for a bunch of Negro nothing-to-America slaves.
Gotta get behind that. Right?"

"I suppose." Curtis sighed.

"But the stuff that I saw going down will scare me
half to death for the rest of my God-given life. Men
without heads stumbling across battlefields like some
possessed haints, with their arms still flailing and crazy.
Burning. And shooting. And you're nothing but goddamn
scared to go to sleep at night, and the same fright to be
waking up in the morning. Never knowing what is going
to hit you. Maybe some sickness that drops a hundred men
dead in a day, or some nigger-hating Confederate who
finds you wounded, and blows your brains out instead of
taking you prisoner like he would the white boys. But,
Mr. Curtis, I'll tell you one thing"—he lowered his voice
to a whisper—"that shit ain't nothing compared to being
a slave."

Curtis leaned deeper into the wall, watching the light
of the room darken to a moldy complexion. Maybe he
could just melt into the wall, and the autopsy would go
on without him, with nobody wondering or caring where
he was, and maybe he could just rest for once.

"The bullshit you have to take," Washington
continued. "Swear the day he made that 'Mancipation
Proclamation, I was enlisted before the ink dried. Had to
get behind it fast because fast wasn't fast enough . . . Hope
every colored person in the United States comes to pay

tribute to Lincoln. Line every inch and corner of Washington, dressed all the best as they can do, and grin and smile a celebration when he rolls by. And when he's gone they should all look up to the sky and say to God, 'Thanks for the loan.' "

Curtis shook his head, *Amen,* and then laughed at his own irony. "I've got to tell you, George D., in my wildest imagination I never could have predicted this conversation. As if the war has not been strange enough . . . But swear by God, when I sat down to eat my supper last night, wondering what we were going to do on Easter Sunday, being glad the week was over because work had been a real grind, I never in a million years could have considered that tomorrow would find President Lincoln's brain in my hand. The only thing making it even a little bearable is a conversation with a Negro half my age. It's no offense, but it's just not what I ever could have imagined."

"You think a white government doctor is the first place I'd turn?"

Curtis laughed, and his eyes met Washington's, swollen and red. "They did it, didn't they." Curtis had to look away, and he heaved a long sigh. "Sometimes this life just makes you feel so tired. Always beating you down. So worn."

The soldier, George D. Washington, stepped in closer and hushed his voice. "He's really in there?"

"Kind of."

Washington offered his hand. Curtis pursed his lips,
and swallowed back a sigh. He gripped the soldier's
hand with both of his, turning the squeeze into a tender
consolation of shared grief. "On behalf of the surgeon
general's office," he spoke as his throat hardened, "I thank
you for your service as an American."

Woodward poked his head out of the guest room with
a slight whistle. "Barnes needs you."

"If you'll excuse me, Mr. Washington."

"Sonabitch if the world don't get stranger every day."

Dr. Curtis turned from the soldier and began the
march down the corridor. Exiled into shock. His feet
sinking into the plush runner, while the walls seemed to
pass him by. He didn't look back at George D.
Washington. Didn't for one moment turn around to take
inventory of the young soldier's distinguishing features.
To imprint his flat nose or his half-closed eyes to memory
in case they met under different circumstances. Curtis
would never see the black soldier again. He knew that.
And the soldier probably knew that too. Because by
tomorrow, the worst would have passed, the shock turned
to confusion, and in short time, no doubt, the confusion
turned to a scrounging memory. As for Dr. Edward
Curtis, he'd probably forget that he ever talked like this to
a black man. Probably wouldn't even be able to tell you
what a Negro handshake felt like.

FIVE

The smell of dry tobacco had made it hard for John Wilkes Booth to fall asleep. The leaves were bundled and stacked at the other end of the barn, but the acrid odor still seemed to hover above him. Nearly making him sick to his stomach.

He was tired.

Run-down tired.

His ankle was still burning, broken when he leapt from the box at Ford's Theater. Throbbing. Despite the setting and wrapping by Dr. Mudd. Whiskey couldn't even kill the pain. His father would have shaken his head in disgust watching John catch his foot in the flag during the grand exit. Know your surroundings. You don't literally "break a leg," you ninny. That's what separates the greats from the rest. They never trip onstage.

He was so worn. On the run for almost a week now with David Herold. The last two fugitives standing. Up and down Maryland. The Union cavalry like bloodhounds. Not a day of rest. If they could just get deep enough into the South they would be fine. Be celebrities. Bigger than life.

Earlier, they had crossed the Rappahannock on a ferry into Virginia. The boat had felt safe. The flowing water all around. The empty land on both borders. Fresh air bathed Booth's face. A care package of guns and two clean shirts at his feet. He and Herold sat next to three ex–Confederate soldiers. David Herold struck up a conversation. "You fellows from down South?"

"Indeed," said the tall one. Older than the others, with a dark mustache that flowed over his wrinkles, hiding the corners of his mouth.

"Whereabouts?" He ran his fingers along his coarse, whiskered chin.

"Georgia. The three of us. Born and raised defenders of Georgia. All three of us. Grown strong by the Okefenokee Swamp."

Booth preferred to stay out of the conversation. He was tired of talking. Tired of thinking.

Herold leaned in closer to the men. A crooked smile etched along his face. "You fellows ever heard of a man named Lincoln?"

The three ex-soldiers caterwauled and slapped their knees. "It's the greatest thing, isn't it?" the tall one said to David Herold. "Justice has been served."

Herold's eyes widened. He dropped his voice to a whisper. Booth grabbed his leg to stop him, but Herold began to talk anyway. Booth wished he hadn't. "This guy next to me," Herold said, "he's the one who done it. Pulled the trigger."

"Well, I'll be," said one of them, a squatty boy no older than sixteen.

Booth shifted along the bench. Tapping his fingers against the splintered wood. They were not far enough from Washington to enlist as braggarts yet. Only time

makes a hero. He tried to nudge Herold to stifle the
conversation, but his foot wouldn't move. Sonabitch ankle.

The tall one leaned across Herold until his face was in
front of Booth, sour breath and all filtering through his
mustache. "Mr. Booth, I presume," he said. "My name is
William Jett, and I cannot convey the honor I am feeling
in being in the presence of such a patriot."

Booth nodded with the same polite grin he reserved
for stage-door fans following a performance.

"You, sir, are a national treasure. You are the light that
casts your father's shadow."

With those words, Booth straightened up his back.
He arced his chin up to take full command of his voice,
and overwhelmed by the conceit of the performer, took
Jett's hand. "It is a pleasure to meet you," he began,
then stopped himself. Of all people, Junius Booth's son
understood the danger of vanity.

"Wait until I tell my girl that I met you. That I met
John Booth."

Booth looked side to side to see if anyone else was
listening. Smile and act casual.

The other two introduced themselves as Mortimer and
Absalom, and both said in their own words that soon
Booth would be rightly recognized as the true hero of the
war. And they'd be the first to shout it to the world.

Booth dropped his smile, and his eyes turned hard.
Henry V hard. "You can't tell anyone anything. We're not
out of this, yet. The traitor army is looking to string us up."

The three nodded an *of course* agreement.

Now Booth really wished that David Herold hadn't said anything. Suddenly they were in it with these three drifters.

More mouths.

More potential problems.

Jett said he'd fix them up. Friend of his named Garrett had a farm. Set deep in the woods. Even the deer didn't venture into those parts. They would never be found there. They could relax. Rest. Then the boys would work on getting them down to Georgia. Sound good?

Herold grinned.

Booth had no choice but to say yes. It worried him a bit. But at least these fellows were fans. True fans. Hopefully tight-lipped fans.

❖ ❖ ❖

The soldiers left Booth and Herold standing in front of the barn while they talked to old man Garrett. Streams of clouds ugly in shape and color smattered the night sky. The big paw-print leaves of the poplars glistened in the moonlight. Garrett kept craning his neck around the huddle of soldiers, catching a glimpse of the two fugitives, and then averting his stare when Booth's dark eyes scared him off.

"Okay." Jett walked over. "All set. The barn is yours. Get some rest. I'll be back tomorrow with Mortimer and

Absalom to help you plan how to get farther south in no time."

David Herold slapped Jett's back. "Talk about your slave railroads," he said, followed by a lone, stupid laugh.

Booth thanked them. Between Mortimer and Jett's shoulder he saw the string-bean face of Garrett poking through the window, balled up and wrinkled in suspicion. "Just remember, no talking. Not yet. We save the speeches for the last act." He turned to enter the barn. Exit stage left. His goddamn ankle ready to explode. So tired he felt sick.

※ ※ ※

David Herold had no problem sleeping. He went out in midsentence. His snoring confirmed it. He was a wet blanket anyhow.

Booth was trapped in insomnia. Flat on his back, with his leg propped over a gunnysack. Unable to reach his cigarettes. Just as well, this tinderbox would probably go up at just the sight of a flame. He tried to plan. He tried to think. The past week was a blur. All over Maryland. Doctors for his leg. Sympathizers who wanted to feel like part of the victory. They all flowed by like a series of extras and walk-ons. And the one crazy thing about the past week was that he had no memory of killing Lincoln. He remembered three things: the blast of the derringer, his spur getting caught in that damn flag, and the sound of his ankle snapping. He couldn't picture Lincoln, the traitor wife, or anyone else in the box. Someone said that he had stabbed some defender of Lincoln, but Booth could only take that at its word. But wasn't that what Junius Booth always said to his sons in his sermons on the craft of acting—"You've played the role of your life when you can't be certain that you were ever there. That, boys, is when you know you have fully surrendered to your character."

Booth closed his eyes. He saw nothing. He hummed a lullaby in his head. He tried to picture tomorrow.

❖ ❖ ❖

Booth woke from a half-sleep. The ground tumbled and shook as if the earth were splitting apart. He turned his head to Herold, but only saw the outline of a lump of sleep. The barn was pitched in night, still and black. But the ground trembled. And he heard the splintered wood siding of the barn's lazy construction start to rattle. "I don't like the sound of this," he said out loud. He rolled to his side and propped himself on his knees. "Get up." He nudged Herold. "Get the fuck up."

"John Wilkes Booth," a voice called from outside. "I know you're in there."

Herold woke when he heard that. His long, drawn face sank deep, and he braced himself, unable to move. "John," was all he could say.

Booth pushed himself up and grabbed a two-by-four to use as a crutch. Goddamn ankle. "Let's just take a little look at what we have here," he said with mock bravado. He hobbled over to the corner of the building where he could peek out between slats of wood. He cupped his hands around his eyes and leaned forward, as if he were peering around a curtain on opening night. "Let's just have a quick little look at what we are dealing with here." His chest went hollow at the sight of an entire regiment of the traitor cavalry surrounding the barn, rifles in hands, shadowed by torchlights and kerosene lanterns. As deep into the forest as could be seen. Even hiding the trees.

"What's out there?" Herold asked, too petrified to move.

"An anxious audience."

"Booth," the voice called, "my name is Lieutenant Doherty, with the Sixteenth New York Cavalry of the United States Army. Come out now. Let justice follow its natural course. Let's not make this worse than it needs to be."

"I don't recognize your army, nor do I recognize your United States," Booth hollered back.

Herold ran over to him. "Jesus Christ, John, you're going to get us killed."

"What do you think they intend to do with us?"

Herold glanced outside. He dropped to the floor. He had trouble breathing.

"Booth, we know there are two of you in there. It's late. The middle of the night. We are going to end this now. One way or another."

"Shit, John," Herold said. "I'm going. Surrendering. I'm not going to . . ." And Herold shouted, "Don't fire! I'm coming out," and he nearly fell through the door, scrambling foolishly against the hay and broken leaves.

Booth looked out to see his lackey comrade immediately thrown to the ground. A boot in his back. A rifle at his head.

It was Act III now. Absolution and resolution. Pathos rife with tension. Where the banter is reduced, and drama flows from the subtle movements, skillful considerations, and empathetic passion. "I don't recognize your authority," Booth called again, unprovoked. He paused for effect, then enunciated the rest of his line: "Mr. Doherty."

A long, silent pause. As though the cavalry and their horses all evaporated into the mist, leaving only the wind and the pine needles. Booth could hear his own breathing. It was strong. In command. He leaned against his two-by-four crutch, broadened his shoulders, and gracefully lifted his chin as a solitary figure in the spotlight. Sensing the audience holding its breath. Feeling the power rising in his lungs.

"Booth, this is Luther Baker." A shrill voice pricked the pure moment. "I'm a detective working with Lieutenant Doherty. And one thing you need to know about me is that I don't have the time or patience to deal with this shit."

Booth hobbled back to the wall of the barn. "Bringing in the loose cannons now, are you, Doherty?" he bellowed back.

"Surrender," Baker ordered, "or we'll fire the barn and smoke you out like a rat."

Booth peered out between the slats. Several of the soldiers caught him eye to eye, and they quickly raised their rifles. Anxious fingers on the triggers. "Well, my brave boys, you can prepare a stretcher for me. I will never surrender." He turned from the wall and limped back to the center of the barn.

Outside there was a count of three, then the sound of shoes pattering closer. He heard the rolling exhaust of a flame catching, and the brittle snapping of dried wood. He didn't smell smoke. See flames. Or feel heat. He just stood in the center of a roaring thunder.

And he wasn't Richard on his knees crying for his horse. Nor either the frail brokenhearted Lear or the helplessly slain Macbeth. Instead a jaunty reel began to play in his head. Fingers tapping drums, and a bow screeching notes from a reveling fiddle. Booth dropped the crutch. His ankle didn't hurt anymore. The pain was gone. Flanked by the adrenaline and the ethereal otherness that takes over when you first touch the stage, he watched a few flames peek through broken wood and taste around before slithering in retreat. That was his cue. Step lightly. Jig while Rome burns.

His placed his hands on his hips.

Feet shoulders' width apart.

Sidestep.

Rise and grind.

And one, and two, and one-two-three-four.

Right out, back hop, step-step.

He danced in small circles. Kicking his right leg forward, then dropping it back behind the left. Housing himself around the burning barn.

Eyes closed tightly.

A lone actor in the footlights. Surrendered to his character.

A Rainy Night in Springfield, Illinois—1849

If any personal description of me is thought desirable, it may be said, I am, in height, six feet, four inches, nearly; lean in flesh, weighing on an average one hundred and eighty pounds; dark complexion, with coarse black hair, and grey eyes—no other marks or brands recollected.

—December 20, 1859

＊　　＊　　＊

The rain seems to fall harder in Springfield. Maybe the clouds are thicker. The sky's ceiling hangs a little lower, and the gray rain clouds mix heavy and brutal, like the mind of a condemned man. It can kind of sneak up on you. A morning blue sky teases with the promise of a cheerful day, and then by mid-afternoon the day turns mysteriously darker, yet there isn't really a visible cloud on the horizon. Then without warning the sun hides or is kidnapped or just doesn't care anymore, and a cannon boom thunders that not only rocks your house, but rocks your nerves. Next come the electrical flashes, dangerously aimed at your window. A tinkling of rain follows that initially sounds melodic, but builds to an evil crescendo that seems full of motive and malice. And just when you finally come to terms with that, the thunder cannon booms again, and the lightning rods spear straight at you, and the best that you can do is curl yourself into a ball on the couch in your sitting room, too afraid to go near the windows and draw the curtains, waiting and hoping for the terror to pass.

✣   ✣   ✣

Mary Todd Lincoln sat on the couch in her sitting room, wrapped in a blanket that was drawn up around her neck, her knees pressed tightly together, while her taut fingers cinched the wool. The wind outside whistled ghost songs, accompanied by the shivering leaves and percussive banging of the oak branches. The kerosene lamps clouded the room in yellow. A big burst of lightning lit up the room, leaving electric shadow outlines as it receded, then returned the room to its faded burning color.

It seemed like it would never end. The rains hitting the flower bed outside like the stamping of angry feet. Then all around the house. Angry feet dancing all around her. She pulled the blanket tighter. And waited.

She had sent her son Robert down to her husband's law office with the urgent message that she needed him to come home, while her three-year-old was long asleep in the back room. "Tell him I don't trust the threatening rain," she told the boy, insisting that he look up at her while she spoke.

"I don't get it," Robert replied.

"Just tell that to your father."

Robert had run out the door, slapping it shut behind him. His mother watched him dash across the lawn,

shielding his hand over his forehead for cover, and out
through the picket gate that he carelessly forgot to close,
leaving the rusted metal latch to bang with each new burst
of wind. His feet managed to find every puddle, stamping
up waves of dirty runoff water that spotted his trouser legs
in thick dark spots. Sometimes that boy didn't consider the
importance of what's around him. Or even care. A lot like
his father in that way.

Mary cuddled herself on the couch to wait. Thinking
to herself that it was strange that she had never feared the
future nearly as much as the here-and-now.

❖   ❖   ❖

Abraham Lincoln leaned forward into the scattered papers
on his desk, resting his cheek in the palm of his left hand.
He looked up at the uneven molding tacked around the
ceiling while listening to the tapping of the rain. Before
him lay the briefing for a typical greed-based case that
involved some combination of land, cattle, and resale
shares. He had taken the case on behalf of a witless
middleman named Earl Muncie who claimed to have been
boned by a big landowner called Toots Johnson over near
Tuscola, just southeast of Springfield near the Indiana
border. This Muncie turned out to be a real jackass, and
hardly the underdog that he had presented himself as
when Lincoln first met him on one of his consulting
junkets. He sang some *poor me the little guy gets fucked again*

tune, drawing upon all the sympathies of this visiting lawyer. But since then it appeared that Muncie had his own lines of illegal networks, including a little side business that cashed in on the dead-or-alive rewards for runaway slaves gone north, specializing in the "dead" part. But Lincoln had already taken the case. Accepted the retainer, an unusually large sum, in retrospect, from a plaintiff in an I-got-screwed case.

The Lincolns could use the money now. His law practice was off the ground, but he still needed to take any case that came in. They had the house at Eighth and Jackson all dressed with its precise decor, the furniture designed in sharp angles, and parlor chairs handcrafted after the classic European styles, a stark contrast to the split tree trunks that his father, Thomas Lincoln, had called furnishing. A showcase for Springfield, where many of the prestige class of the city had milled the single-floor home with a cocktail in their hand at one time or another, making toasts to one another, while Mary individually reminded them that their assistance to her husband's political career would soon be required. He had almost left his Kentucky roots far behind. And one day he would save enough to put a second story on the house, and he would sleep on the top floor, snoring down over the white-trash childhood he had been forced to endure.

But here he sat in the not quite dark, a candle nearly burnt to the tabletop, its spitting wick only threatening light. The thought of this Earl Muncie made him sick—

the same kind of bastard grin as his father's, pulled back
long and slim in ignorant righteousness over mismatched
teeth, spilling out sour breath as he heaved a throaty
laughter in quick spurts. Exactly like his father, whose
main source of power was the unsubstantiated belief that
he had in himself. But unlike Thomas Lincoln, Muncie
had one more secret weapon—a load of cash that he used
to hypnotize the unsuspecting into willing conscripts.

But what did Lincoln care? Take the money and run.
Right? It wasn't as if this Toots Johnson character was any
great prize worth saving. He too was a conniving piece of
shit who used his pocketbook and its complement of
political influence to ensure that things worked out his
way. Plus if Lincoln won the case he'd really be taking
both of their moneys in the end. A form of philanthropic
assistance in burying his past, and molding a future that
would one day leave him more empowered than both of
them combined.

He filed through the notes that he had taken,
deciphering the tall angles of his handwriting. The case
didn't really make sense from a legal standpoint, but he
was sure that if he dedicated himself he could manipulate
some precedent to his advantage, and out-orate any
country sap attorney that Johnson would employ. But
each time he read a direct quote from Muncie, he would
see that bastard face, and his gut would tighten when he
spun a justification to himself on behalf of that clown.

He wished he could just chuck the case. Tell Muncie

to stick the cattle, the contract, and the retainer up his
bony ass. But Abraham had promised Mary a new dining-
room table, long, smooth red mahogany with beveled
edges. It was the last piece of furniture that they needed to
complete their home, and she had already met with a
woodworker named Sam to start the carpentry.

Maybe he could become more selective after this case.
As soon as the verdict was rendered, and Earl Muncie
slapped his overgrown gritty fingernails into Lincoln's
palm in celebration, Lincoln could pull his hand away and
say that he quit defending shit cases just for the money. He
had his dining-room table. His house. His past successfully
plowed under and suffocated so it could never rise again.
He could then take cases based on his own sense of right
and wrong. Become a true defender.

Sure.

He dropped the papers, watching them fall to the floor.
His chest tightened, and he found it hard to breathe, as if
the air in his lungs had turned thick and humidly
weighted in sadness.

He listened to the rain fall harder. Mary would be
waiting for him. The rain terrorized her almost as much as
the fear of ordinariness.

The Muncie papers were scattered at his feet. He
couldn't go on like this. A new life didn't mean anything
if it came at the expense of more assholes like his father.
Wasn't that why he'd left Thomas Lincoln in the first

place? He thought to himself that he was no better than a sonabitch slave who keeps working the same plot of land with the bullshit promise that it will one day be his.

Robert burst through the door, and let his slick soles slide across the hardwood. He landed in front of his father's desk, a thick-lipped grin rising from his fresh, boyish face between flushed cheeks. His dark curls were matted flat and wet, dripping a perfect circle of spent rain around him on the floor. The water ran in a downward stream under the desk, and quickly soaked into the Muncie notes, leaving only splotches of black ink blood.

A smile rose from Lincoln's face as he looked up from the drenched papers. "I'm glad you got the looks of the Todd family."

Robert stared at him, unsure of what to make of that, waiting to see if his father would be mad at him for ruining the papers on the floor.

"You are a handsome boy is all I'm saying. Got a nice round face."

Robert smiled at the compliment, then turned serious. "Mother sent me here."

"Because of the rain."

"She said she doesn't trust it."

"It scares her."

"I don't get it. I told her I didn't get it."

"It's okay, I do."

"She said you would."

"And I do."

Robert remained in place. His arms flat at his sides, looking like he was melting under the dim candlelight. He wore a baffled expression, one that his father recognized as resignation to the logic of his parents. Reluctantly accepting their manner of conducting family business.

"Are you just going to stand there and make Lake Bob?" Lincoln grinned at his son. He reached into a cabinet behind him and pulled out a towel and a blanket. "Put this around you after you've dried off, and just hold tight a few minutes while I finish the last of my business."

As Robert dried his hair, Lincoln bent over and pried the Muncie notes off the floor, the corners of the logged paper disintegrating in his fingers. He balled it up into a mass of pulp and threw it against the back wall, where it stuck with a thud before loosening and sliding down to the floor into a pile that looked like splattered bird shit. And he really should have thanked Robert for his boyish carelessness in ruining those notes, unwittingly stopping the Lincoln tradition of miserable fathers dead in its tracks. Because tonight, on this miserable spring evening of 1849, Abraham Lincoln quit. The ghost of old Thomas Lincoln was howling somewhere deep in the night. There was nothing left to prove. Abe had run from his past, and now that he was a million miles away he was going to quit charging forward with a nervous look over his shoulder. He was sorry for what Mary might think, and the angst it might initially bring her, the shortage of money and the delay of status, but he knew in the end she would be happier with a husband who lived by his own convictions. They were more likely to be where they wanted to be if that place was borne of strength. There really was no choice.

Lincoln ground his toe into the white pulp, mashing it into the floor until it nearly disappeared, and then he kicked it in a thin ragged line along the baseboard.

"What was that?" Robert peered out from under the blanket, his eyes wide and excited.

"Just some junk lying around."

"Do you have any more?" Robert asked, as if intrigued by the new game.

"I hope not."

Robert donned the familiar baffled expression.

Lincoln stood to get his coat and hat. He turned around to face his son. "Let me ask you a question, Robert."

"Dad."

"Do we need a new dining-room table?"

"What's wrong with the old one?"

"I don't really know. Do you like it?"

"It's fine." He shrugged. "It's just a table to me."

"It doesn't make you think of anything?"

"Just eating."

Lincoln leaned over and kissed his son on the crown of

the head. "Thank you, Robert. You have been a tremendous help."

"Sure thing," Robert said, his expression even more mystified.

Lincoln leaned over and blew out the candle. A flash of lightning cracked outside the window, and in the silver light he saw the remains of the Muncie papers, and thought to himself that he felt like he was loading bullets into someone else's suicide shotgun—hopefully his father's.

❖   ❖   ❖

Mary looked relieved when she saw her husband and son come through the front door. She didn't rise from the couch, but instead held her hands out as though she needed assistance in regaining her balance. Lincoln shooed his son off to his room, instructing the boy to get out of those wet trousers and into some dry nightclothes and straight into bed. Robert ran off in a burst of exhausted energy, his shoulders clumsily banging side to side against the hallway walls, as another round of thunder rocked the night.

"Dear God, Mr. Lincoln," Mary cried out. She dug her nails into his wrists and pulled him down against her. She moved her grip over his forearm. "Make it go away."

"Weather always passes. You know what I tell you about that."

She reached up and stroked his hair. "You're all wet," she said. "Go dry yourself off."

"I'm fine, Mother."

"You'd never leave me, would you, Mr. Lincoln?"

"I don't know who else would accept a mug as ugly as mine."

"No." She scooted in closer. Her eyes half closed in momentary solace. "I mean you'll always be with me."

"Mary"—he laughed—"I'm not going anywhere. At least not for another seventy years."

"Because I couldn't handle it. I'd fall apart if you weren't here to hold me when it rains."

He took her hands off his wrist, and held them in his. Her eyes, those bright blues that sometimes looked so lost and gone, stood attentive, maybe on account of the electrical storm. "I came to a decision tonight," he said softly. "A big one."

She laid her head on his shoulder. The rain had stopped pounding, and turned to steady drizzle. "It's so damp," she whispered.

"I can't keep doing what I don't believe in."

Mary dropped her hands and caressed his thigh in short tender strokes.

"I'm not going to lawyer for thieves just for the money." He stiffened briefly, bracing for the reaction. But Mary just reached up and kissed his neck. Her lips felt thin and dry.

"Did you hear me, Mother?"

"I don't know what it is about the rain that frightens me. Maybe it's the thunder."

"We may not have the same amount of money for a while. I'll need to build a new clientele."

"Oh, Mr. Lincoln, it's like you just told me, and always tell me: the weather always passes, and sure enough the sun will shine again."

"We won't be able to get the dining-room table for a time."

"I like the one we have."

Lincoln leaned in and nuzzled her neck, tasting the dry salt that was left over from her fearful sweat. He dropped his hand between her legs, and ran his fingers in short little tickles on her inner thigh, feeling the smooth and spongy flesh that made his mouth water and his teeth ache. She pulled him on top of her and gripped his protruding hips.

He glanced up to the window, at the trickling streams running unevenly down the panes. Lincoln felt good, as strange as that was. Free of his father, and free from the endless burden of escaping him. He wanted to inventory this feeling. Catalog every nuance, from the lightness in his toes, to the thrusting of his pelvis, to the tingling of his brain. It was so foreign, and he wanted to be able to recall it in case he became lost to the darkness that routinely fueled him.

As if reading his mind, Mary cooed in his ear, "I am so happy right now, Mr. Lincoln."

"Me too."

"Let's make another baby right now," she said. "Someone who can capture all of this happiness."

Lincoln started to kick off his trousers. "If it's a boy," he said, "let's call him William—after Shakespeare."

"And every time we look at him, or think about him, we will just know happiness."

"I do love you very much, Mary."

"I'd fall apart if you weren't here to hold me when it rains."

Abraham Lincoln made love to his wife on the couch that night. Thankful that his pain was behind him.

In praise of happiness.

A Word on Researching *Mr. Lincoln's Wars*

Most of the characters in *Mr. Lincoln's Wars* were created (other than people such as Mary Lincoln, John Wilkes Booth, Edwin Stanton, etc.). My need for history was mostly to preserve an accurate sense of the times, as well as to keep the book from becoming so diluted of history that it completely lost its verisimilitude. I was not overly concerned with the historical record, nor about bringing the settings to life—a common characteristic of historical fiction. The true reason I chose Lincoln was for the incredible disparities between the strength of his outer character and the sorrow that resided in his interior world—both as a leader of a bloody war and the father of a son who had recently died. I wanted to find the precise moments when those two worlds came crashing into each other. Sometimes it would be an experience that involved Lincoln directly, and other times it was based on people's views of him. In some cases—such as "The Ward" or "The Undertaker's Assistant"—it was the literal collision between Lincoln's inner world and the way others perceived him. Viewing these sides of Lincoln through fiction allowed me the freedom to invent things off the historical record and to get to places where historians are often not able to go.

❖ ❖ ❖

I drew from a variety of sources for *Mr. Lincoln's Wars*. Initially, there was quite a bit of up-front reading. Although I went through the pages of many volumes, the main books that I kept returning to were *Lincoln* and *Lincoln at Home* by David Herbert Donald. *The Life of Abraham Lincoln* by Stefan Lorant and *Meet Abraham Lincoln* by Barbara Cary and Jack Davis are both books that I have been carrying house-to-house since I was six years old (the former being published in 1954, the latter in 1965). As a child, they played a large part in shaping my mythology of Lincoln, and during the writing of *Mr. Lincoln's Wars* I often referred to them to remember the common knowledge of Lincoln, and how his heroism might be seen both historically and contemporarily. Memories that were also reared during the course of the writing pointed directly to the three volumes written by Carl Sandburg. Lastly, many of the visual and visceral impressions that took shape in my imagination were aided by the documentaries *The Civil War* by Ken Burns and *Abraham and Mary Lincoln: A House Divided* by David Grubin.

Most of the character stories were written with little

heed to history, only to have that filled in later during the numerous rewrites of the revision process. A good deal of the secondary, after-the-fact research was conducted through hours spent on the Internet searching out facts and details from essays, white papers, and collections of documents (including Lincoln's autopsy report) old and new—the products of what is surely lifetimes of work done by others. There were times during this Internet research when a simple fact catapulted a scene to a place that was more daring than anything I might have ever dreamed. An example was a minor fact that I had stumbled upon about John Wilkes Booth. Just before assassinating Lincoln, Booth was having a drink at a tavern next to Ford's Theatre, and had been verbally assaulted by a patron for not living up to his father's acting abilities. From a simple sentence not much longer than that, I was able to envision that man being an old theater critic who speaks to Booth, taking on the role of the demanding senior Booth, thus giving the son his final psychological motivation to follow through with his horrible plan.

✤ ✤ ✤

But even the most amateur Lincoln historian certainly will note that *Mr. Lincoln's Wars* is invention, and because it is populated by mostly fictional characters, the notion of researching human nature, behavior, and psychology cannot be understated. A great deal of time was devoted to understanding the socially abused—the voiceless faces peering from shadows; the battle-weary sons of ruthless fathers; the innocently judged; the wilting faces behind the proud masks. In terms of research, understanding those truths was equally important to the accuracy of this book as the historical details.

❖   ❖   ❖

Many people would think that using a historical subject would hem in a fiction writer, that facts and dates would supercede the fiction process, somehow placing a tourniquet on creativity and imagination. Instead, history and fiction are not so far apart—they are both about taking existing structures and trying to find the meaning inside them, not allowing sepia-toned mythology to take the place of history and the triumph of human endurance. They are about seeing truths, finding and keeping heroes, and not fearing the ugly underneath.

—AB

wm WILLIAM MORROW

Coming Summer 2004
in Hardcover from Adam Braver

DIVINE SARAH
A Novel

A highly imaginative novel about the last years of
Sarah Bernhardt's life, exploring her opium addiction,
her many sexual liaisons, and her scandalous career as
the greatest actress of the turn of the century.

ISBN 0-06-054407-4